FORTRESS OF ANGELS

Additonal Titles by D Dean Boom
Journey to Redemption (Early 2015)
See www.ddeanboom.com for more titles

FORTRESS OF ANGELS

D Dean Boom

Published by Mostly Normal Publishing, Portland Oregon
First Edition, 2014

Library of Congress Control Number: 2014921010
Mostly Normal Publishing, Portland, Oregon
ISBN-13: 978-0692337783
ISBN: 0692337784

Dedicated to my family for always believing in me, with love to Mom, Dad, Nikki, Devon, and Lorna.

Thanks to: Julia, Sterling, DVD, Chris from WWC, Chris from England, Jeremiah, Susan @ Indigo, Vinnie @ Indigo, Wee Jeanie the Great, Karen, Pol, Willamette Writers, Sam, Jordan, Luhmann, Mr. Pease, Mrs. Aragon, Jeff, Stuart, Jeremy, National Novel Writing Month (NaNoWriMo), Oregon State University, and to you, the reader, for helping me fulfill my dream of writing about Holimoren.

Visit www.holimoren.com for backstory, geography, maps and more!

To learn more about D Dean Boom, visit www.ddean-boom.com.

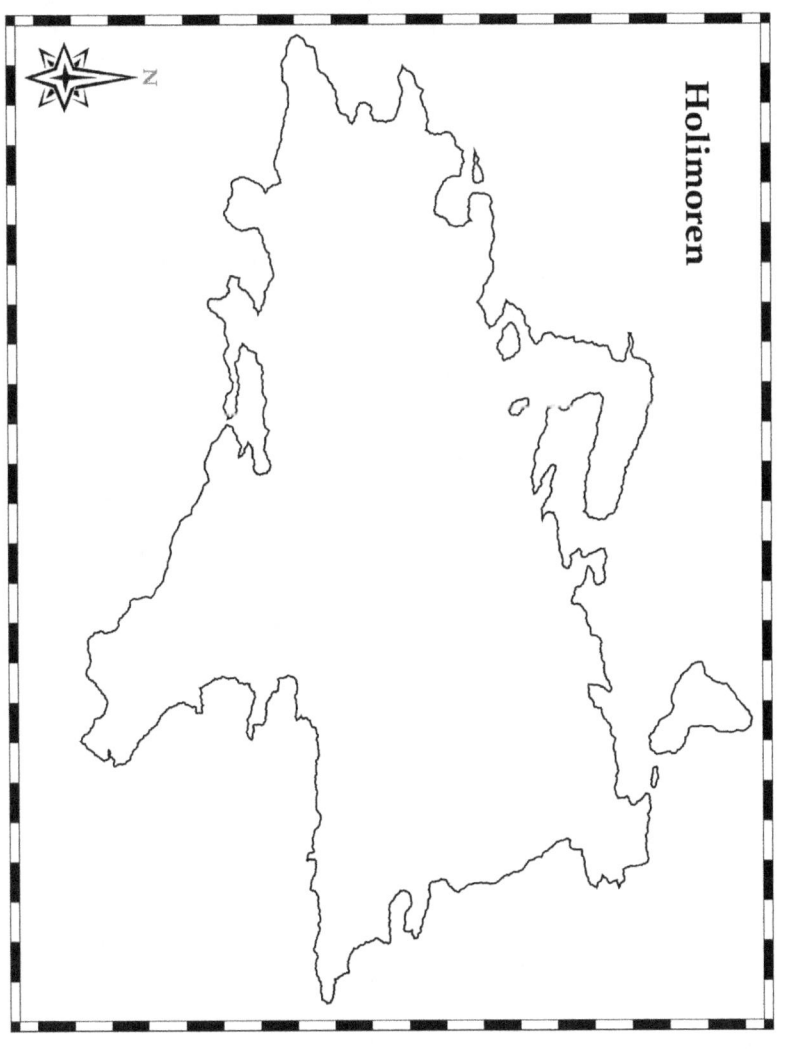

Holimoren

N

ONE

Daybreak

"Nothing ever goes as planned. Not even the planning goes as planned."
—General Groknar

Dar walked up the stone steps to the middle level of the tower that had been his home for the last two years. He could walk there in his sleep, and often he felt like he had done just that. No matter how early Dar tried to get up, it wasn't possible for his body to awaken fully in the stone building. When he was younger, living with his mother's family, he had always slept outside. The warming sun seemed to welcome him each day properly and power him awake. Being an apprentice wizard now, his room in the tower was on the bottom level, a level without windows. The Master's room had windows—slits, really—but even that level of light made a significant difference. Plus, the Master used his spells to give the room even more vibrancy. Dar had not learned enough

1

spells to do that just yet. Dar ran his fingers through his short black hair, trying to make it look nice for his master.

"Good day to you, Dar." The Master didn't look up from his manual. He had found this tome at the market in Magrican some years ago, but was only now getting around to exploring its potential offerings in depth. Master was almost a textbook vision of a mage. Thin, with a delicate body, his face was unusually round, considering his wiry frame. He stood a good two inches shorter than Dar's six feet, but his presence filled the room. When you walked into a room, he was always the first person you noticed. Dar, on the other hand, seemed to blend into the background, even when he stood in the open. Not even his ultramarine-blue eyes (from his elven heritage) could match the intensity of the Master's hazel ones.

"Good day, Master." Dar kept his gaze low, away from the book. Master had warned him that some books were enchanted to be dangerous to those who didn't have the power to master the higher-level magicks.

"I would like you to clean up from my experiments last night." The Master's eyes continued to scan the symbols, but he'd lifted his arm to point to the long wooden table that filled the seaward side of the tower. "Also, I believe that it is time to rotate the tower."

Dar sighed. Tower rotation involved moving everything hanging or touching the walls and putting it all in the center area. All this work so Master could rotate the outside of the tower without destroying his furnishings. Dar knew the next line by heart too; he recited it in his head as the Master spoke.

"We must move the tower to prevent any moss from growing. Nothing attracts Oblivax Moss like a dirty unrotated wizard's tower." The Master pointed at the ceiling. "One thing

I ask from all my charges is to be clean. You, my tools, my tower!"

At this point Dar stood and waited for the next part of the ritual they had acted out every four moons since he had joined the Master. Dar knew it well enough to tell the story himself. Master once had a run-in with Oblivax Moss, which stole his spells and memories, and only by eating the accursed moss did he regain his own mind. But the moss made him terribly sick, and his constitution had since remained weak.

Dar was so lost in his recollection of the story that he didn't feel the weight of his impatient master's eyes upon him. "If you don't remember why we need to rotate it, I'm sure you can find another line of training, since our apprentice relationship will be over."

Dar was dumbstruck for a moment. "I remember, Master." Dar started taking things off the wall. "That moss did you a severe disservice."

"Nonsense, my boy!" Master looked up from the book. (He'd clearly needed to turn the page anyway.) "That was a blessing, not a curse. If I had kept my health, I'm sure I would be out there still, chasing danger and excitement, not here learning and gaining experience through experiment and knowledge. I have tripled my power since I set camp in this tower."

"Really?"

Master closed the book and took up his pipe. He puffed at it, but since it wasn't lit, little happened. Master never smoked the pipe anywhere other than the top level of the tower. The fire hazard from the carpets and wooden interior was too great even for his only vice.

"Dar, I know you're wise beyond your age. Your youthful blood makes your body feel new every day instead of rapidly decaying like mine. But come on, my boy, how could you have assumed that somebody like me, with my frail, wiry body, could have wrestled a tower like this from the forces of darkness?"

Dar looked off into the distance for a moment. "I figured you just attacked it with your spells or had it built with your money."

The smallest glimpse of a smile darted across his master's face. "The money came after the tower, not before it."

"So how did you get the tower?"

A quick adjustment of his pipe showed Dar that his master was going to share a story. "I paid off an adventure party to find me one. They sent me a message, and I made my way here. After enchanting some of their weapons and giving them some training, my debt was paid in full, and we parted."

"How long ago was that?" Master's stories were never very long.

As Dar watched, Master puffed on the pipe. In his head Dar imagined Master counting the years. Decades, maybe.

"Three years ago next time the moon is full."

Dar sat down.

"Yes, my boy. I have doubled my strength since you joined on as my apprentice. I've found myself with the time to spend on my experiments, as well as on solving issues concerning magic force and the relative movements of the moon and its effect on that force, instead of deciding what was for dinner or who was going to clean up the mess."

Dar stood up again.

"I know your studies haven't been progressing as quickly as you would like, and you're barely casting second-level magic this far into your training, but you will master it. And I will master how to teach you."

Dar went back to the wall and lifted off a painting. To his eyes it was just a brown mess on an orange background, with no structure or presence. He never got what this was supposed to be a painting of, and he didn't want to use what few words master would share in a day to find out.

"I'm glad we had this talk, Dar." The Master went back over to the book and opened it where he had left off.

Dar finished taking the various magic paraphernalia (the drying tongue of a Fire Salamander was his least favorite) off of the wall and made a nice pile in the middle of the tower. Then he noticed the table that Master had dirtied overnight. Apparently, Master didn't do much sleeping at times. Apparently, most mages of his master's power didn't. Dar fought a yawn for a while before losing and putting his whole body into it. Obviously, he wasn't anywhere near that level of power.

He moved the scrolls around and cleaned up the two steins of what smelled like mead. Hopefully, Master had remembered to close the spigot, or the kitchen would be afoul with the sticky substance again. It had taken Dar two days to clean it up last time. Dar headed to the stairs to work his way up to the kitchen that was across from Master's room. (Master felt it worked out better to have himself closer to the food than to have Dar closer to the Master.) Finally reaching the top floor landing, Dar turned and worked his way into the kitchen.

He surveyed the kitchen. It was bad, but not as bad as he had feared. The mead spigot was closed, but last night's ham shank was still out, and the bread was hard enough to be used as a weapon. Dar walked to the outside wall and uttered a magic phrase. The air turned electric and created a blue wire that grew into a thin door, and the odd odor of ozone wafted through the room. Dar pull at the door. It opened into a nether-space region the size of a small closet. As the room was on another plane of existence, time and the elements had no effect on it, so he and the Master used it to store foodstuffs like fruits, vegetables, breads, meat, and dairy. But Master had cost them at least one loaf of the bread, most likely the ham too. Dar sniffed the ham, and he didn't like what he smelled. It hadn't spoiled, but it had dried out. The sandwich ham was now a stewing ham or soup ham. He put it into the closet and hung it back from its metal hook.

He walked out and surveyed the bread again. The loaf was from the next town over, some hours by flying spell, or a full day's walk each direction. It was a good size, almost the length of his forearm in diameter. Barely half was used, but the damage had been done. Dar put it into the closet, near the dessert items. Perhaps he could make a bread pudding out of it, or egg bread. Just not sandwiches.

Dar glanced behind him—he thought he heard something. He walked out of the magical pantry and moved into the center of the room.

"I hear my master, and I obey." By uttering the response phrase, Dar activated the Master's spell, which had been magicked into the whole tower.

"Ah, Dar," came the Master's voice. "I'm glad you are using the Tower Talking spell. I believe there is a message arriving on the top of the tower. The familiar won't wait long for somebody to come get it, and I'm in the middle of a rather long glyph sequence."

"Yes, Master." Dar looked at the foods. He hadn't eaten just yet and was peckish. "My master is finished with me, and I obey." The command phrase ended the conversation. Dar walked into the closet and grabbed two hard rolls of bread and slice of yellow cheese. He ripped one roll in half and inserted the cheese. A quick bite followed. He held the other roll while he closed the pantry. Another bite sent more of his cheese roll to its fate as he worked his way up to tower roof, a snack for the guest in hand.

He expected the familiar would be hungry.

By the time Dar got to the roof, a seagull-looking creature was perched on top of the little purple rune-covered box that was the prescribed landing zone for familiars. By decree of the members of the Wizard's Hierarchy, each member had to have a safety zone for messenger familiars to land and rest. No matter the ethics or alignment of the registered wizard, the familiar had to be able to land and survive. Familiars were special creatures, usually from other planes of existence, but their life force was tied to the wizard that owned or summoned them. Good familiars served out of friendship and zeal, while neutral familiars did it more out of curiosity and entertainment; evil ones only served to advance their own grotesque desires.

"I have a message for your master." The bird extracted two short arms from under its snowy plumage and withdrew a small scroll. "It is magicked to only respond to him; do not attempt to read it."

"I understand. May I ask you a question?"

The bird turned its head to look at him squarely with what Dar assumed was his good eye. "You may."

"I am unacquainted with your type. What are you?"

The bird laughed, almost the way a gull scolds someone raiding its food. "I am a Gulull. I am from the plane of Elysium. While I look like one of your native seabirds, unlike them, I have arms with fingers just like yours. I can speak your tongue, as well as three others. I can see in the dark and can use magic and spells. But because I fly like the storm wind, I am often called by my master to deliver callings for the Hierarchy. Today I serve that purpose, with over a score of messages to deliver this morning."

"That won't allow you do fly back to Magrican before dark."

The Gulull emitted a laugh. "I'll teleport back, silly." Then he took to the air and headed toward the interior of the continent. "I only fly because I need the exercise and I love the view," he called back.

"Might I ask you a question?" queried the Gulull from on high.

"It would be my honor!" Dar cupped one hand to his mouth, not sure on how far his voice carried into the sky.

"May I have that snack?"

Dar blushed, as he had completely forgotten about the treat. He reared back and tossed it as high as he could toward the speeding Gulull. It first appeared it would miss, but the morsel changed direction and landed straight in the Gulull's mouth. One flick of its beak and the snack was gone.

"Good day, Gulull!" Dar clenched the scroll, careful not to crush it.

"Good day, Dar. Good day to your master too!"

Dar rushed downstairs to find that the Master had finished his section and had once again closed the book.

"What was up there, my boy?"

"A Gulull! It looks like a…"

"I know that familiar type well. He serves as the companion to Gahngarston from Magrican. He's lucky to have such a wonderful creature as a fellow." The ever-present pipe moved from one side of his Master's lips to the other before he continued. "The bird fellow drinks too much at parties, but then, who doesn't! Tell me, what news did he tell you?"

Dar held out the scroll.

"A scroll." His eyes narrowed. "Interesting. The good news is never written down. Then again, neither is the truly bad news. Word-of-mouth stuff is always more actionable than scrolls. Like the time…well, I suppose that story will wait."

Master reached out and took the scroll. It had barely been larger than the roll Dar had eaten and weighed less than the cheese in the sandwich. But as the Master's fingers came in contact with it, it grew to three times its original size and mass. Master unrolled the scroll and started to read it. "It's a message scroll," escaped his lips as his eyes darted around, taking in every word. Dar looked on—because it was a message scroll, he didn't need to avert his eyes—knowing that when and if his master was ready to discuss the scroll, he would do so. Sometimes it would be days later; sometimes it was never brought up. When the four-legged crow creature had landed last year, the Master took the message personally and stayed in his room for a week. They had never spoken about that message. It must have been bad news, like when Dar had heard of his mother's death.

"Well," the Master said, finally, "I've been summoned to a full vote of the Hierarchy. Somebody has invoked the

Cloture protocol, and all members in full standing must attend and may not take action on a proscribed list of events before attending the meeting."

"What does that mean, Master? Will I be going with you?"

"What it means, Dar, is that you'll be master of the tower for a while. I'm going to Magrican as soon as possible." Master rolled up the scroll and placed it into the pouch at his waist. He strolled past Dar and headed up the stairs to his room. Halfway up, he paused. "Follow me please, Dar."

Dar bounded up the stairs and was only two steps behind the Master by the time he was in his room.

"Here is what you'll need to know to survive while I'm gone." He reached into his closet and took out a several nice shirts and at least three pairs of pants and placed them on the bed. Dar never knew he had this many things to wear. He just always seemed to have just the one robe on. "First of all, let no one know I am gone." Master reached under his bed and pulled out a sack. He gingerly placed all the clothes into the bag. The clothes had at least three times the volume as the sack, though it hung as if still empty.

"And let no one into the tower." He looked Dar straight in the eye. "No exceptions."

"Yes, Master."

"Second, remember to keep everything clean." He hesitated a moment. "Also please get me that staff from over by the door. And grab my protection amulet. And my rings."

Dar hadn't seen Master in a state like this for a while, but did as he was told. He walked over to the door and took the six-foot-tall wooden staff in hand. It throbbed and hummed slightly at his touch; it was as if he was holding a snake by its tail. He then walked over to the dressing table and grabbed a necklace with a small ball at the end of the chain that served as its pendant.

"Not that one!" Master pointed at the other end of the table. "That one."

"What are you expecting at the Cloture, Master? You rarely take so many magic items with you." Dar picked up the correct amulet; this one had two metal swords crossed where the ball had been on the other amulet.

Master stopped stuffing his personal possessions into the bag long enough to tilt his head slightly to one side and then went back to work as he spoke.

"I really have no idea, other than the list of proscribed actions. Spells and combat by Hierarchy members are not allowed until the Cloture is over. That means somebody has an ax to grind. I just don't want that ax sticking out of my back when this Cloture comedy is over."

"So you really have no idea about what this is about?"

Master paused for a moment then continued. "I'm sure some higher member has been caught in a compromising position with a noble's daughter, or went off on some fool idealistic crusade and doesn't want another member ruining their fancy party. Magic users are really foppish fools at heart, me included."

Dar grabbed the Master's ring bag and brought the magical implements over to the bed. The Master emptied the contents of the ring bag into his belt bag and discarded the now empty container onto the bed. He placed the amulet around his neck, and as Dar watched, it disappeared.

"What is that one?" Dar asked.

"Amulet of Backstab Protection. It erects a force field that stops all physical assaults from behind me." He looked at

Dar, beaming in a rare moment of pride. "I made one at the request of the adventure team that emptied the tower for me, and it was an interesting enough idea for me to make one for myself. Mine blends into my clothes so no one will know I'm wearing it." He went back to packing. "Pretty clever, if I do say so myself."

Dar grabbed the empty ring sack and placed it on the dressing table.

"Where was I? Fourth? Third?" The Master looked at Dar blankly before blinking twice and continuing. "At any rate, there is enough food for both of us for a month, so that means you'll be good for two. If I am later than that, I will use my spell powers to put food into the food pantry directly. If you have any special requests, leave a note in there and I'll see what I can do." He stood upright and looked off into some old memory. "Magrican has the most wonderful foods. They have this exotic rice-and-fish concoction where you place the whole thing in your mouth then chew. It has rice on the outside and some tasty snap vegetables next to the fish…"

As the sentence trailed off, Dar noticed the Master's face starting to soften and relax, as if he was coming to terms with some great notion. Dar started to talk but was beaten to it.

"Dar, you've been a great apprentice. I have not always been a great master. I know you will do great things in your life no matter the path you pursue."

Dar felt saddened but couldn't place why. Why was Master talking this way?

They both worked silently, shoving more stuff into the sack. Absentmindedly, Dar almost removed a large mirror from the wall before he figured out that Master wouldn't be here to actually rotate the tower. Instead, he put his time into cleaning up the various dishes that were left lying around, including some dishes that were just about ready to walk off. Dar held his nose a couple of times. Perhaps those dishes were better off destroyed than washed.

"I am ready." Master hoisted the sack over his shoulder and grasped his staff firmly. "How I love a Bag of Holding. The space of a small room, at a fraction of the weight, all loaded nicely into this sack." He took a deep breath and locked eyes with Dar. "Remember, don't let any of the locals know I'm gone, and don't let anybody inside the tower. If you have special needs, leave a note in the food room, and…" He looked off at some point in the air, like he was checking off items from a list that only he could see. "That should be about it. You're a strong lad, and your magic is capable of doing things beyond your reckon, so practice some, but don't try anything dangerous. Remember to keep the tower and yourself clean while I am gone. And no fire spells!"

"Yes, Master."

And with that, Dar's Master looked to the ceiling and snapped his fingers. Before Dar could blink, he was gone. Only the slight smell of ozone was left to comfort Dar as he began his time alone. He hoped that one day he could master the teleport spell. Every time he saw it being used, it left him amazed.

The rest of Dar's first day of solitude flew past like a summer evening. Quick and effortless, it was over and the next dawn came. Not knowing when Master would be back, Dar slept in his own bed, but he was tempted to sleep in the kitchen just to be in the light of dawn again. If the weather would hold for any time, perhaps the tower summit would be an ideal choice. Without Master to make the place a mess, the chores were completed quickly, and Dar needed to find something to do. He practiced a couple of easy spells and used the magic to complete easy tasks. Instead of digging around to find the good bread knife, he cast Locate Object and scanned for it. Dar tried using Unseen Servant to create a butler for him to interact with, but the force from the plane of Air just sat there hovering, awaiting a job. Dar made it carry a table, lift a chair—he even did some experiments with having it put away the dishes. But being a mindless, invisible, floating mule for all intents and purposes, the Servant broke two dishes before Dar dispelled the magic and sent it back to its plane of origin.

Finally, a week after Master left, Dar decided it was time to take up a hobby. His magic skills only allowed him to cast a couple of low-power spells each day before his mind gave out, unable to cast more. This was usually by lunchtime, and then Dar had little to do. A hobby would fill up the afternoon and hopefully do some good. Dar first experimented with clay, but being unable to use magic to fire it, this seemed rather pointless. The tower was otherwise empty of anything he could turn into something fun. There were no painting supplies and very little ink that wasn't magical, which ruled out drawing. Cooking for one eliminated trying haute cuisine, and all the books were magical. Unable to find much else in the way of a possible hobby, Dar retreated to the tower roof and spent the first part of the afternoon of day eight After Master (as he was calling it) just watching the clouds float by. The sky threatened rain, looking all black and foreboding. A roll of thunder echoed past the tower, causing Dar to sit up and search out where the action was coming from. Off toward the sea-side horizon, another flash was followed by the booming noise that was its brother. Dar's gaze shifted from the horizon to the edge of the tower ramparts. The shaded side had moss on it. Dar smiled.

He'd found his hobby.

It took Dar another couple of days to figure out how to remove the moss without violating Master's rules. He built a swing and pulley system. He would use his magic spell of Strength to pull the rope and lower himself down the side of the tower. He also fabricated a return system, so if he pulled the return rope, it would throw a gear, the counterweights would be released, and he would ascend the tower to safety. He would cast the Strength spell while on the swing, lower to his working position, then scrape the moss off the face of the tower. When the spell's magic ran out, he would pull the rope and return to the safety of the tower. Should someone approach, he could quickly pull the rope and duck back into the tower. And since the tower gate remained closed at all times, no one could enter if they came from the side where the tower obscured his vision. It seemed perfect.

After a week of scraping, Dar had barely cleaned off a third of the tower walls. Using a fire spell like Burning Hands would have allowed him to finish the job by now, but Master's rules had to be followed. Dar experimented with various Cantrips, but those minor magic spells were unable to help shift the moss and muck that coated the tower. The Strength spell left his muscles sore and mind weak, so the actual amount of time he spent scraping the moss was little more than an hour.

After another tiring week, his patience was spent. At the end of the Strength spell, he sat on the swing for a while, scraping at the browning moss. Overcome by a fit of frustration, he cast the Burning Hands spell that was forbidden. Flames shot from his fingers, fanning out only a couple of inches, but the drying moss lit quickly. Given the heat from the magic flames, even some of the green moss started to burn, billowing smoke up into the air. Instinctively, Dar pulled the release rope, and he flew up into the smoke and through it, safely away from the flames. But the smoke had made him dizzy, and while he knew he had to get some water to put out the flames, his body betrayed him, and he collapsed to the floor of the tower roof. Between the effects of the Strength spell and the smoke, darkness overcame him.

The next thing Dar knew was that rain was falling on his face. The sudden downpour soaked him, pulling him from his slumber. It was dark now, probably some six hours after his poorly constructed effort. Fearing the worst, he rushed downstairs, expecting to find the fire had destroyed the whole interior of the tower. But everything was exactly where he'd expected, with no signs of temperature issues, smoke, or even anything out of the ordinary. In fact, it smelled like the floor of a large, dark, moss-filled forest. The slightly woody smell chased away the other smells that had long haunted the tower. Dar sighed, changed his clothes, then went back to sleep.

The next day, Dar decided to investigate the damage to the outside of the tower. Following the same drill as before, he cast his spell of Strength and went over the side. Reaching the area where he had worked before, he was amazed at how clean the stone was. Perhaps it was the fire, perhaps the rain, but the original luster of the rock shone brighter than he had ever seen it. Never really having spent much time this close to the stonework, Dar lost himself in examining what appeared to be tiny little animal shells in the rock. He stared at them for a while before deciding they were no more than a trick of the eye..

"Ahoy there!"

Were his ears tricking him too?

"'Allo up there!"

Dar turned and looked down toward the ground. A party of four men stood below, some twenty feet away from the base of the tower.

"Can I help you?" Dar slowly reached toward the release rope.

"We've come to see the master of this tower," said the tallest of the four. Dar sized up each in turn, trying to determine their intent. The tallest wore no armor, and his skin was a sandy tan color. He had a long, slender sword at his hip and wooden sandals on his feet. The other three obviously worked for him. The other three wore chain mail, and their low foreheads and gray eyes suggested magical influence of some sort, probably their leader's. Other than the faraway look of the three, nothing on their faces foretold their intentions.

"I'll get him." Dar reached for return rope.

"Steady on, friend." Dar turned to see the man again. The man's face was stern, with a hint of a smirk on his lips. "I'll parlay you for a spot before you get your master. I wouldn't like you to disappear into the tower and have boiling oil or Magic Missiles or a Fireball be his retort to our gentle inquiry."

"What is your inquiry?" The moisture in Dar's mouth had evaporated faster than a desert rain, and it gave his words a

17

creaky tone. He was exposed, but if he rushed, it would tip his hand and probably lead to an assault on the tower.

"We are looking for volunteers."

"To do what?" Dar shot back.

One of the underlings snickered. Dar's eyes darted away from the leader for a moment.

Then, out of the corner of his eye, Dar saw the leader pull out an ax. Dar reached for the return rope, but by the time he pulled on it, the ax sliced through the rope holding up his left side. Freed from its burdensome weight, the left-side rope shot up while the right-side rope held still. The swing disappeared from under Dar, and he started to fall. Instinctively, Dar used his Feather Fall spell, finishing it just before smashing to the ground below. He beat gravity by mere heartbeats and still landed heavily, which knocked the wind out of him.

"Get him!" the leader cried out, directing his minions to do his bidding.

Dar struggled to his feet, but he felt like a boulder had been placed on his chest. He lashed out with an open palm and connected with the closest underling. The blow hurt Dar more than his opponent. But it did buy him some time. Dar leapt back to the base of the tower and weighed his options. The three minions spaced themselves out, ready to fight. Their purpose clear in their eyes, they were closing in with a deliberate pace. All the while, the leader just stood there and laughed.

Dar used his last spell. He started with the magic-enabling chant, made a soft zzzz sound while lowering his fingers and his eyelids. The final movement was to put both hands together next to his head like some sort of pillow.

Moments after he finished the Sleep spell, the eyes of the three attackers rolled back in their heads as they fell to the ground. The tallest of the three followers was snoring before he even hit the ground. The laugh of the leader stopped. Dar took off running. He would figure out where to run to after he was safe.

He was barely twenty strides from the tower when the leader knocked Dar to the ground. Being almost a foot taller and almost twice his weight, the leader stopped and waited for Dar to make his move. When it came to blows, the brute knew he had the advantage.

"You're a scrappy little one, aren't you?" The leader left his sword still tucked into his belt but placed his hand on the hilt as a reminder of the severity of the issue.

"You'll find I'm full of surprises." Dar got to his feet.

"Oh, you've already surprised me once. I don't like that."

Dar lunged at him, but he just dodged to the side and pushed Dar to the ground again.

"The name is Sh-An. And you are?"

"Very mad at you."

"Nameless or not, you are going to do what I want you to do."

"I doubt it." Dar slowly made his way to his feet. He was glad Master wasn't here. The pure physical strength of this monster would have killed the frail man.

Sh-An rubbed his face. "I'm magic resistant, as your little sleep spell proved." At this distance it was easy to see how nonhuman the monster was. His skin was a pale green, his hair a darker shade of the same. "I'm twice as fast as you on foot, and I can fly." Sh-An apparently shaved, but had left a menacing goatee. His left eyebrow was split by a scar that disappeared under his hair. "I have my own spells, plus the power of my race. I'm an Ogre Magi, clan G'Hai. You have been…"

Dar rushed him again, and Sh-An met the attack with a powerful blow to the gut that doubled Dar over. Dar gasped for air that wasn't coming.

"...an interesting opponent. I could keep beating you until my minions awaken." He pulled out a six-inch-long piece of metal. "But I get paid less for damaged goods."

Dar leapt up, grabbed the sword hanging from his own belt, and took a swing at Sh-An's neck. The Ogre Magi ducked and spun on the balls of his feet, lifted his leg and extended it out at Dar's head. The roundhouse connected with a crunching sound as the heel of the ogre's sandal connected just toward the ear from the apple of Dar's cheek. Dar spun around at the force of the impact and was unconscious before he hit the ground.

Sh-An pulled his sword back from the prone target. He touched the back of the blade softly to each of Dar's shoulder blades.

"I honor you, and I hope your death is swift and with honor."

Then he bent down slightly and touched Dar on the head with a rune-covered metal rod. As soon as the metal touched Dar, he disappeared in a bright light. Sh-An then walked over to each of his minions and looked down at their sleeping bodies.

"Pathetic."

He drove the sword into each minion in turn, severing the spinal cord at the bottom of the neck. They never even moved. He then collected their equipment, keeping what was valuable or edible, and jumped into the air, flying toward the Skyneedle and the other mountains in the center of Holimoren.

Somewhere on the other side of Holimoren, Dar's body materialized on a bed of straw. He was still out cold, and the bruise on his face was growing by the moment. Shortly, a hunched-over, grotesque witch walked up to his limp body and gave it a quick inspection. She placed a salve on the purple mark on his face and then dragged him to the stall at the end of a long row. She placed a small bag of herbs on a string on his nose and tied the ends of the string behind his head. She made sure he was on his side, so that any vomit wouldn't cause choking. But considering the fact that this one didn't smell drunk, it was just out of habit. She paused for a moment, contemplating something beyond her normal routine, like using this one to satisfy one of her many hungers, but she let it slide when the whooshing sound of another arrival reminded her to get back to work. She shut the gate of the stall and proceeded back to the arrival stall, where she cackled and got to work again.

Dar opened his eyes suddenly and panic filled his mind. Not wanting to tip his hand, he quickly closed his eyes again, listening and sensing as much as he could about his surroundings. There was at least one other person in this place with him. He could smell hay, some sort of strong herb or oil, and at least a couple other odors, including excrement. He blinked his eyes open for a second and noticed that a person lay in front of him, unmoving. Then he shut his eyes and surveyed his health. There was something on his face, covering his nose. The skin under his eye was moist, almost slimy. He thought back to the roundhouse kick—his face didn't hurt as much as it should have. The smell from the bag was weakening, or at least was not as effective as whoever put it there had been hoping. He searched his mind. Sleepweed. They wanted him to stay drugged until whoever was in charge was ready to wake him up.

Dar moved his leg slightly, and the body next to him shifted slightly. It was still warm, so it wasn't a body, or at least was a fresh one. Dar was just contemplating his next move when a shot of cold water blasted him across the face. He opened his eyes and shot up to a sitting position. The water was muddy and smelled nasty. Dar wiped it from his face and got splashed several times as the process was repeated for the three others beside him.

"Wake up, scum."

Dar locked eyes with another brutish figure. He was at least seven feet tall and very muscular. He looked to be almost twice Dar's weight. His face was human, but his nose was shaped more like a snout, and his face was too rounded, his ears too short. His hair was thick and coarse, black and uneven. His black eyes pierced into Dar like a knife. He was the man in charge and was letting Dar know it with his icy stare.

"Name is Ocktur. Sergeant Ocktur."

He smiled and showed his sharp teeth, each tooth stained with a touch of black.

"And welcome to your new life as a recruit in the Army of the Protectorate."

TWO

Mice

"To break the spirit, break the body."
–Chapter I, verse 27, The Book of Truth

"You are the newest recruits in our little army. I have been given the task of making sure you vermin give your life to the cause in the most useful way possible." Ocktur scowled. Dar judged that it was probably the natural position of his face. "So our first week together is going to be a review of our objectives, remedial armed combat training, plus teaching you the basic command structure of the Army of the Protectorate. After that we will head to a second line of defense to back the real soldiers in this fight. You live long enough, you might join them."

Dar turned his head slightly as if to stretch. He counted three people to his left. As he went to turn to the right, Ocktur caught him.

"Eyes on me, pretty boy."

Everyone snapped their attention back to Ocktur. Ocktur took two small steps and stood in front of Dar, towering over him. "As your sergeant, I expect that you will be looking at me, listening to me, doing as I command. Is that clear!"

Dar nodded.

"Somebody cut out your tongue? The only answer is *yes, Sergeant!*" Ocktur took a step back and vented his rage a little more evenly. "Let's try it out to see if you kittens can listen!"

A brief pause punctuated his comments while his eyes shifted back and forth over the rabble.

"Are you ready for your training?"

"Yes, Sergeant!" The response, including Dar's, was pretty feeble.

Ocktur rushed forward and punched Dar in the stomach, knocking the wind out of him. As the fist connected with the soft flesh just below his sternum, Dar could tell that this wasn't the fullest application of violence Ocktur could apply. Dar fell to his knees, gasping. He clutched his stomach and grimaced.

"That, ladies, was just a sample of my rage. I can punch so hard as to break bones."

Dar believed him. So, clearly, did the rest of the group.

"Now, let us try this again. Are you ready for your training?"

"Yes, Sergeant!" echoed through the area as each man gave it his all, not wanting to be made an example of like Dar.

"Good."

Dar stood, and Ocktur took a long moment to stare at him. Dar didn't wither under his gaze, and after for a moment, he thought he could see a hint of respect. Though Dar figured that was probably just hoping beyond hope.

"We are Ax Company, part of the thirteen companies of men, misfits, and other types that make up the Army of the Protectorate. The original Ax Company was destroyed in the last raid, so we're all new. There are two groups of twelve of you to the one of me. Our commander is Lieutenant Strlang. As time goes on, I will appoint section leaders—three, to be exact—who will make sure the other three in the section don't get killed without my authorization. We are part of the First Human Brigade, which is part of the West Division. The other divisions are North, Central, and City. You will be expected to understand the chains of command, but that is not our immediate focus. As merit allows, the bold will move up, the weak will die, and the strong will survive. If you are bold and strong, you just might end up with my job."

Ocktur looked around at Ax Company. "Maybe, two, maybe three of you look like you might eventually take a shot at leadership. If you do it while I'm alive, you'll learn I've got plenty of tricks."

Ocktur fixed his gaze on one fellow to Dar's right, but Dar didn't dare to turn his head. A moment later, having finished his stare-down, Ocktur started to pace slowly from one end of the troop line to the other.

"The mission of the army is pretty straightforward. Our city is under attack. An army is trying to take our city and all its possessions, all of its people and all that it stands for. We cannot let that happen. Our division has been given the task of protecting the Abbey. The Abbey lies outside the walls, a half mile away from the city. Its perimeter defenses have been reinforced, but it is up to West, North, and Central to defend the Abbey. The Abbey isn't just a pretty building. It is full of helpless Holy Sisters who cannot leave because of their religious laws or something. The enemy will make short work of these Sisters."

Ocktur stopped and looked up and down the line, as if gauging the reaction to his comments. Whatever he saw seemed to make him happy, because he started his slow pacing again.

"I would rather you died than the Sisters were defiled. Because if you fail, that is what will happen. Those innocents will be on your head. If the enemy gets through, you better be dead, or I will kill you with my own hands. Do I make myself clear?"

"Yes, Sergeant!"

"Good! Currently, Battle and Cutter companies are covering our spot on the line. We have three days to get into some sort of fighting shape before we need to take our place back on the line. Our first goal is to see what kind of shape you sorry pieces of flesh are in."

Ocktur turned to face the group and took a step back. "On your bellies! Let's see how many times you boys can push the ground!"

The group seemed not very excited to get onto the dirt facedown. Ocktur charged, taking two swift steps, leading with his fists. Two quick and savage blows to the faces of two recruits knocked them straight to the ground. Again, they appeared to be measured blows, just enough to really hurt, but not enough to do damage.

Ocktur stood up straight and stepped back to his starting position. "Let's try that again. On your bellies!"

Everyone fell to the ground and kept their eyes on Ocktur. "Now push!"

Dar could judge by those around him that this wasn't a very fit bunch of recruits. He quickly did four push-ups, struggled to complete four more, and by ten was completely spent. Judging from the way Ocktur was pacing from one end of the line to another, somebody was having much better results—probably two recruits, or maybe three. Dar could tell he wasn't the first out, but he certainly wasn't capable of doing the amount these fellows were.

"Excellent. You can stop." Ocktur moved up and down the line. "Some of you are in fighting shape; some of you are in woman shape. We'll fix that quick. Any of you have formal fighter training?"

Dar didn't risk looking around to see how many had the training, but judging by the way Ocktur's eyes darted up and down the line, it was at least a couple.

"Any have Guild training, either as a thief or assassin?"

The pause was short. Dar reckoned nobody did.

"How about as a cleric, druid, monk, or bard?"

Again, another very short pause.

"How about as a mage, illusionist, or any other spell caster?"

Dar raised his hand. He couldn't tell if anybody had as well.

Ocktur worked his way over to a fellow two or three down from Dar. "How much training did you get?"

"Almost two years' apprenticeship."

Ocktur leveled him with blow to the gut. "For being a smart mage, you're not learning, boy. You will *always* address me as Sergeant. Let's try that again."

Ocktur waited for the recruit to get his breath back. Feebly, he stood up and appeared to think a moment before speaking. "Two years' apprenticeship, Sergeant."

"See, boys, that is a smart man."

Ocktur moved over to Dar, taking only a single step.

"How about you?"

"The same, Sergeant!"

Dar swore that Ocktur had the smallest curl of a smile at the corner of his mouth.

"You two are not to use any of your spells without permission from me." He moved until his face was barely an inch from Dar's. The smell of sweat and something rotting filled Dar's nostrils, and he swallowed hard. "Am I making myself clear?"

Dar tried to keep calm. "Yes, Sergeant!"

Quick as a wink, Ocktur spun on the balls of his feet and was in the face of the other lad.

"Yes, Sergeant!" yelled the other recruit.

Ocktur moved back to the front of the line.

"I will be watching you boys. We have strict orders not to allow any magical casting for the next couple of whiles. This is a new order, just about a week, but punishment will be quick and severe." Ocktur paused for a second, either sizing everyone up or considering his next move. Ocktur focused behind the troop for a moment and nodded subtly. Dar wasn't sure he had seen it, but he wasn't going to question it.

"Your training will begin after a short break. First, we will split the lot of you into two groups. Stay here, as anybody caught leaving will be killed for desertion." Ocktur walked through the formation and headed in the direction of the Abbey off in the distance. "Dismissed."

Dar rubbed his stomach, which was still very sore. He turned to his left and watched half of the group as it was led off a bit.

Scanning the area, he noticed that that a pair of recruits were talking amongst themselves. By looking at them, Dar could see they must be brothers. They shared the same nose and brown eyes, with roughly the same underworked physique. They were a couple of inches shorter than Dar, and they each had about twenty pounds on him. All signs of an easy life. The taller one, albeit by only an inch, turned to Dar.

"You okay, buddy?"

"Yes. Nice place we found ourselves."

"Yeah. Name's Deek. This is my brother Zander."

"Dar."

Both boys were blond, but Deek's hair was a little lighter than his brother's.

"Most people call us the Vanander twins, since we're always together."

"But you're not really twins, are you?" Dar looked them both over.

"Deek is a year younger," ventured Zander.

"I'm also the smarter one," Deek said.

Zander countered by punching his brother in the meaty part of his shoulder.

"Are you the one with the magical training?" Dar asked Deek.

"Yeah," he said. "Zander is still thinking about things, but I think he's more of the churchin' type than the magic type."

Zander delivered another mock blow.

"How many spells do you know, Deek?" Zander laughed.

Dar looked inquisitively back and forth between them, not getting the joke.

"He still hasn't learned any."

"After two years?" Dar tried his best to not make it sound mocking, but he fell far short of the goal, and he could tell his words hurt the elder Vanander.

"My sister is teaching me, and she's not a formal mage. She had some training, but she won't tell us where."

"And she's gone a lot," Zander threw in.

"A missing master is how I got here." Dar stopped rubbing his belly. It wasn't helping any, and he felt rather stupid doing so while talking to the brothers.

"We were at a town fair when this bunch of bandits jumped us. We did our best but couldn't hold them off," Deek admitted.

"Doesn't your stomach hurt?" Dar asked Deek. He was remembering when Ocktur had made an example out of the other spell caster.

Deek frowned slightly and made a wry smile. "If Zander has any use in the world, it is that he keeps me tough. Sure, it hurt, but I've had it worse. There was this one time we were running away from our sister and Zander caught a sapling branch in his hand and let it go. Hit me right in the stomach and knocked me off my feet."

"But Sister cast that spell, and you were up and running within just a bit."

"Your sister does both magic and healing spells?" Dar looked at them like they were telling stories.

"Sure." Zander looked at Deek, like it was Dar who was unbelievable.

"She only does magic in public," Zander volunteered.

"Shut it, Zander." Deek looked harshly at his brother.

Dar figured that was enough of this topic. "Where do the Vanander brothers hail from?"

Zander appeared to have recovered his presence of mind. "Cragmoor."

Deek nodded. "I do wonder" He looked around before continuing, "Where here is?"

Dar looked around, hoping to find something—anything, really—familiar, but of course nothing was.

Deek looked at Dar. "Where are you from?"

"My master's tower is just a bit from the Free City of Holin. Away from the coast. It's pretty far from your homeland."

They all stood for a moment to let the bleakness of their situation sink in.

"We're not going to live, are we?" Zander said meekly.

"We will if we stick together." Deek put his arm on his brother's shoulder.

"We will stick together." Dar nodded at each of them in turn. "And we will survive."

The brothers spoke in unison. "Agreed."

Ax Company milled around for a while, not talking, as each person began the process of closing off his old life and gathering the mental strength necessary to deal with this new one. Some wandered off a little, but not too far.

Except one.

A tall, lanky fellow, looking like he had never washed and smelling of dead fish, took it upon himself to see if Ocktur was telling the truth about the path to freedom. After the group went silent, he looked the men over one by one and found them all lacking in any ability to stop him. So he started walking in the opposite direction from the Abbey. After a couple of minutes, nobody could see him, and they continued to just stand around. Dar watched the recruits. They had seen the deserter leave, and it was only a matter of time before another would try the same. They shuffled their feet nervously, and he could tell which were about to ready to leave. They would start pacing and move off a couple paces away from the main body of the group, and then turn around and pace back. But the out leg would be longer than the in leg. And then the pause before turning around became longer and longer. Dar figured another two would leave in opposite directions within minutes if Ocktur didn't return.

"All right, group, form up." Ocktur's voice boomed out of nowhere.

The recruit farthest away bolted. The closest returned to the group. Ocktur spotted the deserter and pulled a throwing knife from his belt. He coiled his body and launched the knife at the target, now a good hundred strides away. The knife altered its course midflight and struck the deserter square in the back. The fellow crashed to the ground, his arms and legs flailing as the violence of the impact tossed him off-balance completely.

"Be in line when I get back, or you'll all wish you'd never been born." Ocktur took off running and quickly arrived at the feeble body of the deserter. Ocktur pulled his knife from the deserter's back as everyone in Ax Company watched. Ocktur raised it over his head and paused.

"Don't look, Zander," Deek whispered.

"I can't not look," shot back Zander.

The blade came down on the fellow once, then again and again and again. Ocktur kicked the body, wiped the blade on his shirt, and walked back to the unit, acting as if nothing odd had just happened.

"So, that means we are starting your training," Ocktur said. "First, we will get you into shape, then we'll teach you to fight, then we'll hope you don't die before paying back that training by defending the Abbey." Ocktur looked beyond the Abbey and licked his bottom lip slowly.

"The lieutenant took the other half of the company. You lot are my problem. Roll call. Say your name twice."

Ocktur stared at each man as they started out. But as each name was called out for the second time, Ocktur would nod and shift his attention toward the next person in line. Dar wasn't really listening until the calling of the voices got near to him.

"Upny, Upny."

"Drots, Drots."

"Zander, Zander."

"Deek, Deek."

"Dar, Dar."

"Gramal, Gramal."

"Modo, Modo."

"Dyo. Dyo."

"Jusin, Jusin."

"Pesha, Pesha."

"Banes, Banes."

"Joolan, Joolan."

Ocktur waited for a moment. "Our little band is missing two." He turned and looked off away from the Abbey. "One is presumed dead. Now where is the other little bird?"

Ocktur pulled the knife out and lowered his head. He switched the knife around to hold it by the blade, and then slowly raised the knife until it was above his head. He gave it a gentle toss, and it flew off like a swift chasing bugs across a fresh summer stream. Darting this way and that, but always forward, always with purpose, until it could no longer be seen.

Ocktur turned and looked at the group again. "I will remind you that desertion from this army will be treated just like desertion from any other army in the history of warfare. You leave, you die. I may not find you today; I may not find you tomorrow. But when I do find you, or when another member of the Army of the Protectorate finds you, you will die. It will not be an easy death. You are better off staying with your unit and hoping that the enemy doesn't kill you. We will win this battle eventually, and you'll be able to go home eventually. But if you leave, you will never see your home; you will never see anything other the Hunter Knife tracking you down and bringing you to me. And your blood will be added to that of the foe's blood already on my tunic."

Ocktur took a couple of small steps to his left and continued.

"Each officer and his sergeant are issued with a Hunter's Knife, or a weapon like it. It exists to hunt and destroy deserters. I predict that within a day my knife will be back. Two at the longest. And the wages of desertion will be apparent to all."

Ocktur looked each man in the eye. Once he had stared at each, checking to make sure his message was received; he stepped back to his starting place.

"Time to make your bodies into living weapons. Then we will give you a steel one."

The rest of the afternoon was a blur. They walked in silence out away from the shadow of the Abbey and the stalls where they had been tossed upon arrival and moved south for a couple of hours. There were fewer people here, as this was apparently some sort of undefended land between the front lines and the walls of the city. Once their unit was about equidistant between the front lines, the Abbey, and the city, they stopped next to a single lean-to.

"This is our base for now," Ocktur said. "Once we are ready, we will take our place on the line and Battle and Cutter companies can move back into their positions. I will also pick three section leaders before we leave for the line. This will mean extra food, extra supplies, and other extras. You will want to be a section leader, so I suggest you work at it. And I suggest you find a nice soft spot on the ground and get some sleep." With that, Ocktur moved into the lean-to and sat down.

Dar looked at the "twins" and watched as Zander dropped to the ground and fell asleep immediately. Deek was more careful, but the result was the same. Dar got onto his belly, put his arms under his head, and blinked twice. He was asleep a minute later. It was a sleepless night, tossing and turning. He couldn't tell if he was awake at times or just in some horrible dream. At one point he was sure he saw Ocktur come out of his lean-to just and head off back toward the Abbey. But that had to be a dream.

Dar was awakened the next dawn by the sound of pain. He opened his eyes and sat up quickly. Ocktur was walking through the recruits and kicking those still sleeping awake. Some got kicked in the head, some in the back. Dar struggled to his feet but stopped halfway to get the Vanander brothers awake. He tapped Deek on the shoulder, but he didn't stir.

Dar shook him, more violently than he had intended, but Ocktur was coming. Dar quickly reached over the awaking Zander and shook him, this time with more fury. Zander just reached up and swatted at Dar. But Deek opened his eyes in time to see the wrath with which Ocktur was hitting the sleepers.

"Zander, get up," Deek whispered.

Ocktur heard the whisper and came running. He put his finger to his lips, and Deek stopped talking. Ocktur stood over the stirring Zander.

"Yes, Zander," Ocktur mumbled, then kicked Zander in the ribs. "Ocktur is coming."

Zander rolled over and struggled to his hands and knees. "Yes, Sergeant." He gasped out, barely loud enough to be heard. Deek went to help him up, but Ocktur tripped him.

"You survive on your own merit here, boys. I don't care if you're twins, lovers, or enemies. You survive by your sword."

Ocktur walked away and put his boot to several of the other members. That gave the Vanander brothers and Dar enough time to get up, get in line, and get ready for Ocktur's next command.

"Today"—Ocktur turned and faced the group—"we will get you into shape. I hope you like pain, because today is pain." He walked up to the line of troops. "We start with running. Followed by marching. Followed by an upper-body workout, followed by running, followed by marching, followed by anything else I want you to do."

"When is chow time, Sergeant?" Upny asked as Ocktur was passing him.

Ocktur spun to his left and connected a haymaker to Upny's face. Upny flew back almost a foot, and blood flew into the air. He was obviously unconscious before he hit the ground; his limp body sprawled on the ground.

"Food is for soldiers." Ocktur walked back to his normal command position in front of Ax Company. "And never question me or my authority. When I want you to have information, I will give it to you." He clenched his fist to remind them of the wages of failing to follow his rules. "You will take turns carrying Upny until he comes to or dies, whichever happens first. Like a dropped sword or misplaced spear, tools you take with you. Until he dies, he will be valuable, if for nothing more than as another target for the enemy's archers. If he dies, drop him and keep moving. I decide when to switch, and I pick Dar to start out with him. Since the magic boys will be soft, this will help him out. And that means you're next, Deek, so stay near to Dar."

"Yes, Sergeant!" chirped both Dar and Deek. Ocktur's lip twitched up a brief moment before settling back into its normal scowl.

"Move out!" Ocktur took off running back toward the Abbey.

Dar and Deek quickly went over to Upny. They hadn't socialized with him much beforehand, and this was their first chance to see him up close. Upny was obviously only partially human. His gray skin was covered in lesions and tufts of hard, coarse hair. His eyes weren't level—in fact, his left eye was noticeably higher than his right eye. Deek recoiled in horror, but Dar pressed on, trying to stop the blood seeping from Upny's nose. Dar inserted a small amount of Upny's shirt into his nostril and started to lift him up to his feet.

"Deek, help me!" Dar struggled with the weight.

"What is he?"

"I don't know, but I know that if we don't get moving, we'll all get a beating. I don't want my nose to look like that." Dar grunted as Upny shifted and almost fell to the ground. Deek lifted his share of the load, stabilizing Upny so Dar could get underneath him and lift him up onto his shoulder. In this position, Upny's face was on Dar's back and his feet hung down his front side. That put Dar's shoulder right in Upny's midsection, but Dar didn't figure he would notice until he woke up. Dar then staggered off toward the rest of the group. The best he could pull off was a jog, but Deek stayed just ahead, just in case. They had jogged for five minutes when Dar started to stagger, and Deek rushed over to help catch the falling Upny. But to Deek's surprise, Upny held out his feet and landed upright.

"Thanks for the lift." Upny took off running.

Dar and Deek looked at each other, completely dumb-struck. How long had Upny been awake? How much longer would the charade have gone on if Dar hadn't almost dropped him? What was going on in this army?

Deek broke the silence first. "That is pretty messed up."

"We need to get back to running."

Dar and Deek were the last ones to get to where Ocktur had stopped.

"About time you joined us. Now we walk back to the camp." And off he went.

Deek and Dar walked slowly, trying to work their way over to Zander. When they reached to him, he was out of breath and obviously suffering. Zander put his arms over his head, but this seemed to make him dizzy, and he fell to his hands and knees and retched. All the food in his belly being a long-gone memory, he just emptied the acids out of his stomach onto the soil. Dar and Deek went over to help him but stopped when they noticed Ocktur had made his way back to their area.

"Zander, I gave an order to walk!"

Between gags, Zander limped as he replied, "I'm trying, Sergeant."

Ocktur pushed him over with his foot and watched as Zander struggled to breathe between convulsions.

"Your enemy will not be as kind. I suggest you get on your feet and get moving." He turned and looked at Dar and Deek. "I suggest you get moving if you don't want a sample of my wrath."

Dar held his ground. "My sergeant said, 'Never leave a good tool or weapon behind.' I don't intend to disobey my sergeant."

Ocktur smiled at that one. "Fine. You get to carry another body, it seems, Dar. I hope you're up to it."

"Yes, Sergeant!"

"But you, Deek, you get to run back to the camp. If you're not the first one there, you will be the first to get special treatment." Ocktur flexed his hand again. "Am I clear?"

"Yes, Sergeant!" Deek gave his brother one last look before he set off running.

Ocktur looked at Dar and narrowed his eyes. Then he too took off for the camp. Dar helped Zander to his feet and the pair walked slowly back to the camp. Partway there it started to rain, and Zander walked with his mouth open. Dar took off his soaked shirt and wrung it out into Zander's mouth. It felt like forever since either had had a drink, and even though it tasted of sweat and mud, Dar imagined it was probably the best water Zander had ever tasted. The water seemed to buoy his strength up a little bit, and Dar was able to let him walk on his own.

They continued to walk as it continued to rain. Time lost all meaning until they saw Upny and Modo running back toward the Abbey. Upny smiled as he passed Dar, showing dark, uneven teeth that were sharper than human teeth. But Dar couldn't focus on him; Ocktur wasn't far behind the two runners. As Ocktur approached, he yelled his orders.

"Once you get to camp, you get to run back to the turn-around point. If you don't finish last, you get a cup of water. If you finish last, you get nothing."

"Yes, Sergeant!"

When they finally they got to the camp, Drots was manning the water barrel. Dar and Zander entered the camp at the same time.

"Zander, you get the water." Drots's skin was pale, but his features were definitely human. Dar figured him from being from the Shadow part of the Skyneedle area. An area of vile humanity, if the legends were to be believed.

"Give it to Dar," Zander protested. "Without his help, I wouldn't have made it here."

"Orders were, if you finished together, Dar wasn't to get the water. Everyone for themselves, remember?"

Zander looked at Dar and then at Drots. "Just give him the water."

"I'd sooner dump it." Drots pulled the ladle out and started to pour a little onto the ground.

"Wait!" Dar stopped him. "Why can't you give us both water, Drots? Ocktur isn't here. He doesn't know."

Drots looked Dar in the eye and sneered, "I'm up for section command, and that means I'll get special privileges like more food and water. You scum will be just troops. I don't want to be troops. I want command. I want that food. If it ever got out to Ocktur that I didn't follow his orders, I wouldn't get the section leader position, I'd get a kick to the head. You're not worth it."

"Take the water, Zander." Dar turned his back. "I'll be fine."

Zander took the handle of the ladle and drank deeply of the water. Dar detected a slight smell to the water as Zander drank it down. It reminded him of the Sweet Water potions master would make to sell to adventurers. Sweet Water potions would make any water pure and would help invigorate the drinker. They wouldn't provide a power up like a Heroism potion, but they would sure make anybody who just ran a distance feel completely refreshed.

After a quick smile for Zander, Dar licked his drying lips and took off running back toward the Abbey.

The second time they returned, it was Jusin at the water bucket. By looking at him, it was easy to see that he was one of the members of the company who had been a warrior. His body was trim, sculpted but covered with scars, including a long one across his abdomen. Zander was the last one in this time, but Deek and Dar both slowed their pace to be close enough that each could let Zander have the water. Dar decided to test Jusin and finished in a tie again.

"Which one of us gets to drink?" Dar asked.

"What do you mean, which one?" Jusin handed the ladle to Dar.

"I thought the last man didn't get served?" Zander chimed in. Dar looked at him with a pained look.

But Jusin answered it for him. "Sometimes not asking why makes everything go easier." He looked at the ladle for a second. "I lost count. You fellows are numbers ten and eleven, and everybody knows that Ax Company has twelve men. So you both drink. Do so quickly and don't ask any more questions."

Dar took the ladle and drank deeply. It was his first water in a long time. Well, other than rainy shirt-water.

"Feel the effect of the water?" Zander nudged him gingerly.

"It's magic," Jusin answered. "Probably spiked it with a Healing potion or maybe even a splash from a vial of Heroism."

"I think"—Dar handled the ladle to Zander—"it's been cleaned by a potion of Sweet Water. My master used to make them. I would think the strong stuff like Heroism would be kept by the cadre for their own use."

Jusin nodded. Zander just drank.

"Done?" Jusin opened his hand and awaited the ladle.

"Yes, I won't forget this."

"The name is Jusin, and you had better not. Ocktur is right, you will survive on your own, but not having extra enemies is a luxury that only kindness can earn. I will expect the same courtesy at some point."

Dar nodded. "It will be granted."

"Then be off."

They did two laps before dark, and two more laps after. Drots and Jusin alternated as ladlemen, and the extra water they got every other lap really paid off. After the first laps, Zander was almost delirious, and Dar was afraid that without the extra water he would not have survived. Deek was in better shape, but not much. He was stronger, but even the likes of Modo and Pesha had started to show exhaustion. Ocktur collected them into a line and addressed them.

"That was the first day. Tomorrow we do weapons training. That will be another workout, I promise. As you might have noticed, two individuals were selected to sit out at times and make sure the water wasn't stolen. These two will be section leaders. I am still working on the last section leader, so keep your wits about you and it might be you. Sleep where you can." He flashed his grin. "My boot looks forward to waking you in the morning."

THREE

Men

"The battlefield is never an easy learning place. Failure means death, and passing just means death tomorrow."

—*Harlec Knight's Army Field Manual*, Chapter 2, Introduction

Dawn came with the same violence as the morning before. Dar heard the grunts and groans of the others and sprang into action. He quickly and silently nudged each brother in turn, and they were both on their feet as they heard the heavy footfalls of Ocktur approaching. Drots and Jusin weren't kicked; Dar noticed they were merely nudged by the foot of Ocktur. Apparently, that was one of the "other" perks.

"Ax Company, today we will conduct weapons training. Now, I know a couple of you think you know how to use weapons. So we will start out with me attacking you, and if you defend yourself well, I'll let you pass, and you can sit out today. Otherwise, it will be drills, drills, and then more drills." He reached down and picked up an ax that was near his feet. It was about three feet long, but the head of the ax looked less like an ax and more like a maul. The edge wasn't sharp, and the mounting point looked cast instead of hammered. "This is a practice weapon. It is blunt and weighs about as much as my boot. It will leave a mark when I hit you with it. You will have one as well, but it won't do you much good."

Ocktur reached down and picked up an identical weapon, then tossed it at Drots. Drots caught it in midair and measured it up. Ocktur raised the ax into a defensive posture. "When you're ready, Drots."

Drots raised his ax into a similar posture, but his hands were higher on the handle, giving him better control. Drots swung for Ocktur's shoulder, which Ocktur blocked with ease. Drots swung again, lower this time, and allowed one hand to come off the handle. With this grip, he rotated the head just as it impacted Ocktur's counterstroke. This caused the head to catch the handle of his opponent, and when Drots pulled his ax back for another blow, it caused Ocktur's ax to slide out of his grasp and down to the ground.

"Stop!" Ocktur held up his hand, and Drots complied. "You pass. You may have the afternoon off, and report to my lean-to for some food. Give your weapon to Dar."

Drots looked smug as he handed his weapon to Dar. "Good luck, rookie."

Dar accepted it and tried to make sense of the weapon. Being a mage, he was not used to smashing weapons such as these—smaller devices like daggers and knives or darts were more the usual fare for wizards. He practiced for a moment, trying to figure out the weight balance of the ax and the best way to use it. Dar had just settled on using it two handed when Ocktur gave him the signal.

"Begin."

Dar eased forward and looked for an opening. The sergeant was just waiting for him. Finally, Dar figured he was close enough and made a wide sweeping arc at the level of his shoulder.

The ax wound up short by almost two feet. Ocktur laughed.

"The wind won't hurt me, fool." Dar could hear Drots and a couple of the others laughing.

"I won't make that same mistake," Dar grunted. He took two quick steps and repeated the move. This time Ocktur obligingly blocked the blow, but still looked disinterested in the whole affair. Dar began his next blow from over his left shoulder and aimed the arc more down toward the ground, hoping to catch Ocktur's deflection attempt either short or give it enough downward momentum to dislodge his weapon. But Ocktur was ready, and again he blocked the shaft of the attacking weapon with the shaft of his own. Dar stepped back and shifted his weight to his other foot. He quickly moved two steps to his right, moving in an arc to keep an even distance. Ocktur too moved, but only by rotating his body slightly. He altered his stance, ready for whatever Dar had ready.

In the time it took for him to move, Dar adjusted his grip on the ax handle. Thinking back to his time in the kitchen, he recalled how changing the grip on his knife changed the leverage and the aiming point. He shortened up his hand position and took a swing as Ocktur settled his feet into his new stance. Ocktur had clearly expected an attack at this opening, as he had lifted his ax handle to block Dar's. But by shifting his grip,

Dar had positioned his ax head at the point where the handle had been. Metal smashed into wood, and a crunching sound told Dar his efforts had been effective. Ocktur's weapon was ruined. As Dar finished his follow through, he barely noticed Ocktur's rage—or the fact that he was now swinging at Dar with his fists. Dar's efforts had forced him to turn his head slightly, bearing the back of his head to Ocktur. Ocktur lashed out with a fist and connected just above Dar's right ear.

The world turned black after that.

When Dar came to, it was well into the afternoon. After the hard work of the day before, his body had just shut down under Ocktur's blow. Dar slowly stood up, his head spinning. It seemed the weapons test was over, and he was hoping to learn the results. A quick glance around him showed that Drots, Jusin, Pesha, and Joolan were missing. It also revealed some fresh wounds, including a nice black eye on Zander. Modo stood to Dar's immediate left, as if he was waiting for something.

"About time." Modo tossed another ax at Dar, but it fell short and dropped out of his reach.

"What are we supposed to do?"

"We're supposed to spar with each other. The four others passed and got the day off. I almost passed, and I got to wait for you to wake up."

"How long was I out?"

"Half the day." Modo started to swing the ax back and forth as if it was a scythe harvesting late-summer wheat. "I needed the break."

Dar looked at Modo. He was another semihuman, like Drots. His skin was more olive, with a hint of scales. He also had thin red lines along his neck, and his eyes seemed a little far apart, bulging out a little. This seemed to give him better peripheral vision, but little else. Modo was almost half a foot taller than Dar and clearly much, much stronger. Dar also noticed his long fingernails and the fact that his fingers appeared webbed.

"Where are you from?" Dar asked.

"Not here" was all Modo offered. "Can we get started? The sooner I put you back to sleep, the longer I get to sit and figure out my way out of here."

"Just give me a second." Dar experimented with this ax, noticing it was heavier and not as well balanced as the first. This ax could be fatal in dealing a head wound, but the blade didn't look sharp enough to cut fruit, let alone armor. This must still be their practice weapon, he figured, but made a note of its fatal potential.

"That is long enough, I think," Modo said, then charged in. He led with a strong overhead blow aimed to split Dar in half. Dar reacted by diving underneath the blow and in between Modo's legs. Modo's rush carried him forward, and Dar dragged his ax a little. The handle caught Modo on the shin and tipped him forward. Dar spun and swung the ax with his own overhead chop but misjudged the distance again and only hit air. Modo reacted by striking out with his leg behind him before spinning on his down leg and swinging widely with his ax. Dar stepped back, and Modo's ax found nothing. Dar stepped in as the follow-through carried Modo out of position again and used a shorter, more controlled swing this time. It glanced off of Modo's naturally thick hide but provided enough blunt trauma to make him wince in pain. Modo stepped out of range, panting. Clearly, he had not expected the battle to go so badly so quickly.

"You got lucky. I went for the kill and left my side open." Modo closed his stance and shifted the ax in his hand. "You won't be so lucky again."

Modo charged again, but this time he planted his lead foot and swung down, much the way Dar had against Ocktur. But Dar was able to counter the move, much the same way Ocktur had. Dar riposted at Modo's shoulder; Modo leaned to improve his position for his next move, leaving his neck exposed. Dar figured a blow like that would be fatal, so he pulled up. Modo countered with his own ax and stopped the blow short. The block and the pull up left Dar open, and Modo punched him in the stomach. Dar stepped back and grimaced in pain. Modo laughed in delight before charging again. He aimed another overhead blow at Dar's head, and just like the first time, Dar ducked under the move. But Modo was ready for that and dodged to the left, not allowing Dar to pass cleanly underneath, or to hit his leg and dislodge his balance. What he did not figure on was Dar immediately spinning and using the force of the spin to get a blow in. During the dodge, Dar had spun the ax head around, and now he struck Modo in the stomach with the blunt end of the head. This knocked the wind out of Modo, who folded in half and dropped his weapon. Dar stood up and lorded it over Modo.

"Surprise! You're dead." Dar placed the ax on Modo's shoulder, who could only gasp for air. As time passed, it was growing clear that Dar wouldn't remove the weapon. As Modo's breath finally came to him, he reached up and pushed the weapon off of his shoulder. "You shamed me, human.

You will pay for that. Nobody makes a fool of Modo and lives."

"I did not shame you. I beat you. There is a difference." Dar made sure his grip on his ax was solid, just in case Modo tried something.

"You are mage. Modo is a warrior. It is shame to be beaten." Modo stood up and picked up his ax. "I will get my revenge."

Modo stared at Dar for a moment, apparently considering his next move. So intent was his focus, he didn't notice Ocktur coming up behind him. When Ocktur pulled on the ax head, trying to remove it from Modo's grasp, Modo reacted by swinging with his free hand to repel the thief. Ocktur blocked it and spun with the ax still in his hand, causing Modo to come off his feet. This move threw Modo on his backside, and Ocktur finished it up with kick to the side of Modo's head. Green blood oozed out of the wound, but Modo's eyes never blinked.

"I said, put the weapons down!" Ocktur glared at Dar, who just let his ax fall from his hands.

Ocktur leaned over to Modo as if to whisper, but his words were loud enough for all to hear. "Attack me again like that, and the least you'll lose is your hand." Then he stood up, yelling, "Ax Company, get into line formation!"

This bellow summoned the rest of the troops. As they arrived, they got into position. Once at full strength, Ocktur sauntered to his normal position in front of the group.

"Your training is now over. We will march to the front. I have already told Battle and Cutter, and they will be gone by the time we get there." He showed his fangs, which Dar reckoned was a grin. "Any additional training will be conducted at the front."

They marched for a couple hours, and slowly the front came into view. The first thing they all noticed was a line of palisades. The landscape was barren of trees, so the logs of the palisades were really the only cover in the area. The line of the palisades was not continuous—there were gaps located every now and again, apparently without reason. Dar had figured they would be living next to the palisades somewhere and was stunned as they walked through a gap and kept going. They were about ten steps beyond the line when Dar noticed a trench dug into the ground. The trench seemed to be as long as the wall, albeit without any gaps.

"This, boys, is your new home," Ocktur said.

The trench had a sloping ramp that faced the wall behind the lines. It allowed for ease of access, not only for troops, but for vermin. The trench was nasty and smelled foul. The ground was black, and even the mud had a veneer of char on it. Dar surveyed the area. Off in the distance to his right was a hill that appeared to anchor the enemy flank. The ground seemed to end far off to the left, a dotting of foliage suggesting a river or creek. Between the hill and the water, this was clearly the best point of attack, which meant the enemy would be back.

Dar hoped Ax Company would be ready for them.

The trench was just about five feet deep, a little bit short of being full cover for the taller members. Ocktur's own head stuck up above ground level, providing a target for almost any archer. As Ax Company walked around their section, Dar sized up their chances. The trench was longer than the opening in the palisades, but Ocktur only expected them to defend the opening.

"All right, Ax Company, listen up." Everyone stopped and turned their attention to their Sergeant. Another grin started across his face. "In celebration of our deployment, it's time for your first meal. Section leaders, go after me. Each section will then eat in order of their ranking. The lower your section leader ranks, the later you eat. If the last section doesn't get enough, so be it. If you take food, you must eat it. Scraps lead to rats, and rats lead to disease, and I don't want a bunch of mold and crap in the trench." Ocktur rubbed his hands together, ready to begin. "We will adjust the rankings as needed, even from day to day if a section's actions require it."

From behind the palisades came the chow wagon, loaded with breads and fresh fruits and stew in a huge kettle. There was fish chowder steaming in the front part of the wagon and a big keg of beer in the back. The cook's kitchen hands dug out plates and utensils for the hungry; the kitchen hands looked like pigs with short, stubby human bodies.

As Ocktur helped himself, Deek and Zander mingled their way over to Dar.

"What are they?" Deek seemed concerned that so many weird creatures roamed the land.

"Orcs," Dar murmured. Not exactly what he was thinking of when the food line started.

Zander mumbled a moment before he found his voice. "Aren't orcs, well, evil?"

Dar nodded. "But they might just be the hired hands, I guess. Although, some armies use prisoners as a work force."

"But as cooks?" Deek looked at Zander, who again appeared speechless. "Either hired or captives, it just doesn't feel right."

Dar agreed. "This will take some getting used to. We can't exactly ask Ocktur about it."

Ocktur's voice boomed loud now that his plate was full. "Drots! In line! First section is Joolan, Dyo, and Pesha. You will be first of the troops to eat."

Ocktur waited while Drots served up his food and the other three gathered next in line, congratulating each other, albeit with what appeared to be a bit of mistrust. Once Ocktur saw Drots had his food, he paused to swallow a big bite of meat. Then he continued with the announcements.

"Jusin! Second section is Upny, Gramal, and Banes."

They too celebrated and got into line, Jusin just behind Drots and Upny, Gramal and Banes tucked behind Pesha in line.

Modo smiled. He was surely the other leader.

"That leaves third section." He grinned. "The other sections should not get used to these individuals. They will probably not survive out here very long." Ocktur paused to shove another big piece of meat into his mouth. "Third section leader is Dar. The rest of you maggots are the leftovers."

"What!" Modo yelled.

"Modo, I don't want to kill you while I'm eating. If you have a problem, take it up with your section leader, who will inform me of the issue. But since there isn't an issue here, I won't hear anything."

Modo turned to Dar. "You couldn't lead a hungry dog to a carcass! I will kill you!" Modo swung at Dar, who just barely ducked out of the way. Dar looked around for a weapon, since Modo was much stronger than he was. Modo had every advantage except one.

The chain of command.

Ocktur rushed in from Modo's blind side, tackled him to the ground, and held his dinner knife to Modo's throat. With all of Ocktur's weight on him, Modo, even with his massive strength, couldn't move.

Modo struggled for a minute, but relaxed when he realized Ocktur wasn't going to harm him. Much.

"We have rules in this army," Ocktur said. "I follow the brigade commander, who follows the division commanders, who follow the orders of the Lord Protectorate. And you will follow the orders of your section order like they were words right out of my mouth. Disobey him and you disobey me. Disobedience is death." Ocktur released Modo and stood up. "Starting now, anybody who does not follow the orders of the section leader has forfeited their lives. We will have order!"

Ocktur flung his knife, handle side down, at Modo. The wood of the handle hit flat on his head and bounced a couple feet away. The message was clear to Dar: blade side down and Modo would have been dead.

As if nothing had happened, Ocktur returned to his plate. "Modo," he said between bites, "you eat last tonight."

After getting his plate, Dar went and sat on the ground next to where Deek and Zander had been standing. They were in line now, but Dar sat with his plate and waited for them. Modo hung out at end of the line, hoping to get something. After what seemed to be a while, Deek and Zander joined him on the ground. Modo sat by himself. His plate had some food on it, but probably not enough, Dar imagined.

"Dig in, guys," Dar said between mouthfuls. He knew none of them had eaten in a couple of days, so they must be famished.

"So, do we call you Dar, or Section Leader?" Deek said between mouthfuls.

"I don't know. Knowing Ocktur, Section Leader, but who knows?"

"You know, the stew isn't that bad." Zander spooned a mouthful from a particularly full bowl of the stuff. "Did anybody try the fish?"

"I saw Modo try it." Deek held a piece of bread to mouth, holding it back until his comment was done. "It was all he took, even though there was very little of it left. There was still a bit of bread left." He ripped off a chunk and devoured it.

"He will be a challenge for me, and for us." Dar bit into a piece of fruit. Only a couple of people took the fruit. It was a little past fresh, but not actually rotten yet. Dar munched on an apple while he looked at everyone's plates. Meat, meat, meat, mixed, meat, mixed, mixed, meat, empty (some people ate very fast, it seemed), another empty, and the plates of the Vanander brothers, who had mostly fruits and breads with a touch of meat. Dar munched on the bread—it was actually very good.

Ocktur had walked up to the kitchen hands now. "Tell the cook that the meat needs to be cooked less. Or just have some raw meat for those that like it like that."

Zander wrinkled up his face. "Raw?" he whispered before cutting off a slice of apple.

"I have given up being surprised, brother." Deek's face had lost all emotion. "You should do the same."

"That's good advice." Dar stared at Ocktur. "But it can be hard to follow."

The meal left the starved recruits a little lethargic. But Ocktur, having been well fed the whole time, was full of energy.

"Ax Company! File into line formation."

The group collected into their line at a relatively slow pace.

"Now that we have the sections numbered and filled, we will line up our formation by section. Drots, you and the rest of the first section come first, followed by second section and then the third." He glanced around. "Move!"

It took a couple of seconds with Modo lagging behind. He stood as far away from Dar as possible.

"Now remember, every time I say 'line formation,' you get into this order. I want to be able to take the first section with me, since I will be at the front of the formation. We can practice more formations later, but this is the one we need for now. If the section leaders want to do more training, that is up to them. You just better be able to do what I want the whole company to do."

Ocktur walked to the front next to Drots. "This is where I will be when we are in battle. We will start in the line and break down in sections from there. When I say 'section one move left, section three cover the rear,' you will do what I order, is that clear?"

"Yes, Sergeant!" cried the whole company.

"I hope so," Ocktur said. "Now I want each section leader to hold section drills until our weapons and supplies show up. This will happen shortly. Once it does, each section will billet on their own in a circle. Since we are at the front line, there will be no fires after dark. Dismissed."

Ocktur walked away from Drots. He wanted to be a little more centrally located so he could watch the section leaders in action.

The Vanander brothers moved over to form a semicircle with Dar. Modo remained several steps away, but close enough for Dar.

"So, what do each of you consider your area that requires the most improvement?" Dar looked at each man in turn, but none offered up. "Perhaps you'd like to go first, Zander?"

Zander fumbled for words for a moment, then found his voice. "I really have zero combat ability. I don't consider"—he dropped his voice to a whisper—"the training that Ocktur gave us anywhere near complete enough for us to survive. I bet he's hoping we won't."

Dar could see the fear in Zander's face. He knew he had to help lift the immense burden he could see Zander was feeling. Dar wasn't sure he was ready for this, but looking at Zander, he could tell the younger Vanander was even less ready. "That isn't relevant anymore," Dar told him, their eyes locking for a moment. "You boys work for me now, and I work for him. So worry about what I think, and I'll worry about he thinks. What about you, Deek? How are you doing?"

"Pretty much the same as my brother. I'm a little better at fighting, but not with an ax. If we get axes, we're going to have troubles."

"Yes, axes are pretty rough," Dar said. "If you swing too hard, it leaves you very exposed. Don't swing hard enough, and you won't be effective." Dar paused, thinking of what he could do. "I'll see what I can do to get something else. What would you guys prefer?"

"Swords." Zander nodded as he spoke.

"Definitely swords." Deek looked off in the distance, then caught Dar's eye again. "Long, short, broad, anything."

"What about you, Modo? What would you like to work on?"

Modo looked as disinterested as anyone Dar had ever seen. Armed crossed, bored, blank expression, Modo's disgust was obvious to anyone who looked at him. "Modo is perfect. I don't need training."

The Vanander brothers looked at each other as each furrowed an eyebrow. Dar, though, was careful to appear unconcerned.

"What type of weapon would you prefer?" Dar's kept his voice flat and without emotion.

"I fight best without a weapon," Modo said, flashing his sharp teeth and scratching his face with his talons. "I enjoy tasting the blood of my enemy as it flows off my claws. Weapons are for the weak."

"I believe I asked you a question that you didn't answer. I order you, Modo, to tell me which type of weapon you will fight with." Dar raised his volume, projecting his voice to where he was sure Ocktur could hear it. Or at least Dar hoped he could hear it.

Modo glanced at Ocktur, who was now staring at third section. "A spear. Or trident. None of your swords."

"Was that so hard?" Dar looked Modo in the eye and only saw hate. "I know you don't like me, Modo. I don't like you. But if you want to survive, we must work as a team, and you must pay attention to my commands. If you don't want to survive, the enemy line is that way." Dar pointed across the trench to the unseen enemy off in the distance.

"Third section will be first section soon enough," Zander offered. "If we work hard, practice hard, and help each other out, we'll be the best."

"Then Modo will become section leader," Modo said, his eyes thinning to slits, scowling.

"Why not?" Dar ignored the implied threat.

"Weapons are here! Form up!" Ocktur yelled so suddenly that Dar almost jumped. Quickly, Ax Company got into formation. The weapons wagon stopped next to Ocktur, and as was the norm, he helped himself first. He pulled out a double-headed ax and a long knife. He then nodded at Drots, who helped himself a shortsword and a dagger. Dar watched as each section leader stood next to the person at the front of the line and approved of their choices. Each man took the exact same combination as their section leader. Then it was third section's turn. Ocktur lingered near the cart.

"What'll it be?" Another orc stared out from the top of the wagon.

"Longsword." The orc tossed down a sword. It had no sheath, and as Dar picked it up, he noticed that it had very little edge.

"Next!"

Zander was next in line. "Shortsword." The orc dug in the pile and pulled out another sword and tossed it to the ground. It was equipped with a sheath. Zander scooped it up and stood behind Dar.

"Next!"

Deek stepped forward. "Shortsword." Again the orc complied. This time the sword had no sheath, and like Dar's sword, appeared to be pretty dull.

"Next!"

Modo stepped up to the front. And said nothing.

"What'll it be, solider?" grunted the orc.

Modo said nothing.

"The solider will have a trident or spear." Dar spoke in a low voice.

"Trident? What you doin'? Fishin'?" The orc grinned.

"Just go look," Ocktur told him.

The orc stepped into the bowels of the wagon and reappeared with a spear. "'Tis the best I can do." And he tossed it down. Modo grabbed it out of the air, then walked behind Dar the way Deek and Zander had.

"Now that we are armed and dangerous," Ocktur said, "we can practice until the supply wagon comes by. First section, you practice here." He pointed to his right. "Second, you're there." He pointed to his left. "And third, you're right here with me." He grinned.

Dar stepped forward. "What are your orders, Sergeant?"

"I have none. I just wanted to watch the soon-to-be-first section practice." He chuckled, his eyes darting in Zander's direction. "So I can learn too."

"Yes, Sergeant." Dar turned, not letting his concern show. Ocktur clearly had better hearing than he had figured. He would have to watch his step, and remind the brothers about it as well. "Okay, guys, get your weapon out. First thing we need to do is figure out how well balanced the weapon is and learn to make it part of our body." Dar presented his own weapon as an example. "My weapon, for example, is a little heavy in the blade." Each soldier of his section took out his weapon and held it the way Dar was holding his. "Modo, your weapon is different than the rest, so you'll need to improvise your own practice regime. But, being an expert with it, I don't think that will be a problem for you."

Modo said nothing. He was just stretching, using the spear more as a staff or stretching pole than a spear. Ocktur observed this with a sour face but said nothing.

"Zander," Dar said, "tell me about the balance of your weapon."

"Mine is light, yet firm." Zander swished it around. "It has remarkable balance and a great feel. I feel like this weapon has been mine for a long time."

"Excellent. Deek?"

"Mine is like yours, I guess. It doesn't want to stay in my hand." Deek flicked it from side to side. It fell out of his hand. The blade fell point first into the ground, but it bounced rather than penetrating the ground. "I rather don't like it."

"It is all you have," Ocktur said, his eyes still on Modo.

"Then we will make it work," Dar said.

Ocktur locked eyes with Dar. "You keep up your efforts until the supply cart comes. I need to see first section."

He walked away slowly, calling back over his shoulder, "Or should I call them second, Mr. Dar?"

"Yes, Sergeant!" Dar chirped.

By the time the supply cart arrived, Deek and Zander thought their sword arms would fall off. As other groups executed practice exercises, Dar made the brothers do them too. Dar had them practice spin moves, thrusts, slashes, overhead smashes, how to quickly pick their weapons up off the ground and how to keep the weapon and themselves always moving. The wagon could be heard before it could be seen, thanks to the palisades, which blocked their view. Dar held up his hand as soon as he heard the clanking of the pots and pans of the cart.

"Okay, everyone, take a break until Ocktur calls us into formation."

"What do you think we'll be able to get?" Zander rubbed his bicep.

"I don't think we'll have much choice. I bet we'll all get the same stuff," Dar said, standing with arms crossed. All the moss work had him in slightly better shape than Zander. While his arms ached too, he didn't want to tip off Modo. Or Ocktur.

Deek couldn't let things be. "Or we'll get a bunch of garbage to share or worse we'll get the sad leftovers and not have enough."

"We'll make do." Dar shot Deek a look that warned him it was over for now.

Finally, the cart came into view. It was a much larger than the weapon wagon, and Dar wondered why it was called a cart. Carts, to him, were small things. This was a house on wheels. It was being pulled by two giant lizards. The scaly creatures looked pretty dimwitted, and only the food in front of their faces seemed to motivate them. The cart was two stories in size, with pots, pans, tins, and ration barrels hanging from every side. The top was covered in a thick cloth, which appeared to be a composed in part of clothes, rather than a single sheet of fabric.

"Ax Company, line formation!" Ocktur bellowed, then moved in direction of the cart. The driver, another Orc, pulled on the food goodie in front of the lizards, and once it was out their line of sight, they stopped. The orc jumped onto the back of the lizard to the left and pulled a strip of black cloth out of his pocket. He shimmed up the neck of the lizard and tied the cloth around its head, covering its eyes. Ocktur tapped his foot, appearing impatient, but the orc simply jumped to the back of the other lizard and slowly made his way up its neck. Ocktur cleared his throat.

The orc pulled out another cloth and started to tie it as he spoke to no one in particular. "If I don't cover their eyes, they will eat your company. Seems to me that I wouldn't be doing my job if'n all of yous got killed."

"Just hurry up," Ocktur huffed.

The orc took his time, maybe just to add insult to injury. He then worked his way to the cart and dug a scroll out. It was pretty sizable. "You want the standard, or do you have any special requests?"

"Standard." Ocktur's patience had clearly left him. "Right away, lackey."

"Yes, Sergeant. Three lean-tos for four, two tents for four, cooking materials for fourteen, two weeks' iron rations for twelve, fresh rations for two, repair tools for the palisades, including ax, sharpening stone for ax, and shovel. I've also got supplies for sending messages back to his Lordship and wound kits to help fix those nasty little cuts those swords will give to you when under attack."

"We will also need some lanterns and oil," Ocktur stated.

"Not all nightseers?" The orc shook his head. "The people they let in this ar…"

"Just get to work, oaf."

As the orc disappeared into the cart, Ocktur turned around and addressed the company. "When he's done, I want you, Drots, to pick your supplies first. Each section gets a lean-to. I get a tent, and so do the extra rations. Each section must take their iron rations. I get the normal rations. Anybody taking from my rations will get killed. Taking another's rations will get you a taste of my fist. Should I need to, I will redistribute the rations and supplies. If you damage, lose, or eat your supplies before the cart comes back, you will not be getting any of mine."

The orc started throwing stuff out of the cart and onto the ground.

"Start stowing that equipment!" Ocktur ordered. "I want the tents behind the palisades and the lean-tos just off the gap. We will billet behind the palisades, close enough to get into the trench quickly."

The first tent set landed on the ground. The sun started to turn the horizon into a sea of red.

Ocktur turned his back to the supplies. "I want to be setup before it gets dark. I bet that tomorrow the enemy will come for a visit."

FOUR

Steel

"Fear is a natural first reaction to almost anything, but it must not last."
—Elader the Old

Being the third section did have some advantages. For in-
stance, Dar was able to hear the kicking and grunts of
Ocktur's normal wake-up routine when he arrived the next
morning at section one, so he was able to wake his troopers
before Ocktur got there.

As he came down the line, their sergeant spoke. "Our
first action today will be to practice getting into the trenches.
Having spent the last day in religious fasting and repentance,
our enemy will come calling today. I want to be ready. It will
probably be a line of skirmishers or a couple of scouts—since
Battle and Cutter was here, the enemy won't send a squad to
attack us directly. Once we beat them off, I figure we'll have
the rest of the day to practice."

Ocktur started to walk toward the trench, then turned around, once again, to address them.

"You must be able to get into the trench in less than three beats. If the attackers are on horseback, you'll be just ahead of them. If they come with arrows, you'll be in the trench safely by then. If they're engaging in skirmishes, you'll have more time. We've been told by command that there will be no magic, so you don't have to worry about that."

Dar looked at the trench. The morning was still a little chilly. The water at the bottom of the trench looked even colder.

"First section! Go!" Drots led them from their lean-to to the trench. Splashes echoed around the area as they jumped in.

"Second section!" Jusin and company ran to the ramp that fed into the trench and then turned away from Drots's team to fill up the other part of the trench.

"Third section!" Dar's heart started beating double time as he ran toward the trench. He counted to himself as he ran.

One.

His eyes darted along the edge of the trench, figuring on the best place to get into the trench. Jump in like Drots, or run down the ramp like Jusin?

Two.

Drots's team had spread away from Jusin's team, so there was space at the ramp. The ramp it would be.

Three.

Dar felt the sting of the cold water as he collided with the front edge of the trench. He had been going too fast and really hit the wall hard. But there was no time to assess the damage; Modo was right behind him.

Four.

Deek hit the bottom of the ramp. Apparently, he had also misjudged his speed, as he too collided with the wall. Dar moved over to give Zander a little more room.

Five.

Zander jumped down from the back edge of the trench straight into the trench. The splash from the water covered all four of them with water, with Deek getting the worse of it. But that didn't matter. What mattered was how long it had taken them to get into the trench. Dar turned to look towards Ocktur.

Ocktur stood in silence for a moment. Then he took a deep breath and then started his critique. "Most of you are now dead. The survivors would be using your bodies as shields. The trench is safety. Get there or get dead. Let's try it again!"

Ocktur waited as Ax Company filed out of trench. Zander, last as always, was just clearing the ramp when Ocktur spoke again.

"Back into the trenches, boys. Our training just turned into the real thing."

Out in the plains leading up to the trenches were three horses, and hanging on behind each rider were two small attackers. They stood on stirrup-like platforms hanging down from each rider's saddle. The force was bearing down on their position pretty fast. The horses were on them by the time Ocktur got them back into the trench.

"Hold until they dismount," he said. "When they come to the trench, let them have it!"

Dar peered over the edge of the trench at the horses. They didn't appear to be slowing down.

"Deek, Zander, Modo, move near the ramp."

Modo turned to Dar. "Why?"

"I don't think they're going to stop before the line."

"Ocktur thinks so." Modo's smoldering anger surfaced as a look of disgust.

"I don't. You want me to make it an order?" Dar stared at Modo, trying to figure out what his agenda was.

"Yes." Modo spoke through clenched teeth.

"I order you to move over there, by the ramp." Dar used his sternest voice.

"Yes, Section Leader." Modo moved, albeit very slowly. Dar pushed past him and met up with Zander and Deek, who were already at the ramp. Dar turned back to the horses, just in time to see them jump over them and past the trench.

"Ax Company, deploy to the camp!" Ocktur screamed, caught in the middle of the trench, next to first company.

"Third section, move! Move! Move!" Dar started to run as he spoke, Deek and Zander by his side.

As soon as the horses could stop after crossing behind the palisades, they did. Quickly, they turned back toward the opening, and the two side-troopers jumped off their stirrup platforms and moved away from the horse. Free from their payload, the horses and their riders raced around, staying away from would-be attackers.

Ignoring the horses, Dar sized up the six enemies as he ran toward their position. They were pretty short, about four feet tall, four and a half, tops. They had clubs, clearly hewn from trees. Their clothes were green with brown trim, and their shoes were made of cloth. As Dar's eyes met those of one of his enemies, he thought the face looked familiar. The ears were longer than human's but softer and flowing. The face looked young, but the eyes had a sense of age about them. If he had met this individual at the tower, Dar would have called him a Gruach, a type of wood elf. But the Gruach were a peaceful, loving race and rarely ventured far from their homes.

The Gruach turned and aimed a blow at Dar's midsection—he had heard him coming. Dar blocked the blow with his sword and countered with a chopping action to the gut. The blade didn't cut through cloth or skin, but the force of the blow knocked the wind out of the little monster. It folded in half and dropped its club. Dar focused on the next one—Deek and Zander were approaching it cautiously, and this Gruach seemed to understand it couldn't take both of them at the same time. It jabbed at them with its club, and they stood their ground. Dar located other four Gruach. They were in Ocktur's supply tent, taking things and smashing up the beer barrel and dumping the spoilable items onto the floor. Dar headed that way.

"Modo! You're with me!" Dar kept up his pace. Modo just walked.

By the time Dar was a couple of steps from the door, the Gruach were leaving the place, arms full of bread and fruits. Dar swung at the closest one and missed badly. There were too many targets, and Dar couldn't get a good swing on any of them. They yelled out something, and the three horses circled back to them. The rest of Ax Company was out of the trench, and Ocktur had them running toward the supply tent. Dar realized they wouldn't be able to catch them, since they were running to the tent and the Gruach were running away from it. So he dove and grabbed one by the ankle. It stopped, regained its balance, and kicked Dar in the face, forcing him to release his grasp. That bought the rest of the group enough time to get onto their rides, leaving only the one facing the brothers, along with the one that Dar had wounded.

The brothers appeared to be locked in a standoff with the Gruach—the brothers weren't willing to charge, and the Gruach was waiting for them to make a move. But where was the downed Gruach?

Dar saw him too late, as the Gruach knocked the weapon out of Zander's hand with his left hand and punched him in the groin with his right. Zander collapsed with a groan. While Deek was distracted by his brother, the defending Gruach threw his club at Deek, which hit him squarely in the head. He fell over backward, and blood started flowing down his face. Now free of their adversaries, the two remaining Gruach jumped onto the back of the closest horse and flew off back toward their lines.

The whole battle had taken less than five minutes, and the tally wasn't pretty. They had lost almost a third of Ocktur's supplies. Deek was down and bleeding, though it wasn't probably serious. They had inflicted no damage on the opponent—well, at least none that was permanent—and only had the two clubs the Gruach had abandoned as trophies.

"Section leaders, in my tent! Now!" Ocktur stormed off to his tent.

Each slowly made his way into the tent, knowing the wrath that awaited them. Dar was last into the room. Each section leader sat on the floor, spaced evenly out, allowing Ocktur room to walk around the tent.

"That was a *disgrace*!" Ocktur began, screaming in a shrill voice. "We were out of position, slow to react, and only the worst leader in the group showed any initiative. If the lieutenant was here, he'd skin all of us."

"That trench really limits our ability to deploy," Drots said in a low voice.

"The trench is our first line of defense!" Ocktur paced back and forth, weaving his way in between each section leader. "Anything that gets past the front needs to be stopped by us."

"Then perhaps we should have another layer of defense behind it?" Dar hoped his voice wouldn't waver. He knew his idea was sound, but he hoped his tone wouldn't betray his nervousness. "We could have a section in the trench and two more behind the palisades. If the enemy stops in front of the trench, the palisade sections can move up to help, and if the enemy breaks through, the palisade groups will hold the line while the trench troops hit them from behind."

Ocktur had stopped pacing. The room was silent. Drots looked at Dar, smiling. It was clear he thought Ocktur was going to level Dar and cement his own position as number one. As time passed, however, his smile started to evaporate. The wrath wasn't coming.

"The idea is interesting," Ocktur said. "We hold the trench as is our orders, but keep the major part of our force back under cover where they can keep their options open."

At that, Drots's face went blank.

"We will try your idea." Ocktur stormed out of the tent back into the area between the palisades. "Ax Company! Form up." The section leaders quickly followed him out of the tent and got into the line. "Based on that horrible performance, I'm changing our rules of deployment. We will now have one section in the trench, third section. The other two sections will locate themselves behind each side of the opening in the palisades. First section will be on the right, closest to the trench.

Second section will be on the left. It will be up to third section to hold the line until first and second can support them. Should another breakthrough occur, first and second will hold the line and third will strike from behind. Am I clear?"

"Yes, Sergeant!"

"Let us test our new stations. Everyone back to their lean-tos." Ocktur paced back and forth, apparently trying to calm himself down. Modo was the straggler again, and again Ocktur watched and waited. Finally, when they were close enough to their lean-tos, he gave them the signal. "Move!"

First and second section moved very quickly into position. Third had longer to travel, but Dar did his best to match their pace, and the brothers followed suit as they ran out into position. As usual, Modo just trotted along.

Seeing this, Ocktur appeared to snap.

He tackled Modo from behind and then pushed him onto his back. Modo raised his hands to protect himself from the blows of the bigger man, who was now positioned on his chest, scratching and fighting back. But he was no match for Ocktur's strength and size, and Modo lost consciousness. Ocktur delivered another couple of savage blows to his limp target, then stood up and then, just for good measure, kicked Modo in the side.

"You will respect me and my orders, or you will pay." Ocktur faced the other section members as he spoke. He was covered in blood, some his own, but mostly Modo's. "You disobey a section leader, you disobey me. You don't give it your all, you're disobeying me. You doubt my word, you disobey me. You disobey me, and your punishment will be swift. You disobey me, and you will feel my wrath. You disobey me…"

He paused and stared each and every man in turn in the eye.

"And you will die."

He kicked Modo again and then turned and went into his tent.

Dar rushed over to Modo. He was still breathing, albeit shallowly. His face was bloodied and his scaly skin was ruptured in a couple of places. Dar wasn't sure what to do. The rest of the company stood around and watched as Dar and the rest of third section decided their next move.

"We need to take him back to the lean-to," Dar said to the brothers.

"He's a troublemaker. We should let him meet his fate." Deek remained standing.

"It's not right to do nothing." Zander dropped to his knees and helped Dar. "Let's carry him together, Dar."

Dar nodded, and the pair lifted. Modo was much heavier than they were ready for. Deek came around alongside to lift his legs, apparently trying to make amends. "Then we'll do the right thing together," he said.

The other members of the sections just watched as the three dragged Modo back to the lean-to, leaving a trail of blood.

"We need to stop the bleeding," Dar said when they had reached the lean-to. He looked around for a rag or towel.

"How about his bedroll?" Deek motioned over to the corner that Modo called his own.

"Better than nothing."

"He's a swamp creature. Should we get him wet?"

"Great idea, Zander." Dar motioned with his head to Deek, who ran off to take care of it. They used a sock to help stanch some of the bleeding around his head while they waited. But Deek had only been gone a few moments when he returned.

"They won't let me use the drinking water for his wounds," he told them.

Dar pondered this for a moment then gave Deek new orders. "Use the water from the bottom of the trench. It's not clean, but I'm guessing he won't mind."

Deek was gone but a moment, and when he came back the rag he'd taken with him was dripping with water. "I tried to dip in a clear part," he said.

"It will do." Dar used the rag to moisten Modo's head, neck, and shoulders. Right away, Modo's skin began to generate a slime that soon covered his wounds and formed a seal. Dar quit dabbing the areas that were already covered or it looked like the slime would soon reach. Dar placed the rag over Modo's eyes and then sat down to figure out what to do next.

Zander was still worried. "If this doesn't work, what do we do?"

"You bury him." The voice was Jusin's. He'd come by to see how things were going.

"I think you're wasting your time." Drots appeared beside him. "Modo's been dogging you since you were assigned section leader. I would have let him die, if that was to be his fate."

Dar stood up. "All due respect, Drots," he said, "I'm not you. I believe every man is important."

"All due respect just means that you're telling me I'm wrong, but you don't want to say it that way." Drots smiled. "We'll see."

"Is he going to make it?" Jusin kneeled down beside Modo, who remained motionless.

"I have no idea." Dar let his eyes drift down to Modo. "I don't even know what he is, so I don't know how to heal him, or what he's capable of."

"Yeah, that isn't good." Jusin stood up. "Ocktur will settle down soon and will be wondering what's happening with Modo."

Dar didn't look at Jusin while he spoke, he just looked at Modo. "He didn't give me any orders to not help him."

"It's your face," Drots said flatly. He turned and walked back to his lean-to.

But Jusin held back for a moment, looking Dar in the eye. "Be careful," he said. "You seem like a good guy. We don't need to lose you too." He pointed to Modo. "He's not worth it." Then he pointed in the general direction of the brothers. "They are. Remember that."

Dar let a moment of hope cross his face as he looked at Jusin. "I will."

Dar and the Vanander brothers went back to the trench ramp to practice with their weapons. Dar started out sparring against Zander, who needed the most help.

After standing around for a while, Deek got a little bored and wandered onto the ramp and down into the bottom of the trench. He could still hear the clunking sound of sword versus sword as he looked for anything interesting. The water was up to his ankles; it was clear until you stepped in it, then it turned brown. Deek could see little details he hadn't noticed the first time they'd practiced in the trench. There were little niches along the front side of the trench. Some had indentations suggesting they were either handholds or footholds. Some didn't have any marks, which made Deek think they were storage cubbies for whatever the last company here had needed to use while stuck in the trench. One niche had a piece of something, probably food, that was now covered in mold and maggots. Deek moved on, farther along down the trench, and eventually found a small rock in a niche at waist height. The stone was slate gray, with what appeared to be streaks of gold wrapping around its widest point. He picked it up and examined it; the stone was lighter than he'd figured it would be. It was warm and quickly made him feel warm too. It seemed out of place here, so Deek placed it into this pocket and continued. He only got a couple of steps before he heard Dar's voice from above.

When he returned to the surface, Dar turned to face him. "Deek, your turn to spar with me." He returned to Zander and said, "You stay here and watch us to see if you can learn anything."

Dar had been practicing constantly since his match with Modo, and only the fact that there were two Vananders to spar with had left either of the brothers any energy. Dar had found that he loved to practice the vicious dance of combat, and he was a natural at it.

Dar sized up Deek. "You ready?"

"Yes." Deek drew his sword up to the defensive position. Dar motioned him to make the first move. Deek obliged, aiming first for Dar's sword. The sword dropped to the ground. Deek stopped.

"That was unusual." Dar looked at Deek.

"Why?" Deek felt a little flush.

"The binding on the hilt of my sword just gave out."

Both brothers came over to look at it.

"Why, it's just twine," said Zander.

"How odd it chose now as the time to fail." Deek looked down at his own hilt, apparently to see if it was wearing out too.

"It came straight off," Dar said, shaking his head. "Zander, check yours."

"My sword is looking great." Zander motioned for Dar to check it out. "The hilt is actually padded, not twine."

"Interesting." Deek reached for the sword. "May I?"

Zander handed it to him by the pommel. "Sure, but it's mine." He smiled.

Deek grabbed it. "This sword is very light." He swished it around. "It almost feels like it's guiding me to strike." He paused and looked at the blade. "It's perfect. I don't even see any marks where your weapon hit Dar's sword." He held his brother's sword away from his body and said to Dar, "Go ahead, hit it."

Dar swung right at the cutting face of the sword and hit it. The sword swung back a bit in Deek's grip under the impact. But when Dar looked at his sword, there was a notch in the blade. Deek held his up—nothing.

"A magic blade?" Dar wondered out loud.

"That's what I would think." Deek changed the way he was holding it so the grip was free and motioned to Zander. As Zander took up the grip, Deek let his hand drop. "I think we should keep this our little secret. Others will want it."

Dar nodded. "It is valuable."

"Sure is lucky we figured that out before our next battle." Zander smiled as he slid the weapon back into its scabbard.

"Sure is." Dar nodded.

"Uh. Dar." Deek had his back to the front lines and was peering out of the opening between the palisades. "Ocktur is coming."

Dar turned around and braced himself for what was sure to be Ocktur's wrath. "Sergeant," he said when Ocktur appeared.

"Section Leader Dar." Ocktur stopped an arm's length away from his charge. "I wish to speak to you."

"Yes, Sergeant."

A furrowed brow showed Ocktur's intensity. He had cooled down to a slow simmer, it appeared. "I am going to the rear to address some issues. I will be in the area of the Abbey, and you will not be able to reach me. I will not be returning until past dawn tomorrow. I want you to have guards posted all night, just in case our friends across the line decide to get interesting. You are not to countermand any of my standing orders, nor are you to post any orders that last longer than I am gone. You are not to touch my tent, my rations, or any of my possessions. When we get a new recruit, you will get a replacement for Modo. And—"

Dar risked it and interrupted. "If I may, Sergeant, Modo isn't dead yet."

"You're treating him?" Ocktur's eyes narrowed and a note of anger back crept into his tone.

"As little as possible, Sergeant." Dar figured that would help him.

"Why?"

"If nothing more than to act a target, as my Sergeant directed me." Dar readied himself for a blow, bracing his chin.

"I didn't give any orders about him, did I?" Ocktur's eyes widened.

"No, Sergeant."

"And so you figured you would do what you wanted." Ocktur's head was tilted slightly to one side.

"All my actions were contained within third section, Sergeant, and Modo will not impact the ability of the other sections to fight."

"See to it that it stays that way." Ocktur straightened up. "Next time he crosses me, his life will be forfeit. Tell him that if he survives. I've had enough of him, and I would rather remove the disease than let it spread."

"Yes, Sergeant." Dar nodded.

"You are in charge while I am gone. I have told Jusin and Drots, and they were, well"—Ocktur looked off into the distance and then back at Dar—"not amused." Ocktur appeared to be fighting off a smile at his own joke. "They will challenge your authority, I imagine, so this is a test for you. I told them specifically not to kill you while I was gone, and should you die, I told them I would make them join you in the afterlife. So know that if you are killed, I will extract revenge."

"Thanks, Sergeant." Dar's words were hollow. He was still trying to wrap his mind around being in charge, and how he would deal with Drots.

Ocktur's eyes darted to the source of the building wind. "With any luck, that line of clouds coming from over the enemy lines will bring rain, and everyone will just stay in their lean-tos and not try to be a hero."

Dar ached to look, but to turn away from a superior was tantamount to disobeying him, and Dar knew what that would cost.

"Enjoy your night, Dar." Ocktur turned and started to walk away, then stopped and called back, "I know I will enjoy mine."

After Ocktur was well behind the palisades, Deek and Zander came over to talk to Dar.

"What was that about?" Zander said.

"I'm in charge for a while." Dar turned and looked at the clouds in the distance. The clouds' bottoms were black like coal, but that black faded toward their tops, which were a perfect white, whiter than anything Dar had ever seen. Noticing Dar's focus on the horizon, Zander turned to look too.

"The top of the cloud is like snow," Zander said to Deek. "Remember the snow back home during sunsrest?"

"Sunsrest?" queried Dar. "You mean winter?"

"We used to get feet of snow sometimes."

"I've never seen snow," Dar said sadly. "Only heard of it."

"It's pretty, but very cold." Zander's smile had too much sadness in it.

"I'm from the southern part of Holimoren. We don't get snow." Dar focused on the coming storm again. "But we do get rain. And we are going to get lots of it tonight."

It was just after nightfall when the rains started in earnest. Dar sat on the floor of the lean-to and contemplated how he was going to deal with the night. "I don't trust anybody but the people in this section," he said, looking at the floor.

"Modo excluded, of course," Deek interjected.

"Modo excluded. But I don't think he'll bothering us tonight." Dar looked up. "Here is what I want to do. Zander, you will take the first watch. Deek, you'll take the second, and I'll take the last shift. We'll do three to four hours each, and that should get us to dawn. Once there, I think Ocktur will be back, and we'll be in good shape. Until then"—he looked to each brother in turn—"I'd be worried about any one of us getting a knife in the back."

"When the lord's away, the drama will play," Deek stated.

"Didn't Aunt Gertrude say that?" Zander was clearly piqued by his brother's reference. "Or was it Mother?"

"It was Gertie, and it was just as true then as it is now." Deek turned to look at his brother. "We could be in trouble tonight."

"The weather should dampen everything down enough to make everyone stay at home." Dar held the eye of each brother in turn. "If we do things right, we should be in good shape."

"What about Modo?" Zander turned to the fallen man. His face was all covered with mucus and the rag they had lain across his eyes.

"Perhaps he would be better out in the rain?" Deek suggested. "He's a swamp creature—I bet if he was awake, he'd already be out there."

"Good idea." Dar stood up. "Then Deek, you and I can get to sleep and Zander can mount the watch."

They dragged Modo out into the rain. It was pretty warm for this time of night, and the humidity of the storm didn't make it any cooler. The rain was tolerable because of the temperature, but Dar imagined that when summer was over, this type of rain could get miserable. He resolved to not be here when that happened.

The sound of a thunderclap reverberated throughout the encampment. There was only a small flash up in the clouds, but the thunder echoed for what seemed like minutes.

By the time the rolling thunder stopped, they had Modo out in the rain. Dar and Deek walked back into the lean-to and tried to find a dry place to lie down. Zander lingered just inside its shelter.

The lean-to was an odd construct. Two shorter poles on one side countered taller poles at the side with the door. A light mesh hung from the canvas roof to near the floor. The mesh only seemed to stop birds, though, and not insects, as had clearly been intended. Barely keeping anything dry, the floor was rapidly turning to mud as water flowed right through the space. Dar looked for a moment to find a dry spot and gave up. He returned his gaze to Zander.

"When you get tired," Dar told him, "come get the next one of us. Remember to look out for the enemy on the south end as well as in at the encampment. Foes are at both ends." Dar settled down on the hard ground and hoped the thunder wouldn't keep him awake.

"I understand," Zander said. "See you in the morning." He walked out into the rain. Dar was certain he could hear Zander say, under his breath, "I hope."

The next thing Dar was aware of was Deek standing over him in the dead of night. Deek was soaking wet, his eyes bleary and showing fatigue. He had reached the end of his endurance, and it was Dar's turn now.

"All right," he said. "I'm ready. Go ahead and lie down."

Deek nodded and lay down. He didn't even bother to change gear. "I found that pacing around keeps you awake longer. Keep moving and you'll keep awake."

"Good advice," Dar said. "Sleep now, you've earned it." He clutched his sword and stepped out into the rain.

It wasn't a particularly hard rain, but a good, soaking one. Dar had barely made it to the opening in the palisades by the time he was soaked to the skin. There was little to see in the direction of the enemy. There was no movement other than the falling drops, no sound but the patter of rain and slightly gurgling sound of the small rivers that flowed into the trench. Dar had excellent nighttime vision, but still, there was little to see. He figured out where the trench was and made sure to stop well short of it. If he fell into the trench face first, that could be fatal—if not the fall, then the water would do it.

Dar turned and faced the encampment, and beyond it by a long distance, the Abbey. It was ablaze with light from inside its hallowed walls; Dar noticed that its gentle features had taken on a dark tint in the gloom of the rainy night. Being the only thing that was illuminated made the Abbey easy to see at this distance.

He paced toward the Abbey until he was well out of the encampment. He paused, let out a long sigh, then turned and headed back. So it would be for the next three hours, until the sun began to bloom on the horizon.

As the sun rose, the enemy side took on some interesting details. There was an encampment well back from the one on the line, and judging by the small fires dotted up and down that line, the enemy troops were having a hot breakfast. The rising sun was to Dar's back as he faced the enemy lines. It occurred to him that was why the enemy would rarely attack in the morning; the sun in their face put them at a disadvantage. Attacking at dusk would be good for the enemy, but operations close to the curtain of night often got swallowed up by the inky blackness. Should something go wrong, or right for that matter, it would be hard to correct that wrong or exploit that right. Should people be left wounded along the enemy lines, they would be as good as dead. Should there be a break-through, night would force an end to operations, with their inability to coordinate making the attackers easy prey. Dar smiled into the lightening sky; he was starting to think like a soldier. And he had to admit it: except for Ocktur's rage and Modo's belligerence, he enjoyed what he was doing. Perhaps mage training wasn't for him.

FIVE

Welcome

"The bottom of every group knows the truth. The top knows only what they want to know. True leadership and vision never comes from the top."

—Elader the Old

At dawn Dar went to sleep on the floor of the lean-to, but not until he had turned over control of the group to Jusin. He needed a little nap, and he needed it before Ocktur arrived. Dar couldn't turn over command to either of the brothers, as it had to be given to another section leader, and Jusin seemed trustworthy enough. Better than Drots, who was sure to be upset over being passed over. Again. Long term this made things worse, but only if Drots made it a problem. For now, Dar just needed some rest. He left strict orders with Deek to wake him up the first sign of Ocktur.

Dar wasn't sure how long he had been asleep, but when he opened his eyes, he saw nothing but Deek's face.

"You gotta wake up." There was a tone of urgency in his voice that Dar hadn't expected.

"Ocktur?"

"Worse." The tone sounded fatalistic.

"What's worse than Ocktur?" Dar sat up and started to look around.

"Modo."

Dar got to feet and looked around for his sword. "Where is he?"

"He's in the trench." Deek started off in that direction. Dar jumped up to join him, and as they walked, they talked.

"He's okay?"

"He's…" Deek turned and looked at Dar. "Well…"

"Dead?"

They got to the trench. It had filled up almost a full stride up the ramp, making the water almost a man's leg deep. Modo was face down in the water, but he was moving around, albeit slowly.

Deek pointed at Modo. "I'm not sure what he's doing, but I am sure that it is not good. He ate some of the food from Ocktur's supply tent, and now he's here floating face down, moving slowly from one end of the trench to the other."

Dar studied the water. The fresh rain had very little sediment in it, so the water was pretty clear; he could see the mud at the bottom of the trench. Dar had to watch very carefully to see Modo moving at all—his movements were confined to just the smallest twitches of his legs.

Dar started toward the ramp. When his foot touched the water, Modo lifted his head, though his eyes were still closed.

"Modo's water," he said. "Stay out. If you muddy the water, Modo will kill you."

"Modo, this is your superior talking. Are you able to get out of the water?"

"You're not my superior, just the little man who is in charge of the third section."

"Ocktur is gone, and he put me in charge." Dar slowly moved his foot out of the water, so as to not stir up any sediment. "And I would like to know if you are better after your wounds and can you resume your duties."

"My healing is not yet over, but I am as you say, able to resume my duties. The freshwater is like from my home, and it helps my jelly to repair the damage. I do not fear Ocktur. Next time he won't be so lucky."

"You can deal with that when he gets back." Dar looked back at Deek, who just shrugged. "If you heal faster in the water, you can stay in there until the signal comes out that Ocktur is coming. Then you have to get out."

"Fine." Modo lowered his head down into the water again and floated away from Dar. As Dar watched, the gill slits on Modo's neck opened up—he could see them wriggling in the flow of the water. Whatever type of creature Modo was, Dar was hoping he wouldn't run into another one like him for a while. He walked up the ramp and ended up back with Deek.

"What did he take from the tent?" Dar asked.

Deek stared down at Modo. "I don't know."

"Why don't you know?"

"Nobody would go in and risk being killed if Ocktur showed up."

Dar furrowed his eyebrows. "So how do you know Modo was in there?"

"His footprints in the mud led from the door to here, and that's when I found him. He was covered in crumbs or something when he came out. I couldn't figure out what he'd gotten into, but I knew he had done something in there."

Dar started walking over to Ocktur's tent.

"You're not going in there, are you?"

"If I'm going to get beat for somebody taking something, I want to know what it is so Ocktur can't falsely accuse me."

Deek shook his head in mute protest. "Fine. Then let me join the watch party to make sure you have enough warning to get out of there before Ocktur shows up."

Dar looked Deek in the eye. "That is a great idea. I appreciate you looking out for me."

"I know you would do the same." Deek ran ahead of Dar, who stopped two more paces along, right at the front door of the tent.

"Remember, nice and loud if you see him." Dar swallowed hard and then went in.

Even though it was almost sunny outside, the tent was dark. It smelled like old, wet clothes, but Dar couldn't tell if that was normal or not, so he decided not to worry about it. He looked around, trying to figure out where Modo had been. A loaf of bread was chewed up, and one of the barrels of drink was off of its holding assembly. Dar shook the barrel. It was a small keg, really, only a couple gallons' worth inside when full. And it sounded like it had been taken for about half of its contents. Dar took a sip from the spigot. It was beer, and a very bitter one at that. Not being much of a beer drinker, he hoped he could water it down and not affect the flavor too much.

The bread was another matter—he figured there was nothing he could do about that, so he picked up the remains of the loaf and walked out. He walked over to their lean-to and hid the bread with their supplies. How he was going to get the water into the other barrel was something he hadn't figured out just yet, but it had to be done. Perhaps not all the way to the top, but enough to keep Ocktur from noticing. Dar grabbed his shirt and their little keg full of water and took off for the tent.

When he got back inside, Dar took the beer keg off of its holder and set it down so the spigot pointed up. He then pulled out the spigot and stuck in the shirt. He picked the cleanest part of the fabric and threaded it into the hole. He then twisted the shirt to make a wick out of it. Looking over his shoulder, he started to pour from one keg to another. The water clung to shirt, travelling down almost like a funnel, and Dar could hear the water working its way into the beer. He was a little sloppy, and some spilled down the front of the beer barrel, but after he judged that it was more or less where it should be in terms of volume, he set the water keg down. He pulled the shirt out and put the spigot back in. He gave it a good whack with the heel of his hand and started to raise it back into position. He was just about done when he heard those dreaded words.

"Ocktur, about two minutes away!" came Deek's voice ringing from the edge of camp.

Dar set the keg in place and made sure it wasn't leaking much. The excess water that had pooled up on the top of the keg flowed off the rim and down onto the floor, but there was no time to clean it up now. Dar grabbed the water keg and the wet shirt and quickly exited the tent. He was just inside his own shelter when he heard Ocktur's voice.

"Section Leader Dar! Report to my tent at once!"

"Yes, Sergeant!" Dar discarded the items he'd used to refill Ocktur's keg and made his way to the tent he had just left. By the time Dar got there, Ocktur was busy looking around for damaged or missing items.

"My keg is leaking." Ocktur pointed at the wet spot directly under the keg.

"Do you want me to push in the spigot better, Sergeant?" Dar left his face blank. Ocktur stared at him, clearly trying to get a read.

"That is not necessary, Section Leader." Ocktur sat down on his bed. "I have command of the unit now. You are relieved of duty."

"Yes, Sergeant."

"The protocol is to acknowledge my leadership by saying, 'You have the command, Sergeant'."

Dar could hardly believe that Ocktur wasn't all in a rage over this issue. But why question good luck? "You have the command, Sergeant."

"Report." Ocktur almost had a smile on his face. What had he done? And why has he in such a good mood?

"We had sentries posted all night, and no incursions occurred. Pretty quiet night, just like you predicted." Dar noticed that Ocktur wasn't looking at him, so Dar started to look around the tent a little.

"And what of Modo?" Ocktur was speaking in what for him were hushed tones.

Dar spoke softly but firmly. "He is doing better. I have him trying to recuperate as much as possible so he can contribute to the total efficiency of the unit, Sergeant."

Ocktur took a deep breath and let it out slowly. It was obvious that whatever had made him mellow was continuing to have its effect on him. "As you will learn when you get your own command, Dar, sometimes, as the leader, we need to do things we don't like. I will be honest and say I enjoyed beating him, but I'm glad that we don't have a man down. I just hope he has learned his lesson."

Dar was about to speak when another voice broke the silence.

It was Modo. He knocked on the wooden frame of the door.

"Permission to enter, Sergeant?"

"If you must." Ocktur put a hand to his head and rubbed it.

Modo's face still hadn't healed fully, but it looked better to Dar since the last time he'd seen him, just minutes ago.

"Sergeant, I would like to apologize to you for any disrespectful attitude and behavior. It will not happen again." Modo bowed his head and closed his eyes to accept the sergeant's judgment.

"I'm glad to see this change," Ocktur replied, "but I warn you that further failures will mean worse punishments." He paused as Modo nodded. "I'll admit I'm slightly pleased you're not dead; it means our unit will be at full strength when his Lordship arrives."

Dar snapped his head around to look at Ocktur. "His Lordship?"

Ocktur put his hands on his knees. "The Lord Protectorate of the City. The general in charge of the army is coming to visit our unit. It is a great honor."

"How soon?" Dar wondered why the usually uptight Ocktur wasn't freaking out about this. Ocktur's face was not betraying if this was an honor or a threat.

"When the sun reaches straight overhead."

"Well, we have our work cut out for us, don't we?" Dar looked at Ocktur. It was obvious to Dar that Ocktur was resigned to his fate at this point.

"I'll take my leave, Sergeant." Modo bowed.

"Dismissed." Ocktur waved his hand at Modo, who turned and exited the tent. Then he turned to Dar. "Get the other section leaders in here."

"Yes, Sergeant." Dar darted out of the tent.

He returned minutes later, Jusin and Drots in tow. Drots spoke for the whole group: "Reporting as ordered, Sergeant."

"His Lordship, the general who leads the Army of the Protectorate, is coming with his group to our company when the sun is directly overhead. That isn't long, and there is nothing we can do to improve our standing."

Drots held Ocktur's eye. "We can try to do something, Sergeant."

Jusin nodded. "Perhaps we could run extra drills?"

"I don't see it happening." Ocktur just looked off into space. "The die is already cast. After he looks at your sorry bunch, I'm sure I'll be relieved of my command."

Dar was silent for a while, then spoke. "Then let us do exactly what we would do if his Lordship wasn't coming. If he must judge us, let him judge us as we truly are."

"And if he finds that wanting, there is nothing we could have done to make him happy." Ocktur stood as he spoke. "That idea I can live with. Live as you are, die as you are." He pulled down a piece of dried meat that was hanging from one of his tent poles, then walked toward the door. "Let's have a normal day, then."

Dar led the others out of the tent. He watched Ocktur wait until his tent was clear of the others before stepping out into the world. Dar noticed he blinked hard; the tent was much darker than the sunny day outside. The troops were mostly just milling around, looking for something to do. Since all the section leaders were gone, they'd become inert. Dar figured the sight of Ocktur would get them active again.

"Ax Company! Fall in!" Ocktur wasn't going to leave anything to chance. He put on his commander face and scowled at anything and everything. "Time for drills!"

Ocktur watched as they darted back and forth, each member falling into position. It appeared as if he lingered on Modo—unusual in that he was actually one of the fastest to get into position—then moved on to inventory each person as they fell in line. As Jusin assumed his position, Ocktur started a short monologue.

"I'm sure most of you know I was at headquarters last night. I'm glad to say your section leaders didn't end up killing most of you for insubordination while I was gone. Today, we're going to do some drills. Each section will take turns being behind the palisades defending, and each will take turns being in front of the trenches attacking. The extra section will stand guard and keep score."

Ocktur looked for a reaction. There was none.

"First section will be the starting attackers. Second section will be defenders. Third section, if you can't figure out what you are, you aren't listening to me and I will correct that issue." He looked at Dar and then back at the whole group. "Then first section will be the defenders, third section will attack, and second will stand guard. Finally, third will defend, second will attack, and first will guard. But you already figured that out, didn't you?"

Ocktur scanned for reaction again. Dar wondered what he was waiting for. A hint of insubordination, maybe? Ocktur was searching for something in their eyes. Whatever it was, Ocktur's face said there was none of it to be found here. Yet.

"Go!"

Drots took first section off to the trench, and each member stopped to look down into the water to make sure nothing was lurking in it before they jumped across it. When they reached the other side, they turned and waited. Jusin led his group to the palisades, then they too turned and waited. Dar walked with Modo and the brothers to the other side of the palisades opening and turned his attention to the enemy encampment, looking for signs of life. He wanted to keep an eye on what was happening over there.

"All right, guys," he said. "I think there is plenty to learn by watching the others, so we'll watch the enemy in pairs and the other two can watch the fun. We'll take turns so nobody has to watch either for very long. Zander, Modo, you guys can watch first. On my signal, we'll rotate one person out at a time. Deek, you're with me."

"Yes, Section Leader." Modo spoke through his teeth, but it was a start. Zander turned and watched the action—careful, Dar saw, to stay just out of arm's reach of Modo. Deek moved to be next to Dar.

Ocktur signaled to Drots, making sure Jusin couldn't see the gesture, and first section sprung into action. Ocktur then signaled to Jusin, and the members of second section took their defensive positions. Jusin had posted a guard at the edge of the palisades, scanning for movement, and kept the rest of his people well behind the wall. Drots moved his team up and had them jump into the trench, hiding his numbers. The second section guard reported the movement back to Jusin, but they didn't do anything about it. Dar glanced over and saw

Zander watching as intently as ever. Dar spared a look at the rest of the drill. It entered into what came across as a stalemate period. It looked like Drots was doing some planning, but it was hard to tell.

Suddenly, three people ran up the ramp of the trench and started to move toward the edge of the palisades. The first section guard leaned back and was joined by the rest of the group, which then stepped into the opening. They were slightly behind the opening, their line of sight to the flank of each side obscured by the walls. Dar and the rest of the third company could see what second could not. During the feint, the last member of first company had come out of the trench farther down and had rushed up to the wall. When the fake attacker yielded the field of play to the defenders, they moved back into their same positions. The guard was slightly behind the wall, more focused on the ramp than anything else.

Dar had enough glancing at the action. "Modo, you watch the enemy, and I'll watch the practice. Switch places."

"Yes, Section Leader." Modo took Dar's position as Dar watched the unfolding drama.

Dar watched as the whole event became a flurry of movement and action. Drots had his men moving forward and backward, and Jusin's team fell for the misdirection. One soldier—Dar couldn't see clearly which one—strayed too far away from his line and the battle changed. Drots screamed a command that Dar couldn't make out, and his team started to run at the isolated man. Jusin's team tried to wheel around to close the gap, but it was too late. Realizing how exposed they were, the attacked unit just collapsed to the ground. Now four on three, Jusin's team was dispatched with little trouble once Drot's team attacked in earnest.

"Stop." Ocktur walked up and looked at Jusin. "Horrible. Your team is dead, the camp is overrun, and the Abbey is now being raped and pillaged. Consider your failure as you relieve third section. First section, you're on defense." Ocktur turned and motioned to Dar.

"Okay, boys, it's our turn to attack," Dar said. Deek and Zander walked slowly the other side of the trench and turned and waited for Dar and Modo.

"Any ideas?"

"About what?" Zander replied. Deek started laughing.

"I don't think this is a time for humor." Modo looked at Zander sternly.

"Suggestions, then, Modo?" Dar still had a smirk on his face.

"Charge and hope our strength and their weakness will win the battle."

"Plan A. Anybody got a plan B?" Dar looked at Zander and Deek.

"Sounds good to us." Deek glanced over at the palisades. "We try the same thing first company did, they'll just eat us up. We really don't have any distance weapons, no spells…"

"That we're allowed to use," Dar interrupted.

"And we don't have horses, like the last attackers." Deek shrugged. "Pretty much a plan-A situation."

Zander spoke up. "I have an idea. We attack second section."

"What?" Deek looked incredulously at his brother.

"Just attack the side they aren't defending. Second section won't stop us, since they are just observing, and by the time Drots figures that out, we'll be in the base and wreaking havoc."

"And if they don't oblige and come out and attack us?" Dar had his own ideas, but wanted to see what Zander had to say about it.

"Well, then it just turns into plan A, and our strength and their whatever makes us the winner." Zander finished with a smile. He clearly thought his plan was pretty good.

"Modo thinks it could work." Modo flexed his hand, apparently warming up his muscles, and smirked. Dar figured Modo was imagining hitting somebody, finally.

"I agree." Dar let the amusement flush out of his expression. Even though this was a practice round, it was still a battle to be fought.

After a brief moment, the signal came from Ocktur, and third section was free to launch its attack when ready. Dar got the brothers and Modo into a close formation and slowly moved them until they were aligned up better with second company. First company had setup two guards, one facing down the front of the palisades and the other facing the front lines. They watched Dar's group appear, then ran to report to Drots, who came over and watched. Even from across the distance, Dar could see him laughing as third section got into position.

"Charge!" Dar thrust his sword into the air and the foursome took off running. Drots's laughter vanished; clearly, he'd realized that he'd figured the angle wrong. He paused, apparently calculating his options, giving Dar's team time, which they converted to yards closer to their target.

"First section, head to the other side!" Drots pushed the nearest man, not looking to see who it was. "*Now!*"

As they sprinted, Dar gave third section orders: "Deek and Modo, when we get to the palisades, you try to hold them off while Zander and I breakthrough and attack the tent. Use the people in second group as shields and blockades."

Zander was just about out of breath. "Take." He panted. "Deek."

"Fine," Dar said. "Deek, you're with me."

First section was about three strides away from third section when they reached the palisades. Zander and Modo immediately stopped and hid inside the group of second section as Dar and Deek raced on. They had broken through.

Dar heard Drots make another call: "Go after the other two!" With that, first company chased off after Deek and Dar. Zander looked over at Modo.

"I think we should take over their starting position," Zander said with a smile.

"I agree," Modo said, then took off running.

Out of the corner of his eye, Drots saw Zander running off behind them. He stopped. He was beaten and he knew it.

"Stop!" Ocktur ended the game before Zander and Modo got even halfway. Ocktur walked up to Drots, his fists clenched. "Why did you stop before I gave the order?"

Drots furrowed his brow and waved his weapon around casually. "I was beaten. There was nothing I could do to alter the outcome. Those two"—he pointed at Dar and Deek—"had broken through, and we had no advantage to help us close the gap. Those two"—he now pointed to Zander and Modo—"had obviously captured our starting position. We'd been outplayed, and the game was over. I knew the quickest way to get you to stop the drill was for me to stop, so I did."

Ocktur struck Drots in the stomach, causing him to fold over and kneel down on one knee.

"You give me your all. At all times." Ocktur turned and faced the others. "Or else."

"Yes, Sergeant," they all replied in chorus.

"Time for second section to attack third section. First section, you man the guard."

Dar and company walked slowly to the palisades. Modo was calm, but Zander was still winded. Deek and Dar were panting as well, but not as bad as Zander. Dar took a deep breath before speaking. "Ideas about this side?"

"So far, the question seems to be how to cover such a large area with such a small force," Deek started. "The tendency is to use the palisades as protection, but I think that isn't helpful, given that the other side doesn't have any distance weapons or horses. I say we just hang out in the dead center of the hole in the palisades and wait. That will make it a straight-up fight."

"And we will win that." Modo did something that could only be described as a smile. But it seemed too threatening to be a smile.

"Good analysis." Dar looked at Zander. "Comments?"

He seemed too tired to even shrug. "It will be good to just stand around for a while."

Dar moved third section to the middle of the gap in the palisades and just waited. Second section was taking its time, planning and talking. Then Ocktur gave both sides the signal, and the game was on. Second section studied Dar's group, apparently trying to figure out what the deal was, and what their secret defense strategy would be. This stalemate was broken suddenly by Ocktur.

"Stop the exercise and form up!" Ocktur assumed a rigid pose, and everyone formed up around him, with second section having to run in from the field.

"Presenting the Lord Protector of the City of Highstar, commanding officer and General of the Army of the Protectorate," a horseman yelled for all to hear. "My Lord, Ax Company, Lieutenant Strlang commanding."

"Sir! I'm Sergeant Ocktur, assisting the lieutenant." Ocktur was as rigid as the palisades behind him. "He is currently away, sir!"

A white horse with a stern-looking fellow in long robes walked up to Ocktur. The general had a short black goatee. He did not appear to be in armor and didn't have any visible weapons. His head was balding, with white hair forming a semicircle from ear to ear at the level of his eyebrows. He looked to Dar more like a mage than a general.

"Conducting field exercises?" The general spoke in a soft voice.

"Yes, sir!" Ocktur kept his eyes forward. He was clearly standing as tall as he could.

"We saw the outcome of your last little jaunt there. That split up was an interesting attack." The general looked over the whole company, stopping at Dar, Deek, Zander, and Modo. "Splitting your forces like that wouldn't work if they had any bows or magic. Any ability to project power over distance really would have finished you off. But given the rules of the battle, it was clever."

Dar wondered if Zander would claim credit for that idea or do some other foolish thing to incur Ocktur's wrath. Thankfully, he stayed quiet.

"I know you boys are still just training," the general went on, "and you're wondering why you're off in some strange land, fighting in some strange army for some strange cause. I'm here to explain it to you." Being on the horse put him high above the troops. Even Ocktur had to strain to look at him. The general's only action was to look from side to side. "Now, I'm not a man of many words, so I'll cut to the chase. You were selected from across all of Holimoren to help protect my prized possession, my beloved Abbey. Since I decided to defend it at all costs, it has become a haven for those that can't protect themselves. Nuns, orphans, women who couldn't flee the oncoming attack, the infirm, the aged. Protect those that need it, and I will compensate all of you who survive the war with one hundred gold pieces to thank you for your service. If you won't fight to save the weak, fight to claim your share of the bounty. Our enemy will not stop until they have defiled those in the Abbey and taken your share of the bounty. Should they get the Abbey, you get nothing. Your payment will be the screams of horror of the helpless." The general looked sternly at a few of the men. Dar frowned, as this was unexpected.

The general adjusted himself in the saddle, trying to get comfortable. Looking him, Dar guessed it didn't work. "As you may guess from my attire, I'm not a fighting man. Well, not a combat fighting man. I fight with magic and I fight with armies." He smiled slightly as he glanced around, looking at the men. "This army must prevail, and it will prevail. History will speak of our army the way it speaks of the Army of Armageddon and the Army of Reunification before them. You must defend the Abbey for the money and for the cause. Our enemies will lose their will to fight shortly, and then you will be allowed to go home. And you will return home with a sack of gold at your side and a heart filled with the thanks of the helpless and meek."

He adjusted himself in the saddle again. "I leave you in Ocktur's firm but guiding hands and look forward to paying you each those one hundred gold pieces personally."

Ocktur saluted as the general pulled the reins of his horse and rode back toward the Abbey. Once he was a safe distance away, Ocktur called out, "Dismissed!" and each section formed up in their own group to discuss things. When Dar's eye met up with Deek's, Deek smiled, but Dar wasn't really sure why.

"That went rather well." Zander laughed.

Dar watched as Ocktur stormed into his tent, pulled the beer keg off of its stand, and let out a joyous yell. He pulled out the spigot and drank the keg dry, then discarded the keg by throwing to the ground. He gyrated for a moment, as if dancing, then the effects of the beer started to tell. Dar could see him inside through the mesh of his tent, walking back and forth, starting to sway as time went on. Eventually he sat down to steady himself.

Just then, Drots yelled out from near the palisades.

"Alarm! We're under attack!"

SIX

Casualty

"First goes truth. Next behind it is always innocence."

—General Groknar

The enemy had sent what appeared to be a gang of skirmishers to attack, and those skirmishers had advanced enough to nearly reach the trench. They were eight strong by Dar's counting, but they were heavily armed and looked more professional than Ax Company. They were walking in two staggered lines of four, with lots of spacing between them to give their weapons room to operate. They had spears in their hands, swords at their sides, and what appeared to be chain mail over their bodies. The front four had shields, but the back four did not. They were human, at least as far as Dar could tell at this range. They had shaved heads and just a small tuft of hair on the back of their skulls. They had managed to make it about fifty paces from the trench by the time Drots raised the alarm. Ocktur sprung out of his tent and rushed to assess the danger.

"Ax Company, it's war time!" He turned to face them. "First section, you take the palisades to the right; second section, you get the left; and third, you man the trench. Everyone, hold your ground. If they attack the trench heavily, Dar, you have authorization to bait them back to the palisades for first and second to attack. I want everyone to look sharp and show them how Ax Company does it."

"Yes, Sergeant!" The sections flew to their assignments. Dar was the last one into the trench, and he began barking out instructions and encouragement as soon as he arrived.

"I want Zander on the left, Deek on the right, and Modo, you're our punisher in the center. I'll stay in the middle to reinforce anybody who needs it." He caught Zander's eye. "Nobody has to be the hero here, so if you can't take your man, ask for help, and we'll take some of the heat for you." He faced Modo. "You're our strongest man, so we'll be counting on you when things get ugly. But don't try to win the war yourself—your still recovering from the beating."

"I know my limits, and I will kill someone today." Modo readied his weapon.

"Deek, you'll be in charge if I go down. If we get pinned, I'll give the order to retreat. If I call it, honor it. There is no shame in being defeated. The only shame is staying defeated!"

Dar stepped to the front of the trench and put his foot into one of the carved notches along the face. His foot was wet from the water at the bottom, but the notch was deep enough to make for a safe lift. He raised himself up so he could see clear of the trench—the skirmishers were almost on top of them. He dropped back down and gave Modo room to operate.

"If they poke down with the spears," Dar told them, "either grab the spear and pull it from them, or try to break the weapon with your sword. Us being up against the front of the trench will make it harder for them to use their spears. If they jump into the trench, call it out. Don't follow them away from where you're standing. By staying close, we can help each other. We need to hold this ramp. The rest of the trench doesn't help them get past the palisades, and the ramp will allow us to escape when things get bad."

Dar stopped speaking when he saw the first spear come over the top. A couple of half-hearted jabs later, it was withdrawn for a moment. When the spear returned, it had three more with it. Zander swiped at one near him, and it did no damage. None were near enough to Modo for him to do much about, and Dar was busy checking behind himself. Deek reached out, grabbed one with his bare hand, and gave it a tug. The weapon came out of the attacker's hand, and now it was Deek's to use. Suddenly, four of the enemies jumped over the trench and turned to attack from the other side. Dar was staring at a foe off to his left; he knew there had to be another to his right. Third section was encircled by attackers, four in the front, four in the rear, one without a spear.

Dar was just about to call out to retreat when he heard the sounds of metal on metal from near the entrance to the ramp. The four attackers on the front side of the trench jumped across, and the ones behind turned to face the other direction.

"Third section, move out to the ramp." This was not a retreat, Dar told himself, just an attack in the other direction. Dar saw second section had moved from their spot on the palisades and had engaged the enemy while their back was turned. One skirmisher was down, stabbed in the back by a knife, which had probably been thrown. Dar saw the knife jutting out—thankfully, there wasn't a lot of blood. It must have severed the spine. He focused on the battle. Banes and the rest were engaged in hand-to-hand combat, and the numbers favored the attackers.

"Third section attack!" Dar cried before charging in. Modo passed him and attacked a nearby skirmisher with vigor and happiness. Deek and Zander were slower on the uptake, but soon were trading jabs with the skirmishers. The brothers stayed together and took on one fellow between them. It was now seven versus eight, and their side was holding even.

"First section attack!" came Ocktur's voice. Seeing how third and second had stopped the threat and limited its movement, Ocktur had apparently decided he could safely commit first company. Drots had already started his men forward, but Ocktur's command turned their trot into a sprint. The skirmishers bunched up and started toward the trench, which was now sealing them in. Modo got a good swing in and knocked the wind out of his opponent. The fellow dropped to one knee, and Modo lurched forward. He punched the attacker's neck right at the apple with such force that the skirmisher flopped forward, gasping for air. It was now six versus twelve, and now the large Ocktur was also coming out to play.

"Kleh-plarg!" one of the skirmishers called out to the others. They turned as one and took off for the trench, coming straight at Deek and Zander. Zander dodged them, but Deek was caught right in the middle of it all. One of the attackers stabbed at him, hitting him in the chest. It made a dull sound, more like steel on stone than steel on bone. Deek fell over; the skirmishers jumped the trench and took off running, not even bothering to look back.

"Hold pursuit!" Ocktur screamed.

Dar moved over to Deek, ready to administer aid if possible. As Dar rolled Deek over, Zander joined him. Together, they examined Deek's chest, looking for the red spot that would show where the wound was. But there was no blood, just a small hole in his shirt—through it, they could see a gold-circled stone.

"Are you okay?" Dar asked Deek, who was blinking rapidly.

"I think so." He pulled out the string he had tied around his neck. It had a small pouch at the end, and the pouch was cut as well. The rock slipped out and landed in Deek's hand. "It hit the rock. I could have sworn that I could feel the blade piercing my skin, and then it stopped. Then the next thing I know, you're asking me if I'm okay."

"That stone," Zander said softly, standing up, "is amazing." He stayed close to Dar to make sure his voice didn't carry. "He found it in the trench, and he's been wearing it ever since. I thought it was just a pretty rock."

Dar looked up Zander. "I sense magic from it."

"You don't say." Deek smiled. "I felt something from it too."

"I'm going to check out the guy that Modo was fighting." Dar stood up too and walked a couple of paces to Modo's victim. His neck was purple and swollen, and he was obviously suffering. He lay on his back, gasping for air. His eyes stared straight up, and his arms and legs lay flaccid on the ground. Dar figured his windpipe had collapsed, which meant now it was only a matter of time.

"Sergeant!" Dar called out, hoping that Ocktur would have some magic to help the fellow.

Dar waited just a moment while Ocktur walked over slowly, his face beaming with pride after their quick victory. "What is it, Section Commander Dar?"

"We have a prisoner, Sergeant, but he needs treatment if he is to survive."

Ocktur's face soured. "Where?"

Dar took a step back and pointed to the helpless skirmisher on the ground. Ocktur looked at Dar, then over at the man. He walked up and placed a foot on the wounded skirmisher's neck, then put his full weight on that leg. A sickening snap echoed off of the palisade walls. The skirmisher was silent.

"We don't take prisoners." Ocktur took his foot off the body. "Ever."

Dar felt tears welling up in his eyes, and he didn't do anything to stop them. Zander fell to his knees and vomited straight onto the ground. Deek had had his back turned, so he just turned his head and winced at the sound. Dar fell to his knees, crying.

Deek looked around at the other members of Ax Company. Upny and Jusin were obviously appalled. The rest were either unmoved, like Drots, or amused, like Modo. Deek could feel the rage building up within him. He stood up and yelled at Ocktur, "You're sick, Sergeant! Sick! You didn't have to kill him."

Ocktur turned to Deek. "Unless you want to be next, do not question my methods or the methods of the Army of the Protectorate. I have my orders. No prisoners." Ocktur looked emotionless. He did not appear to enjoy the killing. But he had done it all the same. "They would have done the same to you. Prisoners mean rescue efforts. Dead bodies aren't worth saving. You don't cry for the fellow that was killed on just the other side of the trench, yet you cry for this one."

"The first guy died in battle, not on his back."

"They both knew what could happen. They knew death was coming along for this trip. If not for them, for you."

Deek started to say something again when Ocktur cut him off. "This discussion is over. You say another word, and I'll teach you a lesson. And you'll wish for the treatment the enemy got."

Jusin walked over, grabbed Deek's arm, and stared him in the eye. Getting the idea, Deek let silence reign. Ocktur turned and walked into his tent.

Deek pulled away from Jusin's grasp and headed over to his brother, who was still on his hands and knees.

"It's okay, Zander." Deek rubbed his older brother's back. "It's okay. He isn't suffering anymore." Zander had always been the more sensitive of the two, more in tune with the emotions and sensibilities of those around him.

Zander wiped his mouth with his sleeve and sat down. "He didn't have to kill him." Tears rolled down his face. "He could have let him live."

"I know." Deek sat next to his brother. "I know."

"We need to get out of here." Zander looked off to the distance. "How do you unsee what you have seen? I'll hear that sound—the sound of crushing bone—until I die." He looked up at his brother. "We need to get home. We need to see Katowyn. I don't want to fight anymore."

Dar came up and sat down on the other side of Zander. He took a deep breath and let it out slowly. "We all need to get out of here."

Deek leaned forward a little and glanced over at Dar.

"Any idea how? We try to leave, Ocktur will kill us."

Dar stared off at the same nonexistent point as Zander. His mind's eye replayed the whole gruesome event over and over. He couldn't do anything else. He couldn't think of anything to say. He knew, as section commander, he needed to say something—his soul begged his mind to figure out something to say—but his heart was in his throat and his tongue was tied.

"I know how." Zander looked at Deek, then stood up. He faced them both, and it was clear that the fear had left his heart.

"We win the war."

SEVEN

Quality Time

"There are two overlooked pieces of equipment that must have frequent care in the successful army: the soldier, and the soldier's weapon."
—*Harlec Knight's Army Field Manual*, Chapter 4, Section 8

I t took what seemed like a minute for the words to finish echoing around in Dar's head. He looked Zander in the eye and felt his own dread leave him, the way he had seen Zander's fear leave him. Deek stood up, and Dar did the same.

Deek said, "You're proposing that the three of us figure out how to win a war that's been going on a while. Months, maybe." His eyes showed he wanted to believe, but he wasn't as optimistic as his older brother.

"I'm saying that every war has a cause," Zander replied, "every problem has a solution, and perhaps violence isn't the best way to solve whatever caused this conflict. If we could better understand it, we could propose a solution. Too often people just get started down a certain road and don't have the courage to find another way. We have that courage. We can be the ones to solve this."

Deek scoffed. "But what do we do, Zander, if the war can only be settled by war?"

"Tell me, Deek, what war didn't have another solution?"

"The War of Reunification."

Zander shook his head. "Holimoren had been separate nations before then, and it is separate nations now. There was no need for unification except in the heads of those would lead the new, unified world. They claimed it was the only for the good of Holimoren, but as history and time have proven, we did just fine without unifying."

"Armageddon." Deek whispered the word, apparently afraid to speak it too loudly.

Zander smirked at his brother. "He was just an evil man with an evil soul who needed to do evil things. A simple flick of the knife and there would have been no need for the war or the devastation that followed that climatic battle with the evil sorcerer."

"Are you advocating assassination?" Dar chose this moment to join the conversation. He wanted to see how committed to this idea Zander was.

"I am suggesting that if someone with the character had stood up to the sorcerer at an early point in his rise to power, or perhaps killed him and him alone, there would not have been a giant clash of armies on the shallow rise to the Skyneedle. Instead, thousands and untold more perished to make him yield his hold on this earth. Would you rather fight in this army and watch the crimes that go on here or kill the evil head that holds it all together?"

"The enemy leadership has methods and practices are foreign to us." Deek was clearly starting to be swayed, but he wasn't going to let his brother know until he had fully decided on his course of action.

"But we should decide today that this is our goal," Zander said. "We work together every day to solve this war. Win it for us, our families, and those around us. I believe the reason they have to steal people to join this army is because they have forgotten why they are here. They're too busy trying not to lose to bother to win."

Dar looked each brother in the eye. "That means that both of you will have to work harder than you have so far. Neither of you have been even average soldiers. I haven't been much better, but if we are going to have time to do our duty *and* end the war, we're going to need to be sharper mentally, sharper physically, and plan our movements."

"I will do it." Zander's face had changed. His eyes burned with a flame of passion and courage. Gone was the jovial smile always at the edge of his lips, replaced with a stony expression of purpose. "Tell me what I must do."

Deek nodded. "Me too."

Dar looked at each brother, then looked around the camp. "As I see it, we need to move up to first section. We need to collect information about the roots of this siege, and we need to stay one step ahead of danger. We have no allies, so watch your back."

"Trust no one, and keep your sword handy." Deek looked at Zander. "This won't be easy."

Zander nodded. "We've lived a sheltered life, Deek. We've always looked to Katowyn, Mother, Father, the staff at the manor—everyone but ourselves to solve our problems. To take care of us. We let Dar protect us, we let Modo bully us, we let Ocktur beat us. We need to use the courage that made Father the great knight he was before his death. We need to show to the world, to ourselves, that we are made of sterner stuff than that we have been so far in our lives." Zander sighed. "We were nabbed by thugs out of a bar, both of us drunk, just after noon. Since then, we've worn out easy. We need to get hard, and we need to end this war."

"That's easy for you to say, brother." Deek folded his arms. "I don't take things on faith or hope. I deal best with matters of the mind, not the heart. And while I agree we need to get out of here, and ending this conflict is the best way out, I don't see what we can do to move things in that direction. You don't need to see the how—you already believe the why. I need the how to make the why make sense. Without how, why is just a dream." He looked to Dar. "We need a plan."

"We have time to make one." Dar put his arm on Deek's shoulder. "The fact that you have a why means you will figure out a how. We will all help figure out the how. Let your mind think on it. I'm sure we'll come up with something."

Zander nodded. "First, I believe we need to start standing up for ourselves, and not let Ocktur and Modo and the others badger us around—"

Dar cut him off. "Those are battles we need not fight now. I believe we need to get along with Ocktur and Modo while we figure out our plan. Ocktur can position us to make it very hard to get anything done. Modo is a wild card, and that's really dangerous. While I suggest we don't actively pursue conflict with either of them, I think we can be a little more aggressive and not be bullied."

Zander sighed. "I guess you're right. The bigger goal is more important than little things like our feelings."

At that, Deek jumped in. "I think what Dar is saying is that when you can get away with it, be yourself. But the goal must come first, and sometimes we will have to do things we don't like to get us closer to our goal." He paused. "Like your comment about having to potentially assassinate somebody to end a great threat. Neither of us would kill like that out of choice, but given the bigger goal, I believe we may have to."

"Deek is right," Dar said. "That is what I meant. Part of our souls may be the cost for getting out of here. It's a high cost, but one we must be willing to pay. It is either that or our lives."

"Then we are in agreement," Zander said. "Everyone, think about how we can end this conflict." He pointed his finger at each in turn, looking for agreement. Dar nodded, but Deek was still struggling with the issue.

"I think we need to figure out why the conflict started before we can figure out a way to end it," he said.

"Then that will be our first point of action." And with that, Dar ended the conversation.

As the day turned to night, the troops were left milling around awaiting some sort of direction. Ocktur had retired to his tent, and nobody had bothered to ask him what his standing orders were. Each section commander had assumed some sort of role in keeping an eye on the trenches and the enemy, but there was no formal structure, and it was clear even this was just about to fall apart as the darkness of night descended. Just as Dar was sure he'd have to talk to the other two section leaders about guard rotation for the night, Ocktur emerged from his tent.

"Section leaders, report to my tent," he said without emotion.

Dar was the first to report, Jusin the last. As he sat down on the edge of his bed, Ocktur began his briefing.

"We were lucky today. We held off a small group of raiders and suffered no losses. But they know we're here now, and they know about how many troops we have in this area. We can count on more attacks in the coming days, and they will involve more troops. We will need to cover the trenches and the entry ways to the palisades both day and night. The enemy hasn't struck at night before, but I don't want to have my soul being judged after my death because I was too lazy to mount a guard." He looked around the line. Ocktur's body language was pretty loose. "We'll do a rotating night watch. Whoever's on it will get the next day off. If we get attacked during the day, they will be woken up, just as if we were attacked during the night."

Ocktur paused and took a drink from a stein near his bed. It was filled with a thick liquid—Dar thought it was probably mead—and he had obviously been drinking it before they came in. Ocktur was drinking a lot, it seemed. Dar hoped it wouldn't impact his ability to lead.

"The first to serve at night will be third section. The next night will be second section. I haven't decided if at that point first should serve or if third should go around again. I want my best troops ready for the most likely combat time, and that is still daylight."

"When will you reassign the section ratings?" Drots asked.

"I reassign every day. Nothing has shown me that any change is required."

Drots smiled at Dar, who did not smile back.

Oblivious, Ocktur resumed his speech. "Once we figure out how thing are progressing, we'll see if changes are needed. This our home for the foreseeable future, so we had better get good at what we do, and get good quick. Any questions?"

Jusin shook his head no. Drots too shook his head. Dar cupped his hands together and blew into them to warm them up, holding Ocktur's eye.

"How did this war start?"

The question clearly caught everyone off guard, but Ocktur quickly covered his surprise with a small grin.

"I have no idea," he replied. "The war was already on when I joined."

"You didn't ask why?"

"I asked what was the pay. Nothing more." His face had taken on a stern look. "You know your pay."

Jusin spoke. "One hundred gold coins."

Ocktur nodded. "Exactly. That is why I fight. I don't know how it started. That doesn't concern me."

"Who does know?" Dar pressed the subject.

"You don't need to know. I don't know who knows!" Ocktur took another swallow of the heavy yellow liquid. Then he appeared to reconsider. "I know the general knows, and I bet somebody at the Abbey or headquarters does too. But you aren't going there, and when I do go there, I have—" Ocktur smiled into his cup before taking a swig from it. "Other things on my mind."

"I think that if we know why the enemy is attacking, we can use it against them."

"Dismissed."

"But, Sergeant…" Dar's voice had a tinge of exasperation to it.

Ocktur's tone became very solemn. "I said, dismissed."

Dar turned and walked out of the tent, a couple of steps behind Jusin and Drots, who had exited at the first utterance of the command. Silently, Dar walked over to the lean-to and broke the news to the section about their assignment for the night.

"We are to guard the base tonight. We are the only ones to be guarding tonight. But that means we'll have reduced duty tomorrow."

"How reduced?" Modo didn't even bother to look at Dar when he spoke anymore.

"He said we wouldn't have any duties, but I think it is best that we consider it reduced—we'll still get extra work, since we're third section for another day."

Zander had been doing something before Dar came in, but quit when Dar walked in. "I'm glad we got watch duty tonight. I think looking at the stars will do me good. Maybe the answer to our problems is up there…"

"Up there won't help our down here problems, brother." Deek nudged his brother gently with his elbow. "But it will give us some time to ponder our next steps."

"What next steps?" Modo quizzed them. "I don't know about any next steps."

Dar cleared his throat. "We are working on a special project, and if you need to know about it, I'll let you know. We need to win the war, and we are going to figure out how."

Modo laughed. "Good luck with that. Just make sure your plan includes me killing. Lots of killing."

Deek's left eye twitched involuntarily. "We'll try to remember that."

"We'll do the rotation just like last time, when Modo was hurt." Dar looked at Modo. "I want you to get extra rest, because you're our heavy hitter when things get bad, and you're still not fully healed. So you can sleep the whole night, and Deek, Zander, and I will split the night into thirds. Modo, you take over at dawn until relieved by the next section." Dar turned to Zander. "Zander, you go first, and Deek and I will rest. Then Deek, then me. Just like last time."

They all nodded, and Zander walked off to the palisades while the rest turned in. It took longer for Dar to get to sleep than it had the night before because every time he closed his eyes the day replayed in front of them. Deek seemed restless too. But not Modo, who'd fallen into a deep sleep quickly and now seemed to be having glorious dreams. Finally, when Dar's head quit swimming, he got to sleep.

It seemed like he'd only taken a short nap when Deek woke him up. It was dark and silent, and Deek was just as bleary-eyed as he had been the night before. "You know..." was all Deek said to him before curling up on the ground and falling asleep.

Dar stretched out the muscles in his neck as he walked to the palisades. The moon was bright, and there wasn't a cloud in sight. Stars blanketed the sky, making all the old constellations easy to pick out. He found this comforting, as they were the same constellations he'd picked out when he used to sneak up to the tower roof and watch for shooting stars. But these stars were a distraction from the job at hand, which was watching the enemy. The enemy. Dar's mind flashed to the bodies of the fallen enemy soldiers from that afternoon's skirmish. He made his way over to where they'd lain earlier, wondering if anybody had done anything about them. Dar wasn't surprised to find both of them exactly where they had fallen. The moonlight gave them a pale coloration, and death doubled that effect. Right then Dar knew what he had to do.

He walked over to the one with the broken neck, put his hands under the dead man's shoulders, and lifted him up to a good position to drag. Dar could feel that the body had already been stripped of all the good materials of war, and he was glad because it made the man lighter. Dar was concerned about the noise dragging the body was going to create, and how he was going to get it over the trench was also a concern. But it had to be done. Dar dragged first the one body then the other to the edge of the trench. He was just about to throw the first one over when a voice rang out in the night, scaring him half to death.

"What are you doing to that body, Section Leader Dar?"

It was Ocktur. Dar hadn't heard him coming, probably because of the noise of the body scraping along the ground.

"I was going to place it in no-man's land for the enemy to recover, so they can give an honorable burial to their fallen comrade."

"You're wasting your time and your energy. You should just leave the body where it fell and get back to watching the lines." Ocktur slurred his words just slightly.

"A rotting body will attract vermin, carrion eaters like vultures, carrion crawlers, and maggots, which may contaminate our water. Never mind the smell."

"But our enemy will see how we treat them and their cause, and they will quake in fear." Dar could see in the moonlight that Ocktur was struggling to remain standing. He also seemed to be blinking a lot.

"If we place the bodies in the middle land, they will know we respect their dead and honor them enough as enemies not to disrespect or defile their fallen comrades. They might even treat our dead with the same respect."

"They are the enemy. They will never treat our dead with respect. The general says so." Ocktur belched, and Dar could smell the alcohol from many steps away. "You're too naive, Dar. You don't know what war is like. You don't know what it's like to have this many people counting on you to lead them. You don't know. You just don't."

Dar felt Ocktur being drunk gave him some leeway. "I know that the enemy troops are better off with this man's body than we are. Either we bury the dead or they do. Which would you rather do the work, the enemy or us?"

Ocktur didn't talk for a while, but as long as he remained standing, Dar knew he was still conscious. The thought of having to drag Ocktur back to his tent while drunk didn't sound like a lot of fun. And if Modo caught on to how inebriated Ocktur was, he would be sure to take his revenge.

"You may take the body to the middle ground." Ocktur turned and headed back to his tent. "And I...you may not tell anybody about this convers...this talk that we had. I will remember enough of this in the morning to back you on the bodies, but if you tell the others about..."

"There is nothing to tell. My sergeant checked on me during my shift. What other details are there?" Dar walked back over to the bodies. He needed to figure out a way to get them across the trench.

"There are wooden boards in the supply tent," Ocktur said. "They were to be used to make a mess table, but I don't want us eating together, so I left it unbuilt. Use that wood to make a bridge to get them across." Ocktur hiccupped. "Just put the boards back when you are done."

"Yes, Sergeant." Dar was behind Ocktur by a couple of steps as he headed to the supply tent. He heard Ocktur struggle with the entrance to his own tent, and he fought back a giggle when he heard Ocktur fall hard into bed. A little too hard. By the time Dar had found the boards and started to head toward the trench with them, he could hear Ocktur snoring.

Assembling the bridge was pretty easy, even by the light of the moon. Dar laid five of the boards together and bound them together with a piece of rope from the supply tent. His plan was to drag each body onto the boards, jump across the trench, then finish dragging it to the middle ground. The boards might not hold the weight of two—Dar didn't want to find out. Falling into the trench at night, in the cold, would not be good.

Carefully, Dar executed his plan, which took just a short while. Now he just needed to get the bodies farther toward the enemy's lines than his own. Taking turns, he dragged one body for a while then the other, so if he had to abandon the bodies, they would be somewhat close together. The moon was Dar's only companion, and he could tell by its nearness to the horizon that the sky to the opposite side would soon be turning the dusty rose of dawn. Getting caught out here in the morning light, he knew, would be fatal, so as soon as he'd reached a reasonable distance into the middle ground, he left the bodies to their fate.

When Dar got back to his own lines, he took the boards that had comprised his impromptu bridge and dragged them back to the supply tent. He took the rope with him, and by the time dawn was budding, everything appeared as normal again. Once he quit working, Dar noticed the chill in the air, and by the time he woke up Modo to take his brief shift, Dar was cold, tired, and ready for bed. He lamented the lack of bedding for moment, pausing to remember his warm blanket in the Master's tower before settling onto the cold ground. He tucked himself as close as he could to the canvas of the lean-to. It wasn't much better, but it was better than nothing. One last thought crossed his mind has he fell into sleep.

What would win this war?

Dar woke to the sensation of something crawling on his face. He wiped at it as he struggled to regain his wits and caught it. It was a tick, engorged with blood and looking for a warm place to call it a day. Dar stood, squished it with his foot, and instinctively scratched his head. When his fingers found a bump. He paused and plucked at it—finding another tick the end of his finger, Dar reacted swiftly. He walked over to the trench and stuck his head upside down into the small amount of water in the bottom. It wasn't enough to cover his whole head, though, so he walked back to third section's lean-to and poured some of their drinking water on his head. Everyone in the group was observing his strange antics with must have been amusement, but Ocktur came over, obviously not finding the same joy in this display.

"Section Leader Dar, what are you doing? Are you wasting supplies?" Ocktur stopped just out reach of the splashing water. Dar was happy he'd stopped that far back; it meant Dar was out of striking range should Ocktur get violent.

"Sergeant, I was just trying to clean myself of parasites. I found a tick on my face and another in my hair, and I just wanted to get rid of them." Ocktur looked at him like he was speaking some strange language. The look of confusion on his face was not a good sign.

"Come to my tent, Mr. Dar, for a…" Ocktur turned around and started walking. "Discussion." As he walked, something else must have occurred to him, since he uttered another order just before entering his tent. "All of the section leaders must report as well." Drots and Jusin nodded. Ocktur ducked inside his tent to await their entry.

Drots got close to the door, but then lingered. Jusin, apparently recognizing that Drots was waiting to talk to Dar before entering, also lingered. As Dar approached, his head still wet, Drots began his interrogation.

"What were you doing?" Drots looked at his wet hair. "Taking a bath?"

"Actually, I was."

Drots blocked Dar's path and poked him in the chest. "Baths are for royals, the rich, and women. Which are you?"

"Where I come from, everyone bathes regularly." Dar was not challenging Drots's physical advantage, and was waiting to see which side Jusin came down on. "So I was taking care of myself."

"Where I come from, every time you cross a river, you get clean. You swim to get fish, and you get clean." Drots turned and walked toward the tent door. He was controlling the pace, and he knew it. "Time is too precious to waste sitting in a pool of water being all pampered."

"So what do you do, Drots, when you find a bug in your hair, or a tick or a flea? Give them a home until they make you sick?" Dar stepped toward the tent door, but Drots was still blocking the way.

"We toast a lot with hard drink and take turns pouring it on each other's heads. So we rarely have travelers on us for long."

Jusin spoke up. "Seems like a waste of liquor. Seems like it would be easier just to wash yourself and drown the little beggars."

"I suppose your sad social group takes baths too?" Drots could barely contain his contempt for the other section leaders. "Am I the only true man in this company?"

Jusin was obviously tired of Drots's ranting. "As a seaman from the Torrents area, we bathe often. If a cootie or some other vermin gets aboard a ship, it can bring a disease that can befall the whole crew without warning. I heard of a ship, the *Exzelric*, that floats around Bywater, cursed and half sunk, because the crew was felled by a rot grub infestation brought onboard by a sick seaman. Since then, the master on my ship has made us bathe just before leaving our home port, just after leaving foreign ports, and just before disembarking for leave."

Drots rolled his eyes. "How would anybody know if the ship was empty if nobody had survived to tell the tale? That story doesn't make any sense. Besides, I know you sailor boys are weak. Not like us ground pounders." Drots lifted the tent flap and walked inside. "We're tough, and once you deal with the wounds caused by swords and axes, little scraps like blood-suckers don't even register."

Jusin and Dar didn't retort as they walked inside the tent. Ocktur was waiting, and by the look on his face, he'd heard the discussion outside.

"Dar, I know you were attempting to bathe. Why did you consider this waste of water worth the removal of a few fleas or ticks?" Ocktur was sitting on a chair, one that looked freshly built—Dar hadn't noticed it the last time he was here. Perhaps Ocktur had been in the supply tent and was still figuring out what, exactly, the orcs had left for supplies. The chair gave him a throne to sit on while the others had to sit on the floor. It reinforced his position of superiority, as everyone had to crane their necks to look him.

"Where I was raised," Dar replied, "ticks carry diseases that can disable even grown men. They get a red circle about a hand's width wide at the bite site, then they slowly lose their strength, and some even go crazy. Only the healing powers of a cleric or druid can cure the disease. Not a minor cure spell, either; only Cure Serious Wounds or Cure Disease or Heal will do it. If it gets to the debilitating phase, the Serious Wounds incantation isn't even enough. It is said that whole towns have been ravaged by it, and only the timely arrival of a group of travelling holy men of a healing faith saved my town."

Ocktur stroked the wiry hairs on this chin. They hadn't changed since his first days with Dar and the rest of Ax Company, so Dar figured he wasn't shaving them. "Disease is a serious issue for you, isn't it?" Dar nodded. "I heard your stand on the issue, Drots, and I heard your story about the ghost ship, Mister Jusin, but I didn't hear what you thought about our little company having bath time."

"Permission to speak freely, Sergeant?" Ocktur nodded, and Jusin continued. "I think it would be foolish not to have the troops bathe regularly. We did it often on our ship and never had sick men. You won't find a lot of clerics at sea, and fewer healers of the sick out in the Torrents area. Prevention was the key, and where we are now, that isn't going to happen. You can't kill all the bugs in the camp, as there will be new ones every day. But with regular washing, you can prevent a lot."

Ocktur nodded. "I'll ponder my decision for a while and let you know. Dismissed." The three stood as one and shuffled out of the tent, Drots leading and Dar at the rear. The door had just barely shut when Drots turned on the other two.

"I know you're both conspiring against me to take over the first section title. You won't get it. This act about washing won't help you. First section and I lead where it really counts, on the battlefield. Just wait until they attack again. You'll see then. First will come out on top."

Dar had opened his mouth to reply when a cry came from the guard area. "Alarm! We are under attack!" As all three ran to their posts, Drots told all who could hear him, "First section will be the best in this battle!" Dar didn't have time to even think about such things. Survival always came first.

This attack was a pretty large one. Ax Company was outnumbered almost two to one. Each section was doing its best. First section was the one already on duty, so they were fully ready for the attack when it came. Second section held the other side of the opening in the palisades. Third section floated around the middle, unable to get to the trench to take their normal position. Ocktur came out early in the battle and was actually contributing to the defense actively, and a good thing too: Ocktur was a very skilled warrior, worth at least two people. But the battle was starting to turn against Ax Company anyway.

Ocktur was in the center at the point where first and third would normally meet. Modo was at the other end, where third and second would meet. As the battle raged, the center of their formation kept getting pushed back. They were yielding ground to stay alive, but yielding much further would mean that the edges would not be at the palisades. Once the corners came off the cover advantage provided by the walls, the enemy would be able to either leak around the edges of the palisades or force the defenders into the gaps. Dar left the center of their formation to help anchor the edge and to get a drink of water. The enemy came in waves, crashing against the Ax Company front line, then retreating back a distance, only to return again, trying to break them. Between thrusts from the enemy group, Dar came back and checked in with Deek and Zander to see how they were holding up.

"Deek, what's the word?" Dar handed him a stein full of water. He drank deeply from it before speaking.

"Doubtful." His face was crestfallen. Clearly, he was trying his best, but it wasn't good enough today. "I keep making good contact, but the weapon doesn't hurt them. The blade is too dull—it hardly even dents their armor, let alone them. I keep getting hit, but luckily haven't been hurt. My shirt has just about had it, though."

"Zander, how about you?" Dar handed him a drink too. Zander was panting, out of breath, having just finished a quick scuffle.

"Pretty good. This sword is really sharp, and it almost seems to guide my hand when I strike. When I think I might have missed, the sword adjusts a little in my hand, or my muscle twitches or something else and I make good contact. And as sharp as this blade is, that's all it takes. I haven't killed anybody yet, but when I land a good shot to the arm, they retreat." He paused and shook his head. "There are just so many of them."

Deek nodded. "I agree—this is a lot of guys. How are you doing, Dar?"

"Same as you, I guess. I'm making good contact, though it isn't doing any damage. But I haven't been hit hard yet, so I guess it's going good at this point. I think the edge of our formation will hold, but we're stretched pretty thin. We started as a line, and now we are more bowl-shaped. Too many more attacks and we'll be done."

"What's the body count?" Deek paused from his drink to ask the question.

"I see four or five in front of second and maybe six in front of first company. Ocktur has killed four, Modo three."

"We aren't very good, are we?" Zander spoke with his mouth hidden by the stein.

Dar smiled to reassure him. "As long as we're alive, we're doing fine."

"What were the Ax Company loses?" Deek set his stein down on the ground, empty.

"I think Joolan has a small wound, and Upny is hurt and had to leave the line. Exhaustion seems to be the bigger issue. These guys are professionals, and they're in shape to keep this attack up for the rest of the day."

Zander finished his statement for him. "We, however, will not."

Dar sighed. "That is most likely true."

"If only we had a way to tell central command that we needed some reinforcements." Deek turned to look in the direction of the Abbey. "What do you think would get their attention?"

"A dragon? Towering wall of water or flame?" Zander's humor lightened the situation, but neither Dar nor Deek actually smiled.

"What if we sent a runner back to the Abbey to get them to come and help out?" Deek looked at Dar as he spoke. "It would weaken our defenses by that much, but the help could turn the battle."

"I'll speak to Ocktur about it right away." Dar patted each of the brothers on the shoulder before walking to where Ocktur was. He was resting on one knee, looking ahead to see when the next wave would come crashing over them.

"Sergeant, I think we need to send a runner back to the Abbey to get reinforcements. The line won't hold."

Ocktur didn't blink. He just kept looking at the enemy on the other side of the trench. "We will not be asking for reinforcements."

Dar had figured this might happen, but still couldn't believe what he had heard. "But Sergeant, the next wave will probably break through. We are exhausted, you included. Second section is down a man, and any concentrated attack along one section will rout them. We need more help."

Ocktur stared out in the no-man's-land. His body language told Dar he had already accepted what fate would bring them. "Ax Company will either survive or it will not. If the protectorate wants to send troops, it will send them without us having to ask. How they know, I don't know, but if they can spare them, troops will be already be coming. Or they will not. So we will not be asking for reinforcements."

"So either we're saved, or we're sunk." Dar tried to read Ocktur's expression.

"I'll bet we're saved."

"How can you be so certain?"

"I hear horses coming from behind us." Ocktur lifted an arm and pointed to the enemy. "And they know it too."

Dar turned to see a cloud of dust clinging to the ground in the distance behind them. Shortly thereafter, the sounds of hooves could be heard sharply as the reinforcements approached. Ocktur stood up and took a deep breath.

"This battle is over."

EIGHT

Supply and Demand

"Whatever is wanted can be removed by a confidence scheme, straight theft, or threat. Violence is ugly and thereby amateurish and should always be the last resort of the professional."
—Centrix Lightfingers, from his biography, *The Thieves' Canticle*

Almost all the grass in the area being defended by Ax Company was already dead before the horses of Lightning Company started grazing. These were the true professionals of the Army of the Protectorate. They all wore custom-fitted plate-mail armor, each suit a beautiful silver with black and red highlights. Even the horses had chain mail and were therefore better defended than the members of Ax Company.

Lightning Company was overstaffed, having twenty-six riders as well as a sergeant leading them. They all kept to themselves, except for the leader of the company, who immediately went into Ocktur's tent as soon as it was clear the enemy had left the battlefield. It had struck Dar as odd that they hadn't pursued the enemy much past the trenches—Lightning could have chased them and routed the enemy, but they'd let them off. As if their orders were to hold the line and nothing more. Dar made a mental note to ask Ocktur what other standing orders they might have. Once again, it seemed as if it would be hard to win the war if they were only trying not to lose it.

"Dar, we need to do something about these weapons." Deek threw his sword down in front of his section leader. "I swear, I hit a guy, like, three times and barely even winded him. We should have killed twice as many, easy."

"My sword worked fine," Zander said sheepishly.

"Yours is obviously magic, Zander." Deek pulled out his stone. "As is this, but it appears to offer more in the way of defense than offense." Deek looked up at Dar. "Unless we get some sort of upgrade, this will be norm for all of our battles from here on out."

Dar nodded and pulled out his own weapon. The edge was dull, not sharp like Zander's weapon. The blade appeared to have been produced from a mold, poured from a blast furnace instead of handcrafted like Zander's magic blade. It was also an amalgamated metal, not pure steel like the other weapon. Probably part iron, part bronze or some other cheap metal. Whereas Zander's weapon almost shone in the dark, Dar's struggled to shine in light of the glorious noon-day sun. "You're right, Deek. We do need some upgrades."

"Let me guess: you'll talk to Ocktur about it." Deek huffed. "He'll just tell us that Ax Company doesn't get any reinforcements in either men or materials."

Dar smiled at how right he was, but countered by saying, "What do you suggest, then? We can't exactly make our own weapons."

Deek crossed his arms. "I think we should take weapons from the fallen enemies. They might not be any better quality than ours, but perhaps we could use them. If nothing more than to trade with other sections."

"Or other companies, if theirs are any better…" Zander looked his brother in the eye.

"You're wise beyond your years, my brother." Deek smiled at Zander. "At least in some things."

"I wasn't wise enough to say no to that succubus who helped capture us."

"Well, we had been drinking, and she was very beautiful." Deek drifted off into a memory. "I can't recall a more beautiful body."

Zander laughed. "First, she was naked, so of course she was beautiful. Second, she had horns. And a tail. And wings. Black, leathery wings. Third, we were drunk—you more so—to the point where she could have been a cow and you would have walked out of the tavern with her."

It was Deek's turn to laugh. "Yeah, I almost forgot about that part. Then she cast whatever spell it was, and *bam*! We're in the army now."

Dar shook his head. "That's a truly fascinating story, boys, but it doesn't help us much right now." Dar turned to Zander. "I think your idea to trade with other companies for better weapons is the way to go. We can collect items from the dead before taking them to no-man's-land and giving them back."

"What are you talking about?" Deek darted a look at Zander, who just shrugged. "We never took any bodies anywhere."

Dar took a deep breath and explained what he had done during his portion of the last night shift. Deek and Zander both nodded as the story went along, and Dar waited at the end for their reactions.

"Sounds pretty risky to me." Deek gave Dar a glance before looking down at the ground.

Zander elbowed his brother. "It was the right thing to do. Ocktur did enough to defile that one fellow—it was the least we could do to return the fallen soldiers to their brothers-in-arms for a proper burial."

"Alarm! Incoming wagon!" The call came from the guard post. It sounded like Drots.

"Wagon?" Deek looked at Zander, then Dar. "That's not something you hear every day."

"Or at all," Zander said. "It's coming from the enemy lines, so it must be a trap. Probably full of fireballs or diseases or something."

Dar went and stood along the edge of the lean-to. The other groups were just as stunned at the news as third section. From where Dar stood, he could see Jusin—his face was a blur of confusion and doubt. And now Ocktur was running out of his tent at full speed.

"This is it, people, let's get up and get ready." Dar turned to his section as he spoke, but something was nagging in the back of his mind. At the sight of Modo gripping his weapon tightly, he realized what it was: Ocktur was unarmed.

"Let's get out there, third section, but let's not overreact." Dar stepped out from under the shelter and headed over to the opening in the palisades. As he walked, he saw Pesha, the least capable member of first section, heading back to the supply tent. He quickly came out with two of the boards that Dar had used to transport the bodies to the no-man's-land. Dar and the rest of third section formed up and headed over to their regular positions, Modo at the rear. Dar could tell from his body language that he knew it wasn't a threat either. Perhaps Modo saw the same behavior from Ocktur that he had, or perhaps something else.

As they got a clear view of the wagon, Dar could see the wagon was driving over the wooden planks across the trench and toward the hole in the palisades. The wagon was a hodge-podge of materials piled as high as a man's eye. It was like the supply wagon that the orcs had driven, but shorter and with only one horse instead of a team. Oddly enough, that horse seemed to hover above the ground, its feet seemingly generating a glittering outflow that kept it in the air. The wood planks bent under its weight but didn't break, and following behind the wagon was an average-looking fellow just a bit shorter than Zander and almost a hand's width shorter than Dar and Deek.

He appeared to be about a decade older than Dar, and his face was worldly looking. His eyes scanned the Ax Company regulars and the Lightning troops with great interest. Suddenly, he bellowed in a voice twice his height, "Items for sale or trade. Items for sale or trade! Buy your scrap, sell you new scrap. Good terms, buy now!" He pulled on the back of the wagon, and the horse in the front slowed down. One more tug, and the whole contraption stopped. "Jesper is the name, and selling is the game. I heard you boys were holed up here, so I came with my good friend Mule to see if you had wares to sell or needed some."

Zander turned to his brother. "A horse named Mule. What's his wife's name? Mother?"

Deek paid his brother no mind. He was too busy staring at the newcomer, trying to figure out what was on the wagon. He saw tarps, blankets, cooking materials, some weaponry, and that was just what was visible—it appeared as if the wagon was filled with more than just the materials on top. That meant there was some internal storage, like drawers. Rings, magic wands, all the small things of interest crossed his mind. If only he had money. If only any of them had money. He thought about trading his lucky rock, but decided against it immediately. That was the type of item a person only came across once a lifetime.

"All transactions conducted in private," the peddler man said. "I'll talk to each one of you, one at a time." Jesper turned and looked around for something in the crowd. "Which one of you strong fellers is the commanding officer?"

Ocktur stepped clear of the group. "I am in command of this area."

Jesper faced him and bowed deeply. "With your kind approval, sir, I will park my wagon toward the back of this area as to keep your opening clear for horse traffic. I'd hate to be in your way as I try to conduct my business."

"You may call me Sergeant, and you may move your wagon, if the price is right."

"Prices, Sergeant?" Jesper looked Ocktur over, apparently trying to read how much of a bribe it would take this time. "Stand loitering fee, then, is it?"

Ocktur smiled, acknowledging that he would be getting a slice of the action. "That would be acceptable."

The head of Lightning Company came over to Ocktur and spoke briefly. The group then conducted a wheel turn, each horse at a perfect distance from the next. They walked out of the palisades opening, turned forty-five degrees, took two small steps, and turned another forty-five degrees, and so on until they were facing back toward the Abbey. They fit perfectly between the walls of the palisades. Dar smiled. The opening was gapped to fit the wheel maneuver of the horses and not for defensive purposes. No wonder the gap was at least twice as big as was needed. And therefore harder to defend. This was designed to keep the horse team more effective than the front-line troops.

Ocktur walked over Jesper, and they started a conversation. It appeared to be going along well when suddenly Ocktur walked away. Jesper pushed the wagon, which gave Mule the hint to pick up the load. A minute or two later, the wagon arrived close to the third-section lean-to. Dar drifted back in that direction and watched as Jesper set up shop. He pulled some items out of a drawer, organized the stacks of bric-a-brac on the top of the wagon, and appeared to do some sort of mental inventory on the whole mess. A moment later, apparently happy with the setup, he looked up, catching Dar's eye. Jesper smiled a kind, warm smile and kept moving until he was facing the opening of the palisades, where most members of the two companies were still milling around.

"According to the wishes of your Sergeant Ocktur," he announced, "we will be doing trade sessions as—what did he call them? Sections. Yes. By section. First section, you're up." Dar watched as Drots and the rest shuffled up. No one in that section had any money either, so they ended up trading things in for credit, which they used to buy other stuff. It looked like some of the items they were trading had been taken from the dead bodies in the last two attacks. In return, they got mostly luxury items, including drink and gambling aids. It seemed as if dice were more important than blankets or tools like whetstones or even jackets. Dar watched Jesper: he looked each man in the eye and watched him like a hawk until he had completed his transactions. Once everyone in first section seemed to be happy, Jesper spoke loud enough for the whole camp to hear.

"Now, once you step away, you can't return during this visit. I'll be back again soon, but once you step away, I won't do business with you further. Is there anything else you want?"

Dar saw some head shakes, and heard what sounded like two "no" replies. First company stepped away, and Jesper turned and reorganized his wagon. Some things were put away, and some new things were brought out. Again, another virtual checklist appeared to be reviewed, and once again, the peddler turned to look out at second section milling around at the palisades opening.

"Second section, please step up. Let us do business."

This round went exactly like the first: idle chatter, product demonstrations, haggling over prices, inspection of trade-in items, review of purchased materials, and then joy on the part of the soldier in acquiring a new distraction from this otherwise dull and deadly life. Dar continued to watch, awaiting third section's turn, noticing that Jesper wasn't tending to the wagon's contents as much as he had before.

"Third section, please." Jesper gestured to Dar. Dar walked over to the peddler's wagon and met Deek and

Zander there. Modo looked over the contents from afar, but went back into the lean-to, obviously disgusted at the lack of items that interested him. Dar was happy to have him elsewhere. It meant they could have a frank discussion with Jesper.

"I'm not sure you have what I'm looking for," Dar began in a smooth tone. He waited until Jesper was looking at him before he continued. "I'm looking for a most valuable commodity."

"I don't have much in the lines of jewelry, gems, magic, or platinum, but I'm willing to haggle over what I do have."

"I'm looking for..." Dar leaned in slightly. "Information."

"The most rare and expensive thing I have." Jesper smiled. "What do you want to know?"

"Will our query be kept private?" Dar held his breath. Jesper closed his eyes and paused. After a long moment, Jesper opened them again and nodded. "Good. I want to know all you know about this conflict. Where are we, and what are we fighting for?"

"You are on the floodplain that leads to the city of Highstar, which is beyond the Abbey toward the sea." Jesper stopped for a moment and appeared to consider this. "Though that is actually a bit misleading, since the sea lies in two of the four compass directions. In any case, Highstar sits on the sea with the river Star running on its flank. As for the cause of the war, if I recall correctly, this war started between two brothers. Each had a claim to the throne of Highstar—the war was very hot for a while, and it looked like the elder would win. But some trickery occurred. The elder brother left, the war stopped, and the younger brother ended up with the city. Why the brother left, I don't know. The younger brother still commands this side, however, that much I know. But all is not as it appears, and you should be cautious."

Dar showed little emotion at this, as did Deek; it was clear that Jesper was watching their faces for any sign of reaction as he told them the news.

"So now it's my turn. I have a question for you." Jesper waited for Dar to nod approval. "Who took the bodies to the middle ground of the war, and what was their intention?"

Dar shifted his weight and stretched his neck. "I took them there to be returned to their brothers, so they might have their fate known to their friends, families, and loved ones. I did nothing to them save look for anything of value, of which there was little. I did not defile, spoil, or soil them in anyway. I was attempting to honor them by returning them." His held Jesper's gaze for a long moment.

"I thought that might have been why they wound up there." Jesper broke eye contact and started to tinker with some equipment on the wagon. "They appreciated it. Not everyone around here treats the dead so kindly."

"You've been on the enemy lines?" Zander blurted out.

"Pardon my brother." Deek elbowed the older Vanander. "Of course he has, he came from the enemy lines, Zander Vanander—he came in through the palisades!"

Deek feigned a smile, which Jesper feigned back.

"Any relation to the Harlec Vanaders?" Jesper eyed the brothers. Discreetly, Dar shook his head.

"I'd rather not say," Deek replied. Dar could tell from the way Zander's face lit up that it was indeed so.

"Of course," Jesper demurred, letting the attempt at obfuscation slide. "Since you are the ones who were so noble, I have been prepaid and authorized to give each of you one item from my store." He lifted up a book and presented it to Zander. "This is a tome of great power. It will only be readable by you, when you most need it. When you are ready, the words will be there." Zander took the book and rifled through it; Dar could see from where he stood that the pages were all blank.

Jesper then turned his attention to Deek. "For you, I have a book, blank like your brother's, but you must fill up the pages. Unlike your brother's, others can read it, so guard it. When you wish, it will grow to full size—when you want, it will shrink to fit into your hand. And while you may not be able to use it right away, it will serve you well." He handed the tome to Deek, but it was Dar who recognized what it was. He would talk to Deek about it later.

"And to you"—Jesper turned and faced Dar—"I give you this." He handed a small white medallion to him, looking him in the eye. "I won't tell you what the medallion can do. I will tell you that as long as you have the medallion and continue with the faith it represents, I will answer your questions. Except about the items I have given you. Those you must figure out for yourself."

"Why?" Dar asked as he inspected the medallion.

"You have proven your worth—now you must prove you are ready. When you are both worthy and ready for the knowledge that will set your destinies in motion, these items will become known to you. As will I."

"How do you know our destinies?" Deek had tucked the book under his arm and was watching Jesper intently now. "What makes you so certain about our lives?"

Jesper took a deep breath and let it out slowly, a slight smile curling up at the corner of his mouth. "I'm not certain.

But I know that people on the other side, ones more powerful than I, have been keeping an eye on you, and while fate has dealt you a hard hand, these items are intended to help to soften the blow. And when you are ready, your hearts will tell you what you need to know."

"Are you a messenger from the gods?" Zander looked up from his book.

Jesper laughed loud enough for the whole camp to hear. He looked at Zander with a twinkle in his eye. "If I said yes, would you believe me? If I said no, would you believe that?"

"I would believe either answer if you said them with honesty." Zander blushed slightly.

"Don't get me wrong, kind sir. I am an operative of the divine, as are we all. But how that divinity is expressed in the world is through each person and through each moment. This is a moment where it sure appears that I am doing the work of the gods, but I assure you that I come at the request of man. They work for the lords of the sky, to be certain, but as for me and my motivations, that is for another time." As he uttered these last few words, he looked at Dar. Dar just squinted at him, wondering what he was talking about.

Silence descended on the wagon. Jesper seemed calm, simply awaiting the next question or the end of the transaction. Deek looked at Zander, and Zander looked at Dar. Dar just looked at the medallion in his hand.

"Any more questions?" Jesper's bright tone roused all three from their momentary funk. "I do have others on this side of the line to visit. You aren't the only interesting people over here. The most interesting, to be sure, but not the only." He smiled, pushing a black cast iron skillet and a feather duster around in the back of the wagon. "Last question."

When Dar caught Jesper's eye again, his right eyelid twitched a little, involuntarily. "Are we in an evil army or a good one?"

Jesper turned serious immediately. He appeared to ponder the issue for a moment, then started to say something three times before finally getting the words out.

"That is a matter of perspective." He pushed on the cart, and Mule started loping off toward the Abbey. "I suggest you check yours. I will return in three days. I look forward to trading with you then. I recommend having something of value then, since you have already expired all the credit due to you."

"Good-bye," Zander said in a weak voice. Deek looked at Zander with scorn, but Dar smirked at his good nature.

"Good-bye, Zander. Good-bye, Deek. See you soon, Dar."

It seemed an odd way to end the conversation. The three of them stood in silence for a while, until Ocktur came flying out of his tent, running toward the wagon. The trio watched as Ocktur rushed up to the wagon and—it appeared from the distance—attempted to strike Jesper. Jesper dodged the move, and both men walked in a loose circle, hunched over, apparently talking or trying to gain an advantage. As quick as it had started, both men came out of their crouched positions and stood upright. Jesper walked back to the wagon, did something toward the back of it, and tossed something to Ocktur. Ocktur then turned and started walking back to the camp.

"Must not have gotten his share of the take," Deek said. "Let's go back into the lean-to and see what new toys we have here."

Zander shook his head. "My book's still blank."

"Just like your head, eh, brother?"

Dar couldn't help it—he laughed out loud. Zander zinged back, "Yours is blank too, brother. So perhaps we both have blank heads." Deek laughed at that, and Zander went on. "As I don't remember most of last year, I think I would agree with you. But this outing we are on—I think it's changed me. I don't think I'll be the same again. And neither will you. Let me see your book."

Deek nodded and threw it at his brother. The throw was short, and Zander misjudged it. The book landed flat on the ground, and made the noise of a book much thicker than of that of the one before them. As Zander bent over to pick it up, his hand stopped just short. He paused.

"What's wrong, brother?" Deek smirked. "Afraid it will be too heavy?"

Zander straightened out. "I..." He sounded frightened. "I don't feel like I should touch it."

Dar rushed over and slowly lowered his hand to the book. "I feel it too. But I think it isn't as strong as—"

"What?" Deek walked up and slowly lowered his hand.

"Nothing," Dar said. "Nothing at all."

Deek picked up the book, flipped it open, and glanced at the empty pages. A grin snuck across his face—clearly, he was amused by their fear of this blank tome.

"It's a spell book," Dar started. "It was obvious to me then and it's obvious to me now. Probably a traveling spell book. It's very powerful, but I thought only magic users could handle them."

"I am not a wizard." Deek's smile faded. "I have thought about becoming one though. Before I was abducted, I was a squire to a magic user, but I have little in the way of formal training."

"I would give you the training I have," Dar told him, "but it would do more harm than good. I was thinking about dropping out of my apprenticeship before I got taken."

The conversation paused. Then Zander tossed his book to the ground, much the way Deek had his. "Try my book, Deek."

Deek lowered his hand to his brother's book. He was still about a hand's width from the book when he pulled his arm away. "It's like it's on fire!" Deek rubbed his fingers, apparently checking for damage. There was none.

"Dar, your turn." As Zander looked on, Dar reached down to touch the book. Expecting lightning bolts or shooting flames, Dar braced himself for pain that never came. He pulled his hand away and struck a thoughtful pose. "Not what I thought would happen. It didn't hurt or burn, but it didn't feel right."

Zander reached down and picked the book up. "It feels warm to me, a good kind of warm." He cradled it in his arms, up close to chest, as he turned to Dar. "What does your item do?"

"I honestly haven't tried." The medallion was a finger thick, white, and about twice the diameter of a gold coin, but far lighter. There was no chain, no clasp, nothing to indicate that it should be worn. Dar lifted it to his nose and sniffed it. "It's soap." He tossed it to Zander. "At least, it smells like soap."

Zander caught it and took a long sniff before he tossed it to Deek. "Yup. I say it's soap."

"If only we were allowed to bathe." Deek gave the medallion the once over himself. "Who gives out soap?"

Dar smiled and took the soap back. "Enough play time. We need to figure out what we know and what our next steps will be." He sat down on the floor of the lean-to and motioned for the brothers to join him.

Deek had begun to speak before his backside landed gently on the floor. "This Jesper fellow knows a lot more than he's telling us. He's connected to the right people on both sides of the lines. He was strong and skilled enough to deal with Ocktur, and both sides let him travel without much restriction. His information and resources are going to be key to our figuring out this conflict and resolving it."

"I agree." Dar nodded. "What do you think, Zander?"

"Jesper meant for us to have these items. He knows more than he is letting on, and clearly, he was trying to help just us. I think somebody knows about us on the other side, and these are tools to help us somehow. Maybe to escape? I think that something has caused the war to ebb, and we need to take advantage of that ebb. If we are fighting day to day, we won't have time to figure things out."

"Good assessment." Dar rubbed his chin. He hadn't shaved in a while and there was a hint of growth. Never one to grow facial hair, the stubble gave him something to expend his nervous energy on. "How do we turn what combat there is to our advantage?"

Deek fielded that question. "I think we need to respectfully remove any items of value from the bodies of the dead as quickly as possible and use them to negotiate for information and resources from Jesper. We know he will transport those items to the other side for possible sale to the enemy, so if they're important to them but worthless to us, he'll make sure they get returned to the rightful parties."

"So we are to become grave diggers and tomb raiders?" Zander raised his voice as he spoke.

Deek stifled a chuckle. "No, brother, we are not going to be necromancers, who gather their zombie horrors after midnight. Jesper has what we need, so we need to get things that he needs. Returning the dead to the neutral area between the two armies gathers us rewards. Watching the other sections, it was clear that he was trading with them for stuff that came off of the battlefield. The items he gave us are magical, so we know he has the goods we need."

Dar jumped in to help out. "We will always do what we do with the utmost care and integrity. We just will do things we wouldn't do normally. I'm not looking forward to this either, but Deek is right. We need more information, and Jesper is the only trustworthy source we have."

"What do you think he meant when you asked if we are fighting for good or evil?" Zander furrowed his brow.

It seemed to hurt Zander to scrunch up his brow like that. Dar guessed it wasn't something he had done a lot of before now. They all were on edge. "I'm not sure. I don't know how to get perspective when you only have one side to talk to."

"I'm pretty sure Ocktur is evil." Zander spat out the words like he had been saving them up for a while. "Nobody who is good would do what he does."

Deek raised his arm and gesticulated at his brother. "He keeps using the 'following orders' line too much to be evil. He didn't enjoy killing that prisoner. He…"

Zander cut him off. "He didn't let him live either. Though you're right, he didn't seem to enjoy the killing." He took a deep breath. "But Modo did."

"Am I evil?" came Modo's voice from behind Zander. All eyes turned to him. He smiled an impish grin, and his eyes widened. "Yes. I am."

NINE

Break

"The worst type of foe is the unpredictable one."
—General Groknar

With second section having the evening shift, third section found itself with time on its hands when the evening gave way to night. After Modo's comments, Dar had a hard time finding sleep. After a while he finally gave up and wandered around the encampment. Jusin was manning the watch, and he nodded when he caught Dar's eye. Again the moon was out in full, or as close to it as Dar could make out. The moonlight was enough to navigate by, but if you were careful enough, you could blend in. Dar softly walked to the enemy side of the palisades and headed toward what he assumed would be the next allied encampment up the line. He alternated walking and running, wanting to get back well before dawn so he could get some sleep, if it would come. He was sure after some exercise, it would.

After what seemed to be a half hour, Dar came upon another hole in the palisades. There was nobody on guard and no activity to be seen. There were some bodies in the field in front of the trench, though.

Dar jumped the trench and headed toward the body closest him. He heard a snore from down in the trench. Dar wrinkled his brow; the guard for this company was asleep. As much as that was good news for his own mission, Dar felt this was bad form.

When Dar reached the first body, he almost retched from the smell. This soldier had been killed a while ago and had lain here rotting since then. Dar felt the body over, searching for something firm to help him orient it for ease of searching, but all was spongy and foul. He figured out the body had leather armor on, and it was probably just a jerkin, since the texture of the torso was different from the legs. The moonlight was enough to see gross shapes, but not enough to tell a sack of coins from a rotting lunch bag, scroll from rotting flesh. As Dar worked his way up to the head, he felt something solid near the neck. Upon further inspection it seemed to be a smooth metal chain. Dar found no clasp, so he grabbed and pulled until it was released from the body. It gave way unexpectedly, and Dar found himself on his backside.

He looked around, as his landing had been pretty noisy. But the snoring continued unabated. He lifted the chain and looked up at it, silhouetted against the midnight sky—it was a small necklace with a gold rose hanging from it. The chain was a barely a wisp of metal—Dar figured that was how it hadn't been spotted the first time by the local company. As he rose to his feet, though, he was hit with a new, more pungent smell.

That's when it occurred to him what had happened to release the chain, though it was still clasped shut: the chain had acted like a garrote and actually severed the head from the body. Feeling sick to his stomach, he ran for Ax Company's base.

He only made it halfway before stopping to catch his breath. He could still smell the foul stench, which he was sure was still on the necklace. He eyed the trench to his right for a moment, then went up to the edge—as best as could determine, given the poor lighting conditions—and jumped into the mud and filth at the bottom.

Even though the topsoil was dry now, the trench still had standing water and mud along its whole length. Dar submerged the necklace in the water and swished it around. It came out clean, and Dar sniffed it gently. It smelled of earth and grass, much better than before. Satisfied with his cleanup job, Dar looked for an exit out of the trench.

He walked down toward the end where Ax Company was located. There seemed to be no exits. Occasionally, Dar would stop and feel around for handholds or ladders or something else that might be lurking in the shadowy darkness that could be leveraged into a way out. After what seemed like a period longer than his initial venture beyond the palisades, Dar came to a ramp and climbed out. His feet were covered pretty well by mud at this stage, and his footfalls were noisy. Hopefully, no one was around up top.

Finally cresting the surface of the trench, Dar could see strange forms moving between the trench and the palisades opening. They were sneaking toward the opening. Dar crouched, assuming they were enemies. Now the mud on this feet changed effect; in the trench it had been a noise generator, but up here in dry conditions, it muffled his steps. So Dar moved to a position behind the man at the rear of the group, trailing behind him by a good two steps. Feeling he had the advantage, Dar pulled out his weapon and leapt forward to close the distance. The mud couldn't keep the sound down this time, but the leader of the group turned before Dar's target could.

"Sil'threll!" shouted the leader, but it was too late. Dar struck, with his blade right at the shoulder of the attacker; the blade just buried itself in the armor and produced a loud cracking sound. The target collapsed to the ground and rolled over onto his back. Dar stood up straight and readied for the next in line to come and pay him a visit. Before the next one could get to him, though, Dar yelled the alarm.

"Ax Company! Alarm! Alarm!"

Dar couldn't say more before he had to focus on his own survival. He blocked a blow to his chest, and his weapon cracked under the force of it. Dar knew that half of the cracking sound was the shoulder of his foe and half was the sound of his sword giving out. His foe's weapon appeared to be the same as his—a longsword—but much more robust in construction. Instinctively, Dar leapt back and ran his fingers across the flat of his blade, looking for the crack. Finding it about halfway down, he figured out how to turn his weapon to minimize the extra damage each collision would do to it—just in time to block another incoming blow.

A light appeared from Ocktur's tent and flooded the area. There were only four attackers, it appeared, and one was already down on the ground. Their leader quickly put away the sword he was carrying and pulled out a bow. Notching an arrow, he let it fly at Ocktur's lamp. The arrowhead pierced the oil store below the wick, and oil flew everywhere. Ocktur dropped the lamp, which fell to the ground, setting the spilled oil on fire. Dar swore he heard an arrow fly past his head, but his attention was still too focused on the target in front of him to figure it out. The light changed from the bright, focused light of the lantern to the more diffused light of a puddle of burning oil.

"Retreat!" the leader of the attackers said.

Dar blocked another blow, and this time his sword gave out, making a sharp sound as the shoddy metal gave way under the force of the more refined weapon. Dar's foe followed up his blow with a rounding kick that struck Dar's leg and knocked him to the ground. Then his foe fled to the safety of his own lines, taking his leave from the battle.

As Dar struggled to his feet, he could make out the outline of the leader and another of the foes making their way across the trench. That just left the one that Dar had wounded in the shoulder. Dar could see him getting up. He ran to grapple with this remaining enemy, but misjudged the distance in the half light, and his tackle landed a little low. Getting his foe's waist instead of his torso, Dar struggled to keep him from moving. He had most of his weight on the sore shoulder side of his target, and with his right hand Dar reached for anything, finally finding a leather strap. The strap led to a pack or cylinder on this fellow's back. Dar could hear shouting, and it sounded like the arrows were flying around again. He suddenly felt his foe spinning around, and then Dar was facing the compound, with his back to the leader with the bow. Since he had misjudged his tackle, his legs dangled free of the enemy, giving the bowman a clear shot.

Then suddenly, Dar felt a stinging pain in his left leg. Summoning all his strength, he tried to pull the man down, but he was just too strong for Dar. Just as Dar was getting ready to release his grip, the leather strap gave way, and he and the cylinder fell to the ground. His foe had escaped—when Dar turned, he could see the man jumping over the trench.

Instead of finishing Dar off with the bow, the archer had aimed several more arrows into the opening of the palisades, and by the sound of it, they'd hit something at least once. Dar touched his wound. Blood flowed freely, but there was no arrow in his leg. It had been a near miss, and while the cut was long—it felt almost as long as Dar's pointer finger—it wasn't very deep. While the scar would look vicious, the wound was not life threatening if properly cared for. Dar waited for a moment to make sure the arrow play had stopped, then rose and walked into the palisades. Where he was immediately met by Jusin.

"Halt!" He pointed his weapon at Dar.

"Jusin, it's me, Dar, leader of third section." Dar put his hands in the air and shifted his weight to favor his good leg.

"Dar? Name the troopers in your section." Jusin squinted at Dar, struggling to make out his features in the dim light of the burning oil.

"My team is Deek, Zander, and Modo. And let me in, this leg wound hurts."

"What's my favorite color?" Jusin let the tip of his sword drop slightly.

"I don't know, you never mentioned it. In fact I don't even know if you have a favorite color."

"It's royal red. Just in case I ask again later when you come back home after breaking up an enemy attack." Dar could hear the smirk in Jusin's voice.

Ocktur walked up, holding a smaller lamp, his hand bandaged. In his other hand he had a pole, probably from the materials tent. He lifted the light up and hooked it on the end of the pole. He then lifted the pole, putting the light to eye level. "Report, Jusin."

Jusin faced Ocktur. "We were attacked. Dar helped sound the signal and break up the attack."

"An attack at this time of night?" Because Ocktur was standing right under the lamp, it was hard to see his expression, but by his tone, he was concerned. "How many did you see?"

"I saw four," Jusin reported. "Dar?"

"Just the four."

"Dar, report." Ocktur sounded much more subdued than normal.

"I was out in the trench for a moment, and when I came out, I saw those four making their way to our camp. I attacked, but my sword broke, wounding one of the enemies. I yelled to signal the alarm and grappled with the wounded attacker, trying to tie him up enough for somebody from second section to help me out."

Jusin jumped in. "But there was an archer in the group, and we were pinned behind the palisades. Dar himself was wounded by the archer, and I think Dyo got hit in the upper arm as he crossed the opening."

"I believe I asked Dar." It sounded like Ocktur was talking through clenched teeth.

Dar sensed Ocktur's rising ire, and since Jusin was one of the few he felt he could trust, he wanted to make sure that Jusin didn't incur his wrath. Especially since Ocktur appeared to be wounded in both body and spirit.

"Jusin had it correct, Sergeant." Dar figured using the command title would appeal to the man's vanity and help soothe any building anger. "That arrow volley would have been fatal if second section hadn't held back. I'm lucky this wound isn't in my back or belly. It could have just as easily killed me."

Jusin chimed in, catching on to what Dar was trying to do. "I felt that risking some of our assets to get one attacker was not a fair trade based on the training and standing orders I have received, Sergeant."

"Did we gain anything from this attack?" Ocktur's tone had gone back to sounding defeated.

"I believe I wounded one," Dar said, "and caused him to leave behind some of his kit. I think that might be valuable. Plus, we stopped an attack, so perhaps they won't try again for a while."

"Or they will be back with a larger force." Ocktur lowered the pole and reached for the handle of the lantern. "What happened to our guards? Why did Dar sound the alarm and not the soldier on duty?"

Dar could see Jusin squirming. "I'm not sure, Sergeant. Banes is the man on duty."

Ocktur stormed off to where the night guard would normally stand. There he found Banes slumped over on the ground, fast asleep. "Banes!" Ocktur kicked him hard in the stomach. Banes shifted a bit, but—strangely, considering the force of the blow—did not wake up. Ocktur cast a glance at Dar. "Get some water." After Dar walked off, he could hear Ocktur tell Jusin, "If he's drunk, he's dead."

When Dar returned with the water, Ocktur had dropped to his knees and was leaning over Banes. He sniffed his face, then sniffed his clothes. Dar offered Ocktur the keg of water, but he lifted a hand. "Don't need it. This is magic. He's not drunk, and he's not just asleep, he's out of it. Only magic can do that. The person who attacked us is a magic user."

Ocktur rose to his feet and started walking toward his tent. "Follow me, Dar. Jusin, find Drots and meet me in my tent. I'm leaving for the Abbey right away." Jusin ran off, and Dar joined him in the tent. He had expected Ocktur to say something to him privately, but no wisdom or orders were forthcoming. Finally, Drots and Jusin joined them.

"Magic use is forbidden by both sides right now. The fact that somebody used it means the current combat rules are changing, and the general needs to know about this. They never attack twice in one night, so I believe it is safe for me to visit him tonight without much risk to Ax Company. I want Dar to be in charge again while I'm gone. Jusin, I would have selected you, but you just came off night duty. And Drots, your team is just heading to night duty, so that wouldn't work either. I'll be back before nightfall tomorrow. Just hold the line, and don't do anything fancy. Any questions?" Ocktur looked at Drots, then Jusin, and by the time he got to Dar, Dar was already speaking.

"A couple of questions, Sergeant. One, can you request better weapons for us? These weapons have failed us and cost us at least three fatalities to the enemy. That will mean failure over the long term, since if we have to effectively kill the same guy three or four times, that multiples their force and makes them nearly impossible to beat. Plus, sharper weapons will make them fear us and allow us to hold the line longer."

"And your next question?" It was clear Ocktur was already losing his patience, probably thinking ahead to his time at the Abbey.

"Please remember to check on permission for us to bathe." Dar had a couple more issues, but he figured his time was over.

"I'll do what I can." Ocktur stood. "Anything else? No? Dismissed." Ocktur hadn't waited for answer. When he was heading to the Abbey, Ocktur tended to be sharp with his words and quick to action. Dar wondered what it was about the Abbey that made him that way.

The three section leaders walked out together, and Drots looked kicked in the ego again. "How do you do it, Dar?" He didn't even bother to turn to look at him. "Find yourself on the right side of the issue every time. I'm still the best, though, and you're still third section. You just wait."

Dar noticed that Jusin had let his hand slip down toward his weapon. Dar knew better to say anything and slowed his pace. Drots kept going, finally ending up at his lean-to, while Jusin headed off to serve as the guard for the next shift. Dar made his way to his shelter and lay down to sleep. Dar had trouble sleeping, half expecting Drots to come in and slit his throat. After a while he heard Ocktur leave, and that restarted his brain. Every sound made him jump, but the effort he'd expended that night finally took its toll. As he drifted off to sleep, he hoped he would wake up.

Dar woke with a start, not sure if the dream he was having was real or not. He had been back at the tower, and Master had visited the magical pantry, only to find that Dar had let all the food spoil and turn moldy. Master was furious with him and was just about to punish him when he woke up. Dar looked around to see what reality he was in.

"Morning." Zander was flipping through his book, each page apparently still blank. Dar's eyes met his. "Bad dream, yes? I have them all the time. In fact, I'm certain this is a bad dream, and when I wake up I'll go have a good cry, a good laugh, and a good bath to wash all of it away. I'll miss you, Dar, but little else."

Deek walked up to his brother. "If this is a dream, it is most certainly a nightmare."

"Always the fun one, eh, brother?" Zander shook his head as he spoke.

Dar was in no mood for joviality or even much talking. His leg had finally stopped bleeding, but it hurt. So did his head; he must have taken a blow during his tackle. Plus, his feet hurt from the dried, cracked mud, and the sweat, dirt, and tears on his face made him feel gross. "Has Ocktur returned?"

"Ocktur left?" Zander looked at him. "I didn't see him this morning, but I figured he was just in his tent."

"We'll just wait it out, then. He's gone to the Abbey and hopefully will return with new orders."

"Great, another variable." Deek huffed. "If we don't start getting answers to our list of problems soon, we'll be here forever."

"I'll settle for the bath and a good weapon, if that's part of our new orders." Dar explained to the brothers about his time on the other side of the palisades. "I'm going slowly mad, and having some sense of trust in my weapon would really help."

Deek nodded. "Yes, it will be nice to get some real weapons. It seems like we got the worst weapons of the company—Zander's excepted."

"Modo is happy with his weapons." Modo always seemed to be heard but never seen. This time he was behind the back of the lean-to, just close enough to listen in but invisible behind the cloth. Why had he commented now? Dar wondered.

"Well, good for you, Modo." Deek was in an unusually bad mood today. "I guess that's the reason why you're so good and everything else is so bad. If only your good weapons were enough to put you in charge of the section."

Modo took a step around the side of the lean-to, toward Deek. "If you want to test my combat power, that can be done right now."

Dar was in no mood for it. "Both of you belay that attitude. We're stuck with each other."

Modo bared his fangs. "If you were not the pet of the section leader, coward Deek, I would have your blood on my hands by nightfall." He clutched his weapon. He had fully healed, and Dar could see that he now felt ready to make his move to take over the section.

"I gave you a direct order, Modo." Dar stood and lowered his tone to what he considered his command voice. It made his voice carry and have more weight, but it was not natural for him, and he had to concentrate on it. "Stand down, or stand charged with disobeying a direct order. Pet or not, you have to respect my position."

Modo looked Dar in the eye with an intensity that matched his own. "I recognize your authority and obey, Section Leader." Modo turned and cast a glance at Deek, but said nothing. Modo walked off through the palisades and headed to the trench, where he disappeared out of sight.

"You really set him off that time," Zander said to his brother. Deek was clearly shaken by the whole event. "I think the next time you should bite your tongue."

Dar weighed in. "I agree. Modo's back up to full strength, so you know he'll be fighting to get into a position of authority, and anybody weaker than he is will taste his wrath. I think he believes both of you Vanander brothers are weaker than he is, which means you'll both be at risk for a while."

"Just what we need." Deek stared off at the horizon. "Enemies across the way that want to kill us, and friends in our own camp who want to kill us too. If this gets worse, I'm not sure what I'll do."

"I'm pretty sure it can't get worse, Deek." Zander smiled at him.

"Modo being in charge would be worse," Deek shot back. "I think we should consider hurrying up with our plans in case he decides to make trouble."

Dar sighed. "What plans? We need to collect more information, then we can plan." He dug around in the supplies for something that could service his wound.

Now it was Deek's turn to smile. "That's what I meant."

They sat in silence for a while as the brothers watched Dar bandage his leg. It took him three tries, because each time he picked off a small piece of the scab, it started to flow again. Finally happy with his bandage, he stood up and walked over to the supply tent to test the it in action. Just as he was turning back to the lean-to, he noticed somebody off in the distance. He watched them approach, and at about one hundred paces, he could tell that it was Ocktur. So he waited. And waited. Ocktur must not be in any hurry today, Dar told himself. Finally Ocktur was within earshot.

"Section Leader Dar." He sounded unusually mellow. "What a good day. Prepare your men and spread the order. We are going for a bath!"

"A bath, Sergeant?" Dar wanted to make sure that he was not hearing things.

"Well, it's not a bath directly—not like I had this morning at the Abbey—but I did get permission to take Ax Company to the river just next to the city and allow you all some free time there. We'll need to double-time march there and back, but we should make it." Ocktur smiled. "It hurt to get out of bed early, but I did get to try your bath idea, and I must say it was nice. Of course she…" Ocktur let the smile melt off his face. They had reached the opening to his tent. "We don't have time for my stories. Get your men ready."

"Yes, Sergeant."

Dar walked over to Jusin and told him the news, leaving him to tell Drots and the rest of Ax Company. Then Dar made his way over to the third section lean-to and informed the brothers. As word spread around the camp, the group began to mill around near Ocktur's tent. Out of the corner of his eye, Dar could see Modo climbing out of the trench to join the edge of the group. After a while, Ocktur emerged and spoke to the troops.

"As you have heard, we are trying out my new concept for keeping you troops in prime condition. We will take a hike of several leagues, take some time out in the river, then march back. We will leave as soon as Killer Company arrives. Killer Company is the reinforced part of Lightning Company, and they should be here shortly. Grab anything you want to take with you and form up. Anybody not ready will stay with Killer and get special attention from me when we return." Ocktur eyed the group. "Go!"

The group scrambled around, and those who wanted to take something with them left, while those without anything to fetch just stood in line. Modo remained, but the brothers went back to the tent—Zander for his blank book, and Deek to keep Zander company. Dar accompanied them and grabbed his soap. Just as Dar was about to turn and head back to the formation area, Jusin walked up, holding a quiver that had six arrows left in it.

"These belong to you, I believe." He held up the item.

"Me?" Dar reached out and took it in hand. "To what do I owe this honor?"

"This is the item that you cut off of the opponent last night. It was found near the trench. One of my men found it, and I figured, after what you did for second company last night, you should be rewarded." Jusin smiled, clearly trying to put a good face on a bad night.

"My actions? I just defended the camp."

"Others would have parlayed second section's failures to their advantage. I know Drots would have blamed us for it so he could get deeper into Ocktur's favor. You didn't, and I wanted to thank you for it. Dace being knocked out could have been the end of my whole section."

"The more Drots works to get into Ocktur's favor, the more he falls out of it." As Dar spoke, he examined the arrows, which appeared to be of high quality. Their shafts were made from black walnut and fletched with goose down, and the arrowheads forged from black steel. They were broad and sharp, looking like they could pierce any armor. No wonder his leg had been cut so badly. The blade of the arrow was almost three fingers wide. "These are impressive."

"There might have been more, but my men might have taken them. I tried to recover other arrows from inside the base, but when they hit, the head breaks off from the shaft. Probably to make extraction from the wound that much harder. No doubt about it, these are finely crafted weapons."

"I am honored that you gave them to me." Dar could hear the thunder of hooves in the distance. "We need to get back into formation, though. Killer Company is close."

Jusin nodded, and they all left to join the ranks. And just as he'd promised, Ocktur left with their formation the moment Killer Company acknowledged that they had command of the base. Ocktur set a slow pace, and after they were a ways out of the encampment, no more than a mile, Ocktur halted the formation and spoke to them.

"Gentlemen." He surveyed the troops before continuing. "I am going to spend the rest of the morning at the Abbey, joining you after noon. I am leaving Drots in command of the company. He will mark you in a straight line to the wall of the town, then head north to the river. You will stay at the river until I come to take you back to our station. Seeing as how there are no questions, Drots, you have command."

"I have command, Sergeant." Drots could barely contain his excitement. "Company, form two ranks and march!" Drots lined them up in pairs and started them off again toward the wall that kept Highstar safe. Drots took a position off to the side of the two columns and set a quick pace. He called cadence only once in a while—whenever, it seemed, he felt that everyone wasn't paying enough attention to him.

They had been marching for a while when Jusin recognized the formation was off step from Drots. Jusin cleared his throat to signal to Drots that he was off time.

"I'm always right, you're always wrong," Drots called back. He watched as everyone else in the formation changed his pace. Then he started changing the pace, and not calling cadence. He would wait for everyone to adjust and then shift it again. It was driving everyone mad. "I'm sure if Sergeant Ocktur was here, he'd be scolding you all for being so slow to acknowledge the chain of command."

"If Ocktur was here, he'd keep an even count," came a voice from the back of the line. Third section—Deek. Dar was marching right next to him, but couldn't seem to stop him in time.

"Ax Company, halt!" Drots walked to the back of the formation. He looked over Dar and the Vanander brothers. "Dar?"

"Yes, Section Leader Drots?"

"Commander Drots, if you don't mind—I'm in charge now." He'd apparently made up the title up on the spot.

"Yes"—Dar let the moment drag—"Commander."

"I heard that remark come from your section. Do you know who it was that spoke?" Drots looked him over, squinting at him. It was clear he was challenging him to do something rash.

"No." Dar knew who it was, of course, but didn't want to rat him out to Drots. Because Deek was right and Drots was way out of bounds.

"No, what?"

"No, Commander."

"I see. I'll make the judgment myself, then." Drots looked at Deek, who was looking more than a little guilty. "Modo. You are guilty of the act, and I will make sure Ocktur punishes you for disobeying orders and not respecting the chain of command." He turned and walked away.

"You need to confess." Modo spoke through his teeth to Deek. "I will not take your punishment."

"He knew it was Deek, Modo." Dar spoke as quietly as he could while still being heard. "He's playing a game, and you're falling for it. He wants you to do something stupid."

"My honor is not stupid."

"Listen to Dar." Deek spoke in hushed tones as well. "He wants you eliminated because you pose a threat to his physical power, and Dar represents a challenge to his leadership power. If you are removed from third section, that makes first section that much more powerful. I'm sorry you got blamed for me, but you know he's being a petty tyrant."

"Enough chatter back there!" called out Drots. He was beaming.

By the time they reached the wall of the city, probably everyone was thinking how Ocktur wasn't that bad. They had changed cadence so many times that most couldn't keep up anymore. Drots only cracked down on third company, though, so the other members didn't even try—well, everyone but Jusin, Dar noticed. When they got to the wall, Drots had them take a rest, mostly so he could get a good look at the fortress that was Highstar. It had taken them almost twice as long as it should have to get there—the pacing had been that bad.

Drots took in the wall and all of its majesty. "I will return here, and instead of walking on the outside, the city elders will invite me in and honor me as the hero that I am."

167

Dar wasn't impressed by Drots's comments. But he was impressed with the wall. Where his tower was barely over forty feet tall, these were at least three times that in height. But there also seemed to be something wrong with them. They seemed poorly manufactured, and the stones repeated in an odd fixed pattern, perfect, without even a slight variation. For a cobblestone-style wall, it wasn't quite right, but it was a behemoth of a fortification.

"Haven't you guys seen a defensive wall like that before?" Deek wondered out loud. "We have walls that size at home."

Zander turned and looked at him. "No we don't. Those are at least one hundred feet tall." Zander's gaze danced up and down the wall, refining his estimate. "More like a hundred thirty."

"No it's not," Deek said flatly.

"Yes, it is," Modo joined in. "I am impressed with the size of the wall. I would guess one hundred and twenty-five. Give or take five."

"Are we looking at the same wall?" Deek clearly couldn't believe what they were saying. "That wall is fifty, tops. When we first came into view of it, it looked bigger, but as I looked at it, it didn't look right. It seemed to lose height at we moved up toward it. At this distance, I think it's just fifty feet."

"Are you calling Modo a liar!" Modo got right into Deek's face.

"No, Modo!" Dar forced himself between the two.

Drots watched from a distance as Dar interjected himself between Deek and Modo. This was too perfect. After all the setbacks, things were finally going his way. Perhaps third section would entirely implode and solve all of his troubles.

"Ax Company! Form up!" Drots gave them just a moment to get into place. He noticed that Dar had paired up with Modo, while Deek and the other Vanander brother we together behind Modo and Dar, making Deek diagonal to Modo. Meaning, if Modo went after Deek, both of the others could jump in and break it up. Time to make sure things weren't that balanced.

"Dar, could you join me up front? And Modo, you haven't corrected your shame, so you get to march last in the organization. Here, right behind Deek." Drots couldn't contain his feelings and let out a small cackle.

"I know what you're up to, Drots." Dar said as he walked to the front of the formation. "You're trying to break Modo or one of the brothers so you can blame me and eliminate some competition."

"I know, isn't it a wonderful plan?" Drots was beaming. "The best part is, you can't do anything about it."

"We'll see about that. Modo knows what you're doing and won't fall for it."

"I agree. He won't do anything until we get to the watering hole." Drots turned to face the troops. "Ax Company! Double time! Quick march! Go!" They took off in a trot. Soon both Vanander brothers were slowing down, unable to keep the pace, forcing Modo to modify his gait to avoid knocking them both over. Drots was pleased to see him glower at them.

The whole company was pretty winded when they crested a small sandy ridge that shaded the river from the floodplain that lead up to the city. They were still in the shadow of the large defensive walls—as high as they were, it was hard not to be. At the place where the walls turned to follow the river, there was a small beach that formed a small bend in the river. The river itself was a monster here. It was a mile wide, as Dar judged it, and he could see something that looked like an encampment on the other side. The river flowed pretty fast for its size, and by the looks of the whitewater, it was pretty shallow at least part of the way across. It was probably too fast for crossing by horse or walking, but not deep enough for crossing via barge, boat, or skiff. Like the defensive wall, there was something odd about the river—Dar had never seen one this broad that was so fast. Or so shallow. But the area where they'd stopped was pretty calm, and as they got to the river's edge, they could see the sandy part was an island, just about a twenty paces away from the shore proper. The channel that created the island was slow and gentle, though the river on the other side of the island was rushing. Dar figured the channel was the best place to wash off.

"All right, boys," Drots called out from next to Dar. "We are here. Time to do whatever you're going to do. Dismissed."

Dar rushed back to Modo and the rest of third section. Modo had already walked away from the formation, and while everyone else stopped in the channel area, Modo headed into the fast part of the water. Dar had to run to catch him. "Modo! We need to talk!"

"You do not need to worry about me, human." He dove into the water head first, quickly disappearing from sight. Apparently, Dar couldn't read rivers very well. It seemed there were three channels in the water. The river went shallow, deep, shallow, deep, shallow, and then there was the channel that formed the island that most of the company was already resting on. Dar hadn't noticed it at first, but it was like the water was different every time he looked at it. This whole area wasn't right.

"Hey, Dar!" Zander called out. "Nice river here, isn't it. The rapids in the middle look nasty."

"Yes, they do." Dar looked out in the river. He thought he saw something in the far channel that looked all dark and menacing like Modo. But that couldn't be him, since he would have to get out of the water to get to the rapids in the other channel. "Let's get to work, Zander." Dar fished out his bar of soap from his pocket and went to hand it to Zander. "You can go first."

"I'd like to sun myself a little first."

Dar looked into the sky. He was so busy worrying about Modo and Drots he hadn't noticed how beautiful the day had turned out. He put the soap away and enjoyed the moment. The sun was shining hot and bright, bathing the land in a radiance that was almost intoxicating. Being stuck behind the lean-tos and the palisades and in the slum of the trenches had been hard on him, he realized. He had always been a man who loved the beauty of the land, and perhaps that was what had been distracting him back at the tower with Master. He enjoyed the physical work of his apprenticeship, and the spells were fun, but there was another side of him that hadn't been getting attention. He realized he needed more than wizardry could offer. But being a cog in a big army or hired sword wasn't attractive either, and he didn't have the boundless faith and wisdom to be a cleric. And being a druid was just tipping the balance the other way, giving up the city for the woods. Dar wanted to be part of the world and to do good in it. But he wasn't sure, at that point, how.

"You have any idea where Modo is?" Deek interrupted Dar's daydreaming.

"Umm, what?" Dar shook his head, as if physically trying to dislodge the thoughts from his head and get his mind back into the present.

"Modo. Have you seen him?" Deek sounded concerned.

Dar tried to reassure him. "I haven't seen him since he dove into the river. I don't think he's going to bother you. He can vent his anger on the river. He can hunt and kill the fish or whatever is in there. I just hope he doesn't get caught up in the rapids." Dar looked out on the water. "Of course, he can breathe underwater, so I guess it isn't that big of a deal."

"Rapids? What rapids?"

Dar turned, looked at Deek sharply. "What do you mean, 'What rapids?'"

Deek just stared at him blankly.

"Tell me," Dar said, "what do you see out there?"

"An idyllic river, broad, deep, and with a fairly good movement to it. Why those guys on the other side don't just a sail a boat over is something I don't understand." Deek said it like every idiot should see it the same. Then, clearly, it hit him. "What do you see?"

"Well, rapids, obviously." Dar stared at the river.

"Magic?"

"Magic."

TEN

Versus

"Reality is only what you believe. What everyone
else believes is the illusion."
—traditional start of the opening speech at the
annual gathering of the Hierarchy of Illusionists

Dar sat down hard on the sandy bank, kicking up a little sand in the process in Zander's face. Zander kept
his eyes closed as he reached up and brushed the sand off.
"Nothing can bother me right now. This sun is too enjoyable,
and this sand is just right."

Dar turned to Deek. "There is really sand here, right?"

Deek crashed down on his backside too, kicking up a little
sand onto his brother as well. "It is lovely and easy on the skin.
I've never seen finer sand."

"So we agree on something. It's hard to have a conversation with somebody when you're seeing two different things."
Dar leaned back and rested on his elbows.

Zander opened his eyes. "Different things?"

Dar sighed. "According to your brother, this area is covered in magic, and we aren't seeing what's really there."

"How do you know that we aren't seeing the real thing and he's the deluded one?" Zander closed his eyes again. "Deek has always thought the world began and ended with him."

"As do you, brother." Deek picked up some of the sand idly and let it slip out of his fingers. "Which is more likely, given the landscape here? A fast river with two deep channels to scare off crossing and a fast, shallow section to scare off boats—or an easy, gentle river?" He turned over his hand and let the rest of the sand escape. "Or how about a city that has to go around Holimoren pressing people into their army but can afford walls as tall as twenty-five men? I just didn't believe it when I saw it, and I guess I still don't. So I guess the illusion doesn't work for me at all."

Zander let him finish before retorting. "But since you've told us that it isn't real, why hasn't it changed for us? How do you know I'm not an illusion?"

"I think it hasn't changed for you because you believe your own eyes more than you trust my words. Words lie easier than your eyes, and you've lived your whole life trusting them. Your eyes have delivered you from evils that your ears enjoyed. I could tell you that I'm a kitchen table, but unless your eyes believed it, you won't believe me."

"So it's a matter of faith, then?" Zander sounded more skeptical than when the conversation had started.

"I think so. If when you first see it you believe it, you're done; your mind won't be turned against it unless something you can see changes it for you."

"So if you threw a rock at the wall a hundred feet in the air, it would dispel the magic?" Zander sounded interested, but not interested enough to actually open his eyes.

"I don't know." Deek sighed, clearly frustrated. "I don't have formal magic training. And definitely not training in illusions." His eyes drifted to Dar.

"Don't look at me—I don't have illusion skills. I mostly did abjuration and enchantment stuff. Locate Object, Burning Hands, Strength, combat spells mostly." Dar shrugged. "I wouldn't know how to dispel the magic. I'm sure whoever did this must be very powerful."

"The general?" Zander opened one eye and focused on Dar.

"That would be my guess." Dar nodded slightly. "Should we ask him?"

The comment brought a hush over the group. It was clearly the thing to do, but gaining access to the general via the chain of command would be hard, if not impossible. They had only seen him once—would they even know him if they saw him again? And what if he *wasn't* the source of the illusion? Dar's mind raced with all these questions and a thousand answers to them, none of which he could prove, and only a handful of which he liked.

They let the time pass in silence for a while, enjoying the calm, the lack of a threat, and the easy sunshine. It was almost like there wasn't a war—like death wasn't waiting around the next corner—like they were back where they belonged. Finally, Deek ended the silence.

"I'm going to go wash." He stood up and held out his hand. "Where's your soap, Dar?"

Dar reached into the pocket of his jerkin and pulled out the medallion-shaped bar. "Don't lose it."

"As long as it doesn't float away, I'll be fine." Deek chuckled. "Here, keep an eye on my lucky rock." He took out the gold-trimmed stone and tossed it to Dar, who placed it in his jerkin where the soap had been.

"Be careful, Deek." Zander had opened his eyes and propped himself up on his elbows. "This isn't home."

"I know, big brother." Deek walked off to the water; Zander closed his eyes and resumed his prone position.

"Dar! Come here!" Dar looked up. It was Drots.

"I wonder what he wants." Dar cast a glance at Zander, who had perched up on his elbows again.

"I bet it's no good." Zander grimaced. "You be careful too."

"I know, big brother," Dar said playfully.

"He only says that when I'm annoying him." Zander lay down again. "Which also happens to be only when I'm right."

Dar nodded and walked over to Drots.

Deek had started out in the water pretty close to where Zander was lying. As long as his brother was in sight, he figured, he would be fine. But the water here was pretty shallow, only just above the ankle. That would be hard to get wet in, let alone wash. So Deek wandered toward the main channel, which put him out of sight of the main group. He figured he was still within shouting distance, so that was good enough. The water here was a bit deeper, almost to the knee, but the water was silty at the confluence of the channel and the main river. He looked over to the side of the channel closest to the wall—there appeared to just be rocks there, so the water was bound to be clearer.

As Deek waded to the other side, the water grew deeper. He had to swim for a moment, and then his foot found a large rock. He waded forward to another rock and sat down. He thought he heard a splash out in the deeper water, but saw nothing. The river was sure to be filled with fish, he told himself, and they were probably jumping after their lunch. Deek watched the bugs skim and dance upon the surface of the water, something that he figured Zander and Dar couldn't see because of the illusion. Seeing rushing water, the magic would hide any still-water background details. He looked over at the island where the members of the company were sunning themselves. It was pretty far away—farther than he had intended—so he started washing. The quicker he was done, the quicker he could return.

Dar was now close enough to Drots to see his smug expression. He was most certainly up to something.

"Commander."

"I have sent for you because I wanted to take this chance to let you apologize for your section's horrible performance during my tenure as commander." Drots stared at Dar, clearly hoping to catch him at something.

"And what exactly are your charges?" Dar didn't make eye contact with him. That smug look of his was sure to drive Dar to violence. And straight into Drots's hands.

"Disobeying a direct order, behavior not fitting for a section leader—I could go on."

"Please don't," Dar said wryly.

"I will if I want to." Drots smiled. "I don't like you, you don't like me. You need to recognize that I am superior to you, and I always will be."

"Why do you have that view?" Dar choose his words carefully. "What makes you think that you are superior to me?"

"You don't see it?" Drots's smug look had been replaced with one of incredulity. "You don't have any idea how bad you really are, do you?"

Dar faked a slight smile. "Apparently not."

"First of all, I'm stronger. Second, I'm smarter, more talented, better looking, more skillful, the list goes on. If I was you, I'd kill myself, because I could never handle being second in anything."

"You seem to be handling it pretty well."

Drots hit Dar across the face with the back of his hand and knocked Dar to his knees. "I see you need a lesson." Drots rubbed his hand. It had probably hurt him as much as it hurt me, Dar thought. But Drots continued. "I have had a setback or two. Mostly your doing, I'd say. But I've taken a couple of steps to make sure third section won't be bothering me much more. I've got you here, and I hope nothing happens to Deek or Zander while you are gone." There was a glint in his eye. "But I think something will. At least, I hope it does." He beamed. "I set it up so it would."

Deek had finished washing his legs and body. Now he rubbed the soap over his head and let the bubbles run into his face. He then rubbed those too. The soap made him feel good. It reminded him of better times, when he was younger, taking the occasional bath when Mother made him. He would sit alone in the wash room, only the noise of his own giggling and splashing to keep him company. As he used the soap, a chain worked its way out of the bar. Finally, enough was exposed that he put it around his neck. The river gurgled softly in the background, and he thought he heard a noise. He quickly dunked under the water and worked his fingers through his hair and over his face. Coming to the surface, he used his fingers to get the excess water out of his eyes then scanned the area. There was nothing around.

He picked his clothes up off the rock and put them back on. (Sure, they would be wet, but after sunning with Zander for a while, they'd dry.) Deek tucked the soap into the pocket where he usually kept his lucky rock, realizing that he missed it. He felt vulnerable without it, almost invincible with it. Oddest thing, that rock. But maybe being away from his brother so long was just making him jumpy. Deek waded out to the deep part of the channel, then dove underwater for the short swim to the other side of the channel.

Dar was looking Drots in the eye now. "Are you threatening me?"

"I'd never make a threat, Dar." Drots looked off at the river. "But wouldn't it would be a shame if something in the river came up and bit somebody? Or killed them." Drots flashed his smirky smile again.

"Modo." Dar's heart sunk. He knew Modo would do something if given the chance.

"He's your problem child. I just gave him enough rope to hang himself—as well as you and hopefully one of those damned Vanander brothers." Drots turned his back to Dar. "I figure if I hold you here a couple more minutes, that should let things take their natural course. I'll be horrified, then stick you with all the blame, since it was your man killing a man from your section. Shoddy leadership, Dar. Not good enough to lead Ax Company at all."

"I'll stop you."

Dar could hear the evil joy in his voice. "You don't have the power to do so."

Deek's foot connected, once again, with the bottom of the river. But just as he went to put weight on it, something grabbed it—a hand with sharp claws, pulling him down deeper. He kicked with his free foot and got loose just long enough to kick to the surface. Deek took a deep breath and started to yell when the hands pulled him down again. Whatever it was, it blended into the dark river bottom, and Deek couldn't get a good look at it. But his mind raced, trying to figure out a way back to the surface. He kicked again. This time, however, the hand didn't let go, and the surface drifted farther and farther away.

Zander was finally starting to get bored with being in the sun. He sat upright and looked around for his brother. He didn't see anybody in the water—at least from where he was sitting—and it looked like everyone was doing like him, sunning himself. He saw Dar on his knees in front of Drots, who was looking out at the river. What had happened? Zander made a mental note to ask Dar later. As long as it wasn't bloody, it was probably okay, he figured.

Finally, Zander took out his book and started flipping through it, expecting to see the usual blank pages. But this time, there were words. On a few pages, at least. He flipped faster, counting the pages, finally giving up once the number went into the twenties. His eyes were wide and joyful—the magic of the book had finally been activated, at least in part. Zander looked around for his brother again, wanting to share this news with him. Where was Deek?

"So, Dar, I win." Drots turned to face Dar. "You just don't know it yet."

"I know that I will save them." Dar moved to stand up, but Drots put his arm on his shoulder.

"I didn't say you could stand."

Dar grabbed Drots's wrist and twisted it to force Drots's palm to the sky. Continuing his move Dar end up behind him still holding onto Drots's arm. The speed of the attack pushed Drots over. By the time Drots hit the ground face first, Dar was on top of him, pushing Drots's wrist and arm up toward his shoulder blades. Dar could see Drots wince in pain as his shoulder started to give from the pressure.

"I could break your shoulder right now. I could step on your neck, or I could strangle you." Dar lowered himself down to Drots's ear level, using his weight to keep the larger man pinned. "But I don't want revenge, I want justice. And I'll have it after I rescue the Vananders from Modo."

Drots started to laugh. "Assaulting a commanding officer? This really doesn't have a down side for me. Any way this works out, you lose, I win. Go ahead and try. You'll probably just get killed too."

Dar pushed Drots's head into the sand and stood, then quickly took off running.

"Dar assaulted me!" Drots started to yell, quickly drawing attention of all of first and second section. "You see him running! He attacked a superior officer!"

But Dar paid him no mind and headed back to where Zander had been.

Deek's lungs were just about to burst when he kicked at the hands again. This time he used his own hands to propel himself down a little deeper, and he kicked more at the arms than the hands. That seemed to do the trick. Released, he pushed toward the surface and broke it. He quickly released the air he'd been holding and took in another breath. But before he was done, he was dragged under the water again.

Deek noticed the water was more silty here, which meant they were probably closer to the island, but the speed of the current meant they had switched sides. He was now on the side away from the channel. They would be looking for him in the channel. So this is death, he said to himself. He tried to thrash around enough to get away, but it wasn't working, and his lungs were about to burst. Whatever was doing this was just toying with him and enjoying it.

Zander thought he heard a splash and a gasp for air, but when he looked into the channel he saw nothing. He stood up and looked around. That's when he spotted Dar running toward him. Zander held up the book.

"It has words now!" Zander said with pride. "I think if I look at it long enough I can make it out. The cover reads, *Book of Miracles*."

"Zander, focus! Where is your brother?" Dar panted, frantically looking around. "Where is he?"

Zander was now alarmed as well. "I don't know. What's going on?"

"I think Modo is trying to kill him."

Zander rushed to the edge of the water. "How do we find him? If Modo has him in deep water, we won't be able to find him."

Dar rubbed his face, hoping for a miracle. Something, think of something, he told himself.

"Do you remember any of your magic? Can you use Locate Person?" Zander looked back at Dar, his book in hand.

"We never did people. Only objects." Dar rushed from one side of the island to the other before stopping to think. Then it came to him. And Zander. The two spoke in unison.

"The soap."

Deck's lungs finally gave out, and he let in the water. He felt a strange euphoria replace the fear and the dread. As the oxygen in his system finished its work, his mind floated away, and without fresh oxygen to replace it, his body started to shut down. He was oddly buoyant, and he could feel the hand at his leg let go. His arms floated away from his body, and he could feel his soul leaving him for the heavens. At least he hoped it would be the heavens.

"I'm trying to remember the spell, but I didn't study it today. I barely remember it." Dar was panicked. Water could drown very quickly. And Modo, being a water creature, would know exactly how long that would take.

"Give it a try and hope you'll get lucky." Zander slapped the water, hoping to get somebody's attention.

Dar started the movements and struggled with the incantation. He felt the memory returning to him and accelerated his movements up to the speed the spell required. He closed his eyes, tilted his head back, and finished the spell. He clapped his hands, and a beam of light shot out from his chest, seeking the bar of soap. It angled toward the water next to Zander, just ten paces off of the island.

Dar opened his mouth to speak, but Zander had already tossed the book to the sand and dived in.

Dar followed him, running into the water as far as he could, then diving down below its surface. The guidance of the spell would continue for just a minute more after he quit concentrating on it, so they needed to move quickly. The path to the soap was moving at the speed of the river, so Deek had to be floating free. Dar's mind raced as he swam. He could feel Zander's movements before him, and he could hear Zander rising to the surface to take a breath. Dar took one of his own, then dove after the slowly fading glowing path. When he opened his eyes underwater, and saw the path was now pointing to the shallows and up. He followed it, breaking the surface. Zander was holding Deek's lifeless body.

"Help me take him to shore!" Zander yelled.

Dar grabbed one arm, Zander held his brother gently by his shirt, and they quickly made it to the shoreline just a bit down from where they had jumped into the water. Zander pulled the limp body of his brother out onto the sand and rolled it onto its side. He hit Deek's back hard right in the middle.

"He's not breathing!" Zander sat back, looking stricken.

"We need to start his breathing again." Dar took over and started to work at Deek's chest.

"Do you know any spells?" Zander had started to cry. Dar shook his head. They had been too late, he feared.

They had placed Deek's body next to Zander's book. Zander picked it up. "*Book of Miracles*," he said. He opened a page and started reading.

"The true follower of the Energus Posivista the Undeniable will give of themselves not for glory but for the great love of brotherhood, health, and peace."

At the words of its master, the rest of the medallion of faith cracked through the soap, allowing it to glow in the sun.

Zander swallowed visibly and spoke out loud. "The Undeniable, I swear my life to you if you will save my brother." He placed his hands on his brother and continued to read from the book.

Dar recognized it almost immediately as a spell of healing. The *Book of Miracles* was a magic book of scrolls and religious texts. Zander was almost already a cleric, and Jesper had given him the final push toward becoming one with this book. Once the spell was done, the page went blank, as did Zander's face as he lost consciousness. Brother landed on brother, and Dar was afraid that Zander had gone to join his brother in the afterlife, whichever one they had earned.

But Zander's momentum caused him to roll off his brother onto the sand, and Deek coughed. Dar's heart raced as he moved closer to Deek. A strong cough was closely followed by another, then Deek vomited onto Dar's leg.

"It's okay, Deek," Dar said softly. "You're going to be okay." Deek vomited again, this time on the sand. "You need to purge the water. Let it all out." Dar looked back at Zander. His face was peaceful and calm. Too peaceful. Dar looked at his chest. He watched and waited and watched and waited. Finally, it rose and fell.

Neither Vanander would die today, it seemed.

Dar turned to face the river and let his legs collapse under him. He took a deep breath and slowly let it out. His mind turned to Drots. Dar was just starting to think of a plan to deal with him when Modo started to splash his way out of the water.

"So the little vermin didn't die." Modo watched as Deek once again wretched water out onto the sand. "And it looks like I might just get both of them." He grinned, showing his teeth, as well as a noticeable amount of drool.

"You'll have to kill me first, Modo." Dar stood up and looked Modo in the eye. Dar noticed they were hazy; apparently, his kind had an extra eyelid that sealed out the water, but not the light.

"Then it will be all three." Modo's hand rose to his mouth and wiped away the drool. It was thick and stuck to his hand. He motioned to Dar, who took a short step back. "You know I'm stronger than you."

"I don't care." Dar's mouth had gone dry. His mind raced to figure out where his weapon was. Where any weapon was. He needed some time. "Tell me, why do you hate us?"

Modo scoffed at Dar's lack of understanding in the ways of the world. "I don't just hate you. I hate everything that doesn't serve me. You're all food for me. Ocktur, Drots, the two on the sand, all of them. It's been...odd to work with and talk to what I normally would kill for fun or kill to eat." Modo took a small step, really just shifting his weight a little bit, but it made Dar move back. Modo didn't seem to notice.

"I'll eat the one I already killed first. Shame to get him living again just to have me kill him again." Modo tilted his head slightly. "Actually, that's better. I get to enjoy killing him twice. I should thank you."

"Let's do this." Dar had run out of patience, options, and ideas. Whatever was going to happen with Modo was in fate's hands now.

Modo lunged clumsily at Dar, who sidestepped the attack with ease. Modo overshot him and was now partway up the embankment. Dar spun around, as did Modo. Modo lurched suddenly at Dar and then planted his lead foot, spun his weight on it, and connected with Dar's chin with a roundhouse backhand. Dar landed on his stomach almost a full stride away from where he had been standing.

Modo strolled over and walked around him where he lay—Dar could tell what was happening, though for a long moment, he wasn't quite conscious. Before he could fully regain lucidity, Modo picked Dar up in his mighty arms and flung him toward the water. But Dar was more alert than Modo had counted on and sprang to his feet. He stood facing the sand, with the walls in the distance and his back to the river, which spelled a sure death.

"My mother said it was bad to play with my food." Modo laughed. "But in this case, I don't think she would mind. Would you rather die on the sand or die in the river?"

Dar spotted something behind Modo. It was large and moving at amazing speed. Dar wasn't sure he was seeing right after the blow, and he strained to make out the creature. Modo saw the look on Dar's face and turned his head slightly to see if he was bluffing.

He wasn't.

Now it was clear to Dar who it was. Ocktur. And in two quick strides, he entered the fray, tackling Modo to the ground. Ocktur, moving like lightning, clenched Modo's chest with his legs, allowing his arms to remain free. But Modo had barely gotten his claws up when the sergeant grabbed his head with both hands and gave it quick twist with all the force a man his size could muster. Dar could see the veins on Ocktur's head as the larger man put all his hate into twisting Modo's neck. Time seemed to stop—Dar watched Modo's eyes widen as his head was turned beyond its natural radius. Dar had just barely managed to avert his eyes before the snap of Modo's spine marked the end of his control of his body.

But Ocktur apparently wasn't satisfied with that. Because when Dar looked back, he was squeezing Modo's skull between his hands, which made another sickening crack as it gave way to the massive pressure. Blood erupted from Modo's eyes; finally, Ocktur opened his hands and let the tension in his legs go. The body slid away with almost a slither, and the silence of the moment was only broken by the sound of air rushing from Modo's lungs. Ocktur stood on his foe's neck and pulled out his dagger. The violence was too much for Dar—he collapsed to the ground. The last sound he would remember was that of knife hitting bone.

ELEVEN

Afters

"In this world, the dead have it easy. They're
dead. Living is suffering."
—Musdave, one of the first preachers of *The
Book of Truth*, while on his deathbed

"Dar."

Sounds were the first thing to return to him. He
could hear the river off in the distance, and the voice was that
of Deek. He opened his eyes.

"You're okay?" Dar spoke weakly.

"I could ask you the same thing." Deek was kneeling next
to Dar.

"Is he awake now?" came the sergeant's voice.

"Ocktur." Dar moved to sit up, but his body didn't like the
idea. So he propped himself up one elbow instead and looked
toward the booming voice of the sergeant.

"What was that?" the sergeant asked.

"Ocktur, sir." Dar overemphasized the *sir*. "I'm reporting for duty."

"Like the Nine Hells you are. You got one Vanander"—he pointed over at Zander—"laying flat out, sleeping, unable to be woken." He pointed at Deek. "Another is covered in vomit and scratches. And now you have a missing trooper."

"And he struck me while I was in command," added Drots, whom Dar was suddenly aware of. Dar pushed himself to a full upright sitting position and finally took in the whole scene. The whole company was standing around him—some up on the sand dunes, some barely a stride away. Dar noticed that Drots was well out of Ocktur's reach, and probably not on accident either.

"Shut up, Drots." Ocktur crossed his arms. "Dar, do you remember anything about what happened with Modo?"

In response, Dar just lifted an eyebrow.

"I should say, do you remember anything else that Deek didn't already tell us."

Dar looked over at Deek. Deek slowly raised his chin while shifting his head from side to side just slightly. Dar turned his attention back to Ocktur.

"Depends. What did Deek say?"

Ocktur nodded. "I figured you might say that." Ocktur rubbed his forehead. "He said that you and Zander were looking at the book, it knocked you both out, and Deek almost drowned after his foot got stuck on an underwater snag. But he freed himself." Ocktur narrowed his eyes and locked Dar into his stare. "And Modo is missing."

"And you have no idea where he is." Deek nodded slightly. "He…" Dar studied Ocktur's face. Why was he doing this? He looked at Deek again. Deek was rubbing his neck, but as his hand swept across his skin, he narrowed his fingers down to a single thin line. Dar turned to Ocktur again.

"I was knocked out. I have no idea what happened to him."

Ocktur took a deep breath. "Fine. We'll look for him for one hour, then we'll march back to our station." He let the rest of the breath out and took another breath, a little shallower this time. "Well. Start looking!"

With that, he turned and walked away. The show apparently over, the rest of the group split apart, searching the spit, the dunes, and the nearby shore for Modo. Deek leaned over Dar and offered his hand.

"Can you stand?"

"I think so." Dar looked around. Once everyone else appeared out of earshot, he grabbed his friend's hand and rose to his feet. The world spun a little, but his interest in what had just happened overwhelmed his dizziness. "What happened just now?"

"Are you questioning charity?" Deek stayed close to Dar, keeping one hand on his back and his voice down low.

"I'm not questioning charity, I'm questioning reality. The reality of the situation is that Ocktur attacked…"

"Ocktur believes there is a spy for the general in this troop, and he didn't want this event to hurt his career." Deek and Dar held each other's gaze for a moment. "So he encouraged me to keep quiet."

"Drots?" Dar stretched his arms and neck. His head seemed to vibrate on his neck. This long day would only get longer, it seemed.

"Who can tell?" Deek stepped toward his brother, still lying motionless on the sand. "Do you think he'll be okay?"

Dar's eyes locked on Zander. "Is he still breathing?"

Deek kneeled next to his brother and got right up close to his face. "Yes. It's not very regular, though. It's like he's busy doing something while he's sleeping."

"How long was I out?" Dar walked slowly over to Zander. "About an hour, I gu…"

Zander's eyes popped open, and he sat straight up, almost knocking over his brother. "I understand!"

Deek stood up and looked into his brother's eyes. "You okay, brother?"

His face was pure joy. "I have never been better. I had the most wonderful experience."

Deek helped Zander to his feet and brushed the dust off his back.

"I met with an angel…well, technically, she was a planetar, the second level of holy minions of the Gods of Good, between Deva and Solar. She was speaking to me as a messenger of Energus Posivista the Undeniable. She told me the tales of the creation of the lands of Holimoren and my role in the saving all that exists in this life and the next. I have to meet with the nearest Patriarch of the Undeniable, but that will wait. I have seen the world in a whole different light. I see so much I can do. And…"

"And you're babbling, brother." Deek placed his hand on Zander's shoulder. "But it is good to hear your voice."

"You can tell us your stories while we walk back to the base." Dar started to walk away from the river.

"I've got plenty of them!" Zander called out from behind him.

"You were asleep for a less than an hour, brother!" Dar could hear that Deek started after him.

"I know now that I was asleep for most of my life." Dar heard the smile in Zander's voice. "But I'll spare you for now. I'm not even sure I understand all that I saw."

The trio walked around for a while, during which time the rest of the company searched in vain for Modo. After a short debrief in which nobody seemed interested, the company headed out toward their outpost. Missing a man, third section was stuck at the back of Ax Company. Ocktur marched at the front of the line, with Drots immediately behind him. Even from his location at the very back of the formation, Dar could sense something was different. There was an easy chatter amongst the middle ranks, with only the known troublemakers like Drots keeping their silence. Ocktur let them talk, which was a bit unusual, but Dar was okay with it. The three members of third section just walked in silence, thinking. Only Zander seemed to be better off for their travails, as Deek seemed to have lost a little of his soul. Dar just kept moving, lest he stop for the rest of the day.

After a couple hours of marching, the company arrived at the region between the city and outpost they were fighting for. The Abbey loomed large in the distance, and the pace seemed to slow. Dar came out of his walking trance and focused on their surroundings, taking in the details of the Abbey. It had large, sweeping arches and tall spires. There were no external indicators of the attending deity, and the facade seemed a little dark for holy ground. It seemed to have two or more stories, probably three above ground and at least one below it. And like the wall and the river, there was something that was just not right about it.

"What do you see when you look at the Abbey, Deek?" Dar kept his voice down, trying to keep from being heard over the conversations around them.

"It's not what I would expect from an abbey, but, I don't know—what are you looking for?" Deek squinted at it.

"So it's really there, not some illusion?" Dar was still staring at the building.

"Looks real to me." Deek shrugged. "There isn't a reason for me not to believe that is what it appears to be."

As Ocktur called for the team to halt, Dar looked over to Zander. His face had an odd expression, one Dar hadn't seen before.

"That's no house of the holy." Zander spoke quietly, but the anger was clear. "That's a house of evil."

"Interesting," was all Dar could say.

"Attention, troops!" Ocktur turned to face Ax Company, halting all conversations. "We are about to be inspected by the protectorate before continuing back to our station on the line."

There was a momentary twitter as everyone got excited about this new turn of events. Ocktur let it run loose for a moment before getting them all back on the task.

"Silence!" Ocktur yelled. "I want the company to form up per section, with section leaders at the front of their section. You will not speak unless spoken to, and you will answer 'Yes, Lord Protectorate' or 'No, Lord Protectorate' or something equally harmless. You will not embarrass me, because I know you want to live to see another day." He scanned the troops, apparently looking to see if anyone had that fire in their eye that meant trouble. "Right, then! Form up!"

The troops of Ax Company placed themselves in parade formation, a box of two by two for each section, with third section missing a man. Ocktur stood in front of them about four full strides. A gray-and-brown horse about fourteen hands high rode out from the Abbey, and atop it was the Lord Protectorate. The horse walked up to Ocktur and paused.

"Ax Company, ready for your inspection, sir!" Ocktur stood rigid. Dar kept his bearings, but his eyes drank in the scene, trying to understand the dynamics of the situation. The Lord Protectorate seemed to say something, but Dar couldn't hear what it was. Ocktur turned around and walked alongside the Lord Protectorate's horse as he eyed the troops. The two came down the line, then stopped suddenly in front of Dar. Dar swallowed hard.

"You're missing a man here, section leader." The words were a whisper, but Dar could hear them perfectly.

"Yes, Lord Protectorate." Dar kept his eyes front and his back straight.

"What happened to this missing man?" The words seemed to blow to Dar's ears on the wind.

"Fatality, Lord Protectorate." Dar couldn't see Ocktur's reaction to the comment, but he hoped he had picked something nonoffensive.

"That happens." There was a sense of softness in words of the protectorate. He started to move down along the line, and Dar allowed his eyes to flick over the man. He was not exactly has Dar remembered him from the brief glimpse he'd had before. This was clearly a man in his fifties, a little overweight and well groomed. What little hair he had was gray, almost metallic looking. He was wearing full plate armor, but no chain mail jerkin underneath, meaning the armor was largely ceremonial. Dar didn't notice any weapons on the man, and a light scent of flowers surrounded him, probably from the feed of the horse. But just as the word *horse* crossed his mind, Dar noticed the horse was backing up.

"One last thing, solider." The protectorate paused to allow for acknowledgement.

"Yes, Lord Protectorate."

"What is your mission?" The words rang out, unlike his previous words. These were more forceful, with more conviction and a sense of urgency.

"Anything you order, Lord Protectorate."

Out of the corner of his eye, Dar thought he saw the Lord Protectorate smile.

The rest of the inspection went quickly. Once clear of the main body of the troops, Ocktur and the Lord Protectorate continued for a while until they were clear of earshot. There they had a quick exchange of words, and then, with a jump, the horse was galloping off toward the city. Finally, Ocktur walked back, and as he passed third section, he slowed.

"Well done" was all he said.

At the front of Ax Company, Ocktur held the silence for a moment. Then he said, "We've earned a new benefit! We will have helmets waiting for us when we get back to camp. So let's break ranks and get home, boys." He turned toward the outpost and started walking. Apparently using the sound of footsteps as his guide, he let the rest fall in behind him. Ocktur was smiling now. It seemed that he'd had a positive review.

Ocktur's good mood seemed to hold for the whole rest of the journey. He let the company chatter again, but once more third section was quiet. When they finally got back to their lean-to, Dar and Deek curled up on the ground and quickly fell asleep. They'd arrived in the last moments of twilight, and Dar and Deek knew their turn at guard duty would come quickly enough. But Zander still felt light as a feather. As the sky grew more and more full of stars, he cast his thoughts to his newfound lord and said a quick prayer. He felt he should be doing more, but he wasn't sure what. He closed his eyes, feeling the gentle breeze and the lightness of the evening air.

But there was something a little out of place, and Zander opened his eyes. Off in the distance, he saw a flash of lightning, and slowly, a wave of thunder rolled across the field in front of the palisades and past the encampment. Zander watched and listened as the apparent battle in the sky continued, moving toward them. Knowing that the rain of the storm would be here soon enough, Zander lay down on his bedroll and closed his eyes, shutting out the battle between his brother's snores and the lightning's vengeful-sounding thunder. There is beauty in everything, he said to himself as he drifted off to sleep.

The falling rain tapped on the top of tent and harmonized with the dripping water right near Dar's ear. His body had recovered enough to come out of his deep sleep, and he found the world around him dark, much darker than just night. He looked skyward and, not seeing any stars, it all made sense to him. It wasn't a shower, but a deluge going on. The rumble of thunder confirmed it. A hard, soaking rain was covering the area. He wasn't exactly sure of the time, but he stood and headed out of the tent. He was only five steps away from the spot where he'd fallen asleep by the time the rain had soaked him to his skin. By the time he reached the normal muster spot for the nighttime guard detail, the water dripped from his arms and weighed down his every movement.

"Hello, Dar." It was Ocktur.

"Sir?" Dar felt he had to speak up to be heard over the pounding rain.

"Looking to see if it's your shift time?"

"Actually, yes." Dar didn't bother to try to hide his surprise.

"Nobody is coming over the field tonight. Nobody is doing anything tonight."

Dar let a rumble of thunder finish before he spoke. "How do you know?"

Dar could hear a tone of humor in Ocktur's voice. "Only Modo would enjoy this weather, and only he and his kind can actually move and fight in it." Dar could barely make out the head of his commander. He was reclining on the ground, propped up on his elbows. His feet pointed at the battle lines out in the distance. "Look at you, you're soaked, and you traveled less than a hundred steps. March a mile or two in this stuff, and you'll be so weak that a single foe could crush you."

Dar wondered why Ocktur was out here in the rain. Then another thought crossed his mind. "Why did you kill Modo?"

"I figured you'd ask why I covered it up." Ocktur still had a lilt to his voice.

"Are you drunk?" Dar asked softly.

"Why, aren't you?" Ocktur giggled.

"Right." Dar was trying to think of how he could use this moment for his advantage.

"I killed him because I wanted to. And he deserved it. And he would have killed everyone and anyone who stopped him, displeased him, or just made him hungry." Ocktur reached over and grabbed something, then lifted it to his lips and raised the bottom up. Ocktur swallowed hard and put the object down. "He wasn't anything this company or this world needed anymore, and I did what I had to."

"But you enjoyed it, didn't you."

"I enjoy many portions of my job."

"You did evil."

"I did justice." Ocktur shifted his body so his hands were free. It was almost a cross-legged position, but much more clumsy. "If I have a choice between me and him, I will always choose me. The fact that I enjoyed killing him is irrelevant. He earned his punishment, just like you will if you keep questioning me. You've earned a night off; so have I. Now go back to your tent and wait for the end of the storm."

"Yes, sir." Dar turned and walked off.

After a bit Ocktur yelled after Dar, "And I never said I wasn't evil."

Dar heard Ocktur mumble something off in the distance as he reached the lean-to. The rain was just as heavy and just as loud here as out at the guard spot. Once under the cover of the tent, Dar shed his clothes and went for his spare garments. A little smaller than his field clothes, they didn't fit very well, but at least they were dry. As Dar worked each button from his belt up, memories came to him. Modo, Deek's near drowning, the violence, the constant brutality, the endless danger. Each thought seemed to have a tear with it, and by the time he was fully dressed, his cheeks were soaked, as was the collar of his jerkin. He laid down on his back and pulled up his blanket. Tomorrow he would be resolute. But tonight, the tears kept coming down.

The next thing Dar knew, it was light. Though that might have been too strong a word for it. Clearly, the sun was shining somewhere in Holimoren, but the sky was still too full of black rainclouds for it to make an appearance here. Pools of water were everywhere, and water was flowing into the tent like a small creek. Dar was at the high spot of the tent, and the water flowed around him, turning him into a small island. He looked around and saw Deek and Zander tying something together.

"What are you doing?" he asked.

"Zander had a great idea." Deek didn't look up, but continued struggling with the rope. It appeared he was weaving something out of the rope.

"We're making hammocks to sleep in so we won't be down on the dirt while it rains," Zander explained.

"That's a great idea." Dar sat up and noticed his was the only dry spot in the tent.

"I know." Deek had a lot of pride in his voice. "He came up with it out of nowhere."

"It came to me while I was meditating this morning."

"That's a new thing he's doing, by the way." Deek looked at his work approvingly and nodded at his brother. "Finished."

"Only one real test." Zander put his hands into the hammock, testing it and steadying it all at once.

"If you bring down the tent, we'll all get wet." Deek put his weight against one of the poles of the lean-to. "Dar, you get the other one."

"Okay." Dar rubbed the sleep from his eyes and went to the tent pole at the other end of the hammock. "Ready."

Zander leapt into the hammock. The ropes creaked and tent poles groaned, but they all held.

"Looks like we should add more reinforcements outside the tent." Deek looked at the poles. "Just a couple more should do it for all of us."

"If we hang the hammocks from a center pole to the end poles, we can all have one." Dar looked at Deek. "Having them hanging from side to the side means all the weight is off the center."

"But we have an odd number of people."

"We can make an extra and hang our supplies in it." Zander chimed in, demonstrating he understood Dar's concerns. "That will get all our stuff off of the floor."

"But the tent doesn't have a center pole!" Deek looked at Dar like he had gone crazy.

"Yet." Dar smiled. He reached over to the corner that Modo had called his own. He grabbed one of his spears and took off the spear point. He grabbed another and repeated the process. He then stuck the two notches for the points together; they mated fairly well, but not well enough to hold the weight of the canopy overhead.

"I hope you have some idea for how to improve that," Deek offered.

"I do." Dar started to whisper the words of the mending spell. The two spear shafts became one.

"You really need to teach me some of that," Deek told him.

"I'm not qualified." Dar peered up at the tent. "But my master is. When I get home, maybe I can ask whether he would take on another student." Dar pushed at the center of the tent with the pole, but quickly ran out of strength. The shape of the tent had been a lean-to when they started, with longer poles at one end and shorter poles at the other. The new center pole pulled the canvas off center. The whole roof would have to come down, and the canvas would have to be adjusted.

"Um…can you help?"

"Who?" said Deek.

"How?" said Zander at the same time.

"You help me lift the center," Dar said to Zander. "And you shorten the sides of the tent enough to make the center take the load."

Quickly enough, they had it finished, and the four-pole lean-to was now a five-pole tent. They moved on to stringing up their hammocks, and soon the three were so lost in their efforts that they failed to notice the small crowd that was gathering. All the off-duty people stood in the rain, watching the changes in third section's tent.

Zander noticed them first. "Dar. Deek."

Each stopped and looked around. Deek was first to say something to the crowd.

"We needed a hobby to keep us busy in the rain."

Dar was going to add something when Drots jumped in.

"I doubt this tent is regulation." Drots stepped into the tent. "Be a shame if somebody reported you."

Dar turned and squared his shoulders to Drots. "It's pretty hard to miss what we've done. Report it. It's not like Ocktur can't just look at it and see what we've done."

"For a…" Drots paused and rubbed his cheek, then his chin. "For a fee, I might not make it worse for you. Ocktur doesn't check tents very often, and he might not notice."

Deek seemed to sense what Drots was trying to do. "Are you asking for a bribe, Drots?" Deek turned his head slightly to the side and narrowed his eyes. "Because while I don't remember Ocktur mentioning much about our tents, I'm pretty sure bribery is out of the normal conduct for somebody in command, even if it is just a section."

Drots smiled. "Nice try."

Zander waved his hands. "If you boys are going to carry on with your little pissing contest, I would like to try my hammock out by sleeping in it." Zander put his rear into the sling and tested his weight against it.

"You know, Drots," Dar said, moving toward the center pole, "if he breaks it, you'll be caught in here with us."

"I do think it would be wise of you to leave." Deek continued for Dar.

Drots looked up at the center pole and then down at the way Zander was weighing down his hammock. "You just watch yourselves," he said. Then he walked out.

Deek joined Dar at the center pole and watched as Zander leaned back and let the hammock take his whole weight. The end pole creaked a little under the load, but otherwise nothing changed. Deek moved to his hammock opposite his brother's and worked his way into it. Again the wood strained but held. Dar loaded up as much of the gear as he could into the hammock opposite his own and then went to lie down in it, first testing it out with his hands before placing his full weight into it. When he leaned back into his hammock, the end pole gave another creak, but quickly enough, the only thing Dar could hear was the easy rhythm of Deek's breathing, Zander's light snoring, and the constant drone of the rain. The hammock started to sway slightly in the winds that occasionally breezed through the campsite, but it was perfect for sleeping.

TWELVE

Changes

"The only thing that changes more than my wife's moods is the weather!"
—Elader the Old

"Dar."

It was Ocktur, and Dar could tell that he was really close to him, probably even in the tent. Dar opened his eyes and looked around. It was still dark, probably near dawn.

"Sergeant Ocktur?"

"You need to come with me." Dar couldn't smell any alcohol on Ocktur's breath, so this must be several hours later. He had slept well.

Dar could hear Ocktur moving back then toward the opening in the tent's mesh sides. Dar swung out of his hammock and rushed to gather his weapons. He had to run to catch Ocktur before they reached the guard post where Dar had last seen him.

"The weather is shifting, so the enemy will be attacking shortly." Ocktur didn't look at Dar, just continued toward the center of the camp. "I want you to wake up the troops quietly. I don't want a full muster call."

Dar worked the scenario forward in his head. "You want the enemy to think we're still in bed."

"I want them to think we aren't doing what we will be doing." Ocktur looked at Dar. "Killing them."

"Have they attacked like this before?"

"Not here, but I've heard of them attacking just before either the weather or the dawn broke. By the time both have, the enemy will be here attacking us."

"But we'll be ready."

"Not unless you quit jabbering at me and get to your orders!" Ocktur waved Dar away.

"Yes, sir!" Dar took off to the nearest tent to wake the troops.

"Quietly!" Ocktur hissed.

Dar had the whole company ready within minutes. Drots and first section gave him a little trouble, but once Drots saw the rest of the company readying for muster before the battle, he quickly got his team working. Dar watched for a minute. Drots was effective as a leader. He got his troopers up and assembled quickly, with minimum of words and minimum of noise. They were just lining up to march out when Dar decided to return to Ocktur's position to see if anything had developed. He reached Ocktur just as the horizon started to show signs of the rising sun.

"They ready?" Ocktur was focused on the enemy lines somewhere out in the inky blackness.

"Yes, sir."

"Have Drots and first section take the left side of the palisades. Have Jusin take second section and hold the right side."

"What of third section?"

"You're the bait."

"We stay in the camp?"

"I'll be with first section, and I want you to stay in the middle here and wait for the enemy to arrive." Ocktur stood up. "Once they do, I want you to fall back to second section."

"And you and first section will attempt to strike from the rear."

"Yes," Ocktur said. "If you think it will sell the trap, you can run for the camp, but I want you to pair up with second section. Jusin and his team will need the extra help."

"So we are to engage the enemy?"

Ocktur snickered. "I want you to run, you idiot, not fight. I'll give you a minute, then I'll leave this post for the first section position. Have Drots meet me there. Don't bother explaining it to Drots—I'll do that. Tell Jusin to hold his part of the position until first can hit the enemy hard. Once Jusin is briefed, get your team to its spot." Ocktur started counting—quietly, but Dar could see his lips move.

"Get moving. Eight."

Dar ran for the tents. He ran into Deek and Zander just before reaching the spot where he expected to find Drots—his lean-to.

"You need to follow me; we're getting ready to hold off an attack."

"Nice." Zander looked a little sad, and it showed up in his voice.

"Let me guess. Are we the bait? Or the sacrificial lamb?" Deek didn't sound much better than his brother.

"Bait." Drots chimed in as he walked up to third section.

"Hello, Drots," Dar said. "I have your orders."

"Let me guess." Drots looked Dar in the eye. "Right side palisades, be the hammer to second's anvil."

"Totally wrong," Deek offered.

"It's the left side," Dar said meekly.

"Enjoy running." Drots turned and motioned to first section to follow him.

Dar took off running to second section's assigned duty station within the camp. Jusin had his team assembled, but his wasn't as ordered as Drots's.

"Jusin, I have orders from Ocktur."

Jusin turned and acknowledged Dar by nodding just enough to be noticed.

"He wants you to deploy second section to the palisades and hold the line. During the battle, third section will most likely be joining your lines."

Jusin nodded. "Let's go, boys." He clapped his hands. "It's showtime."

Dar grabbed at Jusin's elbow. "Keep it quiet."

"Right."

The three members of third section stood in the guard post spot. Sitting would have been more comfortable, but the soil was just too wet. Dawn would be coming at any moment. The horizon had changed from mostly dark to mostly light. The sun pushed the darkness back little by little, and it seemed to be taking the rain with it. By the time Dar saw the first gleam of the sun on the horizon, the rain had stopped completely.

"What was that?" Deek dropped to his haunches.

Zander hunched over, but not as far as his brother. "I didn't hear anything."

"I thought I heard something too." Dar dropped to one knee and cupped his hand to his ear. He heard a faint whistling noise.

Dar looked out towards the enemy lines just in time to hear a high-pitched whistle.

"Arrows!" Deek lowered himself to the ground and scanned the sky for the shafts of death.

Each time an arrow hit the ground, it buried itself deep in the mud and quivered under the impact. Dar heard more whistling—another batch was coming.

"Move back, toward the camp."

They took five solid steps back, but remained facing the enemy lines—and hopefully, the unseen enemy.

"Ow!" Zander clutched his head but remained standing. Something had struck his helmet and struck it hard.

"Are you hurt?" Dar's gaze darted over to Zander.

"It came from behind!" Zander whispered to Dar and Deek.

Dar looked at Zander for a moment.

"Run toward the camp!" Dar pushed each of them toward camp, and they all broke for the cover of the tents. Dar paced himself at the back, turning occasionally to see what, if anything, was coming after them. Deek was out in front, moving quicker than Dar thought he had in him. Zander was a little slow, his lack of dexterity making him less light on his feet than his brother.

Once they were behind the line of the palisades, Dar called out again. "Turn to the side so we can use the palisades as cover."

Dar could now hear the people chasing them. When he had broken cover, so, apparently, had they. He couldn't tell how many there were, but he could tell they were a lot closer than he had figured. Every now and again he could hear an arrow whistling by, but it was a rare moment now. Dar could see Deek slowing to turn the corner of the palisades, then he was out of view. Zander came up on it next, electing to dive around the corner rather than slowing to turn the sharp corner. Just as Dar came to the corner, Jusin wheeled his troops out of their positions and faced the oncoming threat head on. Dar darted between Banes and Upny, who closed ranks and allowed Dar to slow until he too turned and faced the lines.

Dar scanned in front for the enemy, which turned out to be a troop of six. They looked like woodland people, with green garments over ring mail. Each had spears, as well as bows slung around their torsos and quivers on their backs. As soon as Jusin and his team had appeared, the enemy stopped and formed up. They placed their spears on the ground and took their bows in hand. What appeared to be their commander looked behind them and uttered some sort of command in a language Dar didn't recognize. The enemy responded immediately, stowing their bows and grabbing their spears.

"They've seen Ocktur and Drots," Deek explained to his brother, who was still behinds the palisades, trying to catch his breath.

The gang of six took off running, and the chase was on. Drots trailed Ocktur but was a full two strides in front of the rest of first section. The invaders were smaller than Ocktur but were too fleet of foot for the trap to be closed around them. The ambush petered out after a couple of minutes of full-bore fighting. And while there were some enemy losses, it wasn't as big a victory as it might have been. Dar watched as Drots came to a stop alongside his commander.

"Jusin came out too early." Dar could just make out Drots's comment as he took his place at Ocktur's right.

"Sometimes the rabbit sees the hunter coming, Drots," Ocktur said, winded.

"Sometimes the hunter's friends give the hunter away." Drots turned and started walking back to the camp.

Since his group had done less fighting than the rest of them, Dar and the brothers had to go out into the field and clean up the dead bodies of the few enemies they had managed to slay. Normal procedure was to take any scavengable items for Ocktur to divvy up. Before, they had just ignored the dead after that, but now they had to figure out what to do with bodies.

When Modo had been alive, it seemed, the bodies took care of themselves, but Dar figured that he had probably been eating them or using them as bait. There had been the orcs that had occasionally come and gone, and Dar was sure they'd taken their share of scraps too. Dar took a shovel for each man.

"So, what do you want to do with the bodies?" Deek asked Dar as they walked.

"The peddler gave us credit for taking them out into no-man's land."

Deek winced. "I don't think Ocktur would allow that during the daytime."

"But we can't leave them out in the open. It's not proper." Zander frowned as he spoke.

Dar looked at him. He'd been hoping to have more time to figure out what to do. "What do you think? I say we bury them."

"There are a bunch of them, so I guess that would be okay."

By then, they'd reached the site of the battle that morning. Zander grabbed one corpse by the arms. He was an elf, so the body was pretty light. "There are only three bodies total, it looks like."

"Look at that breastplate on that fellow," Deek commented. Dar turned to look. The breastplate was a polished silver, gleaming in the transient light of the passing clouds.

"Looks magical." Dar commented. Deek rolled his eyes.

"Of course it's magical." Dar removed it from its former owner. "But how magical?"

"If you're done stealing things from the recently deceased, maybe we can honor their sacrifice by putting them into the ground." Zander scowled at his brother. He threw a shovel at him, and it landed a little too close for comfort.

"That could have hit me." Deek jumped to his feet. "You say you're sorry."

"Are you boys really picking a fight with each other now?" Dar stepped between the two of them. "If we're going to bury these bodies in the area outside of the palisades, we'll be at risk of attack. I say we do this and get back into cover." Dar staked his shovel in the earth. "Then you can bicker at each other."

"Sounds fine to me." Deek dug down into the earth and moved aside a shovelful of dirt. Zander joined in, and before long, they had a good-sized hole. The corpses were all elves, which meant the holes could be slender and barely over five feet long. After the first hole one was finished, Zander took the first body and placed it gently in the grave. Then he looked a bit startled. A moment later, he was sitting with his feet in the hole and flipping through the pages of his book.

"What are you doing?" Deek asked him.

"I felt something move, but it wasn't the body. It was this book I got from the vendor." Zander turned a page. "The first pages were just purple blurs, but then about halfway into the tome, I found a page covered in this finely lettered black script. I'm pretty sure it wasn't this way before. Listen." He read aloud: "*As the body is consecrated to the ground, the soul shall fly up to the heavens and start a life anew.*"

Deek stopped digging the next hole and looked at his brother. "What?"

"*The sins and actions you have committed are left in the ground, allowing your spirit and soul a new beginning.*"

Dar stopped as well, and watched as Zander and jumped into the hole. Dar and Deek abandoned their shovels and headed over to it.

"You okay, brother?" Deek was the first to arrive.

Zander was leaning over the body as he placed his lips to the forehead of the dead elf. "May we meet and be friends in the kingdom of the gods." He closed the book and looked up at the two. "What's going on?"

"We were going to ask you that." Dar held out his hand, and Zander used it to climb up and out. "What are you doing down there?"

"The book told me to do it."

"The book?" Deek looked at his brother like he was a talking carrot. "It has more in it now?"

"It does." Zander flipped through the pages and showed them the new lettered page.

"It's purple and there are no letters on it." Deek said, pointing the book back at his brother.

"Interesting." Dar looked at the book. The pages were still purple to him, but he swore he could almost see some black letters in that soup of swirls. "Perhaps the book is tuned to you, then?"

"It would seem so." Deek was staring at his brother.

"Or he's getting tuned to the book," Dar offered.

The trio sat in their tent and wasted the day away. Ocktur seemed oddly busy, and the rest of the unit just milled about doing not much of anything. The weather had stayed clear the rest of the day, and other than the normal changing of shift for the guards, little else happened. Dar tried to keep busy organizing the supply hammock, but gave up after a while. Zander read his book, occasionally closing his eyes to mumble something before resuming his studies. Deek kept busy trying to figure out how to make the magical breastplate fit him. He was bigger than the elf who had worn it, and he had pulled the straps out as far as they would go.

"Can you give me a hand, Dar?" Deek looked up from his tugging at the straps. "I need that mending spell of yours to graft some extra cloth onto these straps."

Dar chuckled. "You'll have to wait. I only have so much power, and without regular study, it's gotten weaker. Maybe tomorrow."

"Maybe?" Deek frowned. "But I want to use it now!"

"Then use it as a mirror," Zander said, his eyes still on the book.

Dar laughed. "Hang it from the tent post so you can see how pretty you are."

But Deek wasn't laughing. He headed over to the pole and rigged the plate to hang from the center, then looked into it and smiled. From where he was standing by the tent pole, Dar could see that the magic metal reflected Deek's face perfectly despite its curved shape. But then Deek leaned closer to it, blocking Dar's view.

"Look, somebody is looking at the armor!" echoed around the tent.

"Who said that?" Dar looked around the tent.

"It came from the armor." Deek pointed at it. "I saw people in it! It was a bunch of elves and a couple humans. I couldn't make out any faces exactly, but clearly, somebody else was on the other side."

"What?" Dar stepped to Deek's side.

"Do you recognize them?" came the voice again. "It is one of the targets. We must be careful."

Dar grabbed the armor and threw it to the ground. It landed face up, and now Dar could see the faces Deek had been talking about. "I think they're onto us," stated one of the voices. Then came another voice: "We are coming for you."

Dar flipped the armor over. "This thing will get us killed." He grabbed a sack from the supply hammock and placed the armor in it. "I'll put it with the bodies, and hopefully that will be the end of it."

Deek followed a couple of steps behind as Dar walked to the area where they had buried the bodies and placed the plate next to the grave of one of the dead elves. Dar was aware of Deek hovering nearby but paid him no mind. A few moments later he had dug a small ditch with his hands. They had few sacks, so he quickly transferred the breastplate, from its bag into the hole and filled it up. As he finished patting the dirt down to finish entombing the armor, though, Deek descended on him.

"I'm going to miss that armor," he lamented. "It looked really powerful."

"It was being used as scrying portal. My master has used them before. The enemy was looking into it, seeing you, me, and all of us. They're probably looking for information to use about when to attack here again. Maybe they'll be after us, since they know we killed their buddy." Dar frowned and walked back to the tent.

"And I'll get the blame!" Deek sounded dejected. "I didn't do the crime, and now I'll get the blame."

"Is that all you're worried about? We could get killed." Dar was almost all the way back to the tent before he saw that something was up. "Where is everyone?"

Deek pointed over near the road in the direction of the city. "They're mustering over there."

The two took off running, and when they reached the others, they quickly and quietly snuck into their ranks, forming up with their unit. Ocktur stood in front, and royal guards were scattered around the area. Dar stood with a horseman behind him. The horse breathed on his neck, and Dar turned to make eye contact with the solider on the horse. He smiled feebly at the rider, whose helmet covered his eyes. But it didn't cover his frown, which turned into a snarl. Dar turned back around and hoped the next sound he would hear would be the sounds of the horse moving away. But nothing of the like happened. Instead, he caught the conversation at the front of the group.

"So, Sergeant Ocktur, your group was the only one that held the line in this sector today. All other units collapsed and had to be either reinforced or retaken. How did you do it?"

Ocktur tone was as rigid as a stone. "We set up a trap, so when the enemy came behind the palisades, we could strike their flanks."

"You didn't encounter the enemy in front of the wall?"

"No, sir."

"Interesting. It was a dawn attack—you were awake in time for the assault?"

"Yes, sir."

"So, you practice normal military discipline here?" This sounded to Dar like an insult. Was he trying to imply that Ocktur had lucked into success?

"I try, sir."

Dar couldn't tell if Ocktur was responding in such an abbreviated way to keep the conversation short or if he was scared of the man. Dar couldn't see him, but judging by the guards, it was a general high in the protectorate army.

"How many men have you lost to disease?" the protectorate's emissary queried.

"Only one loss by all causes in total in the unit, sir."

"One?" The voice was clearly impressed. "What was the cause?"

"Suicide." Ocktur paused. "Sir."

"Amazing."

Dar couldn't see what was happening, but it sounded like the officer was moving away.

"Congratulations, Sergeant Ocktur," the general said. Dar watched as he climbed onto a horse. "Perhaps sometime you could join me at the mansion for some privileged time."

"It will be an honor, sir," said Sergeant Ocktur. The general nodded and took off toward the fortress.

The company held formation until all the horsemen could not be seen. Ocktur turned to face them. "Good work today. Dismissed!"

THIRTEEN

Promotions

"Easiest way to make a man lazy is to make him
an officer."
—said by many a private

It seemed as if the week flew by after that. There were no
attacks in their sector, but news came that other sites were
constantly under pressure. They would drill, but the tedium of
not seeing any action led to some fights, which were quickly
settled by their participants or by Ocktur. He would smash
into the fight, delivering blows that would typically knock out
both fighters. Ocktur never cared about who started what,
or who did what—he would punish both the same. After his
third fight that week, Upny had to dig another latrine, a hole
some twenty feet deep. He had to climb out by himself, and
he wasn't allowed out of the hole until he finished. Drots had
joked about using the facility while still under construction,
but Ocktur had not allowed that to happen.

Another storm was rolling in when a flag officer from the rear units came to visit. Dar and Drots were lingering in the command tent when the man came in. This officer was all pomp and procedure; Dar could tell he had never seen combat in his life. They sat and watched as the man handed a paper to Ocktur.

"Your new orders are contained in the paperwork," he said.

Ocktur read the paper, but after a while, it was clear that the officer was growing impatient. "You're being promoted to battalion commander, Colonel."

"Colonel?" Ocktur lowered the paper. "How do you go from sergeant to colonel in one piece of paper?"

"You apparently impress the general, who influences the protectorate, and outlive all the other company commanders. Or something else, like blackmail or extortion." The orderly paused meaningfully. "Which is clearly not the case here."

Drots smiled. "Congratulations, sir." He paused to salute Ocktur, then turned to the flag officer. "Who is to be the replacement for the colonel?"

"The order leaves it up to the colonel."

"How much is the pay?" Ocktur squinted at the paper, then looked up at the bureaucrat.

"Three hundred."

Ocktur winced. "A month? That's not much of a pay increase."

"A week, Colonel." The flag officer smirked. And that's when it became clear to Dar, the way it was apparently already clear to him: Ocktur really couldn't read.

The flag officer dug into his coat and produced a sack that jingled. "Here is your promotion bonus."

"Bonus?"

"The protectorate thinks you've got some innovative ideas, and is interested to see if you can put them into practice along this side of the fortress. You'll have four companies reporting to you, and so that comes with a bonus. Four thousand gold, which, for ease of carrying, I've put paid out in eight hundred platinum coins. They're easier to carry, and most vendors will change them out for gold if you'd rather."

Ocktur was speechless. Even Dar, who had seen a lot of money working for his old master back in the tower, knew that was a serious amount of coins.

"When does the colonel leave for his assignment and need to have a replacement picked out?" Drots was still smiling. Dar couldn't help but be galled at Drots's naked ambition.

"The colonel must meet with the protectorate tonight at the fortress. And he'll need that money if he's going to pay for his evening's activities." The flag officer smiled. "The ladies don't work for free."

Dar's ears perked up. "Ladies?"

Ocktur finally emerged from his coin coma. "Don't bother your head, Dar. My problem now, not yours."

Dar opened his mouth to say something but figured he shouldn't. Ocktur turned and considered the two of them. Clearly, command would come down to one of them. Ocktur looked both of them up and down, then turned to the orderly.

"Dar will be in command."

Dar couldn't tell who was more surprised, him or Drots.

"Congratulations, Sergeant Dar," the flag officer said. "I will record back at headquarters that you're now in charge. Your pay will be two hundred a month. You will receive it next month."

"What?" Drots shook his head, as if trying to make sure his ears were working right. "You're putting him in charge?"

"Watch yourself, Drots." Ocktur poked him in the chest. "Dar's in command, so deal with it. And if I catch you not obeying his orders, I'll come and sort you out." He poked again, hard enough to make Drots take a step back. "And it's colonel now, so you had better respect the rank."

"Yes. Sir." Drots stood rigid and scowling.

"Colonel, are you sure about this?" Dar asked.

"Deal with it." Ocktur turned to the flag officer. "Let's go."

Drots didn't open his mouth until Ocktur was well out of sight. Dar figured an attack from either the enemy or Drots would be coming soon, so he put his hand on his sword hilt.

"I don't think you should be in command," Drots said. "I'm the superior warrior. Who knows what you've been doing for Ocktur that convinced him to pick you."

"Well, Drots, you have two choices." Dar unsheathed his sword and held it up. "You can either leave the unit, or you can obey my orders. Which one, I don't care."

"Leave? Like in a casket or a transfer?" Drots crossed his arms over his chest. "Are you threatening me?"

"I think the enemy is about to attack, and I want to be ready for it."

"I'm not your enemy, Dar."

"I think you are, Drots." Dar meet Drots's steely gaze with an intense look of his own. "Otherwise you would be following my orders the way you did Ocktur's."

"I think we both know that I only followed his orders enough to met my needs." Drots let his arms fall to his side. "I'll only be doing the same with you."

"As long as you follow them, I don't care why." Dar let the tip of the sword drop a bit before righting it again. "And know I'll be keeping an eye on you. You get out of line, and we'll have more than words."

"I can assure you that won't be any nicer than if you'd done the same with Ocktur." Drots smiled. "I think you over-estimate your abilities."

"I think you overestimate yours." Dar started to put his sword away. "And unlike you, I have friends and allies. Admit it: If you did take over from me, it wouldn't be long until you were deposed. You help me by accepting my authority, and I'll make you second in command."

"Second?" Drots rubbed his chin. "That means if you get promoted or killed, then I'm in command. I like it."

"You kill me, and you'll get nothing. My allies will strike you down." Dar pushed his sword into his scabbard until the hilt hit the metal top but didn't latch the strap. "If we work together, we can get more done than if we battle. Your time will come; I'm not planning on being in this war forever."

"I accept your terms." Drots held out his hand. "For now."

Dar took his hand and shook it.

Drots turned and started to walk back to the main group. "Corporal Drots, eh, Sarge?"

Dar smiled. "Sure thing, corporal."

Dar let him get in front a ways before heading out after him. He had just about reached his tent when he heard the sound of incoming arrows. He heard no alarm, so he called it himself.

"Incoming! Duck and cover!"

Men poured out of the tents and headed for the palisades. Drots ended up on one side of the opening and Dar on the other. Dar did a quick head count and was relieved when he came up with the right number. He worked his way to the front of the opening in the palisades and looked out: the area just in front of the opening was full of enemy troops. The tent area was still being pelted by arrows, but the rate of fire seemed to be slowing.

Dar made an X shape with his arms to Drots and was relieved when Drots replied with a thumbs up. Dar peeked around the palisade wall again and noted the number of the approaching enemies. Which, as far as he could tell, was just about the same as the number of men in Ax Company.

Dar held up a fist and looked at Drots.

He pulled it down quickly.

Both sides stormed out from behind the palisades and into the opening, and a quick skirmish ensued. The enemy quickly bunched up and formed a defensive arc, which Dar's men could not safely attack. Drots swung a harsh blow at one of the opponents, and the target blocked the blow with his shield. But the leather arm strap of the shield didn't hold, and it fell to the ground. Their line, apparently spooked by this, beat a quick and orderly retreat back from the opening. After Ax Company got a little too far into the open for Dar's liking, he called them back to the safety of the palisades. But they stopped to collect the dropped shield on their way back.

Dar ducked behind the wall and leaned out to see the enemy force retreat all the way back. The arrow attack ended, and another round of the battle was over.

Dar could feel somebody lean on the wall next to him.

"That was too easy. Why didn't the archers attack us when we were in the open?"

Dar was pleased. The voice was Deek's.

"Look at the placement of the barrage," Deek went on. "It's well behind any place we might actually be effective."

"You think they're distracting us?"

"Or trying to engage with us, but not kill us."

Dar watched the battlefield. "They drew us out, but then didn't put us to the quick. They turtled up into defense almost as soon as we came out. It doesn't make sense."

"Maybe it doesn't have to. I like living, and maybe I'm just overthinking it."

"Let's see that shield." Dar took off toward the tent of the last person he'd seen with it. His heart sank a little when he saw Drots now had it. He was apparently figuring out the lengths of the straps by fitting it to Upny.

"Corporal, I would like to see that shield." Dar used his best in-command voice.

"Sure, Sergeant." Drots handed it to him.

Dar looked at the front of the shield. There was a crest of a golden-headed eagle holding a rose with thorns between its talons. The workmanship was beyond anything they had, but it didn't feel magic.

"Anybody recognize the crest?" Dar looked around the crowd. Nobody said anything. Dar met Deek's eyes, and Dar thought he saw a slight nod. It looked familiar to Dar, but he could not place it. He handed the shield back to Drots. "Carry on, Corporal."

Drots smiled. "Sure you don't want it, Sergeant?"

Dar continued to walk back to his tent, Deek in tow. "You do with it as you see fit, Corporal."

But as he walked away, he could hear Drots say to Upny, "See, I told you he'd let me deal with it. It'll cost you sixty-five, mind you, but this beauty will keep you in this war until the end."

Deek was almost ready to explode, it seemed, by the time they got back to the tent.

"Go ahead, tell me where you saw it." Dar settled into his hammock.

Deek reached over and took Zander's book. "Zander, quick, what is the crest on the pages you can read?"

"A golden-headed sea eagle holding a rose with thorns." Zander looked confused. "Can I have my book back?"

Dar almost fell out of his hammock. "What?"

"Golden-headed…" Zander started again.

"He heard you the first time, brother." Deek tossed the book back to him. "What I can't understand is why a shield of the enemy would have that crest on it."

"Given that the Sea Lord is the good God of the Sea, it is clear the enemy took it from someone who is of the faith." Zander said with a tone that made it clear he felt the answer was obvious. "Why else?"

"Why else, indeed." Dar stared out into the distance

"Cart!" A loud, familiar voice boomed across the whole site. "Selling items for ready money!"

"You guys stay here, I want something from the cart." Dar stood up and headed to the door.

"If they have any more items like my book, let me know," said Zander, without taking his eyes off of the pages of his tome.

"I want a magical scroll," Deek said as he worked his way back to his part of the tent. "What are you going to buy, Dar?"

"Answers, I hope."

"Hello, Dar." Jesper spoke with a low voice. "Mule missed you, so we've come for a visit."

"Hello, Jesper." Dar kept his voice low too.

"I heard you are in charge now." Jesper handed Dar a piece of canvas. "And Ocktur is the battalion commander. How are you dealing with it?"

"You sure know a lot." Dar looked over the canvas and faked interest in it.

"Just like you, I'm more than I seem." Jesper took the canvas and handed over some other bauble to make it look like they were haggling over materials, should anyone be watching them. "You seem troubled."

"I'm not sure I'm on the right side of this war," Dar blurted out.

"The sharp end of a war is rarely the right end to be on." Jesper considered him kindly. "But you're good with the sword and quick-witted. You'll do fine. You still using your magic?"

Dar reacted like he a bucket of cold water had been poured on his head. "How did you know?"

"I know lots of things." He handed Dar a piece of linen. "When you hold young Zander's book, do you feel any power from it?"

"I do." Dar was starting to get worried now.

"Clearly, you are truly a man amongst boys, then." Jesper took back all the items he had handed Dar.

"I didn't mean it that way." Dar looked sheepish.

"I know you didn't. I did." Jesper moved to the far side of his cart and crouched down for a moment. Dar thought he heard him say something, but he couldn't tell what it was. Just as Dar's curiosity was getting the better of him, the older man stood up and returned. "I need to ask you a favor. In two days, I want you to release this bird."

The bird reminded Dar of the Gulull who visited his master before this all started, though he couldn't imagine that something as powerful as a Gulull would allow itself to be placed into a small wooden cage. The cage was barely larger than the bird. "Why do you have a seagull in your cart?"

Jesper took on a serious look for a beat. "I don't ask you many questions, so I'll give you fewer answers."

Dar bristled at the retort. "I was just curious."

"Fair enough. Here is another book for Zander." Jesper reached into the mess that was the cart and pulled out a hand-bound blue book. "Tell him to read it all before attempting to use it, and not to let others read it."

"How much will it cost me?" Dar held the cage in one hand and the book in the other.

"You let the bird go in two days, and we'll call it even." Jesper looked sternly at Dar but with a twinkle in his eye. "But if he isn't released in two days, he'll take it upon himself to get out, and I'll find out. Then you'll be in trouble." He winked then pointed at the book. "That tome costs a thousand gold pieces, and I'll make you and your troops pay back each one."

"I'll do it, don't worry." Dar was confused. "No need to get mad at me."

"Don't confuse mad with direct." Jesper smiled. "Action leads to reaction. When you don't know what the action is, you won't know what the reaction is. I want the correct reaction, so I need to provide the action. Understand?"

"Sure." Dar said. His tone probably made it clear that he didn't, but he smiled nevertheless and headed back to the tent.

He tossed the book to Zander. "Jesper said you should have this."

Zander looked at it for a moment, then he held it to his chest with both hands and closed his eyes. "There is a lot of power in this book," he said.

"Jesper said to read the whole book before you try to use it." Dar looked around for someplace to put the birdcage. "And don't let anyone else read it."

"What's up with the bird?" Deek joined the conversation as Zander dropped out of it and into his new book.

"He gave this to me too." Dar looked at the beast. "I'm not sure why."

Deek got up and got closer to the bird. "A seagull? Odd taste in birds."

The gull nattered its beak like it was going to either bite one of them or speak. It did neither. It just looked at Dar, then Deek, then Zander.

"I have to release it in two days' time," Dar said. He set it up so the cage would hang from the mended joint in the central tent pole. "Hopefully, he's okay up here."

"Hopefully, he's pretty quiet." Deek inspected the bird. "All in all, he's a pretty fine-looking seagull."

"You know much about them?" Dar worked his way back to the hammock and started replaying the whole conversation with Jesper in his head.

"Only read about them in books, really, but this fellow looks like he's all business." Deek worked his way back to his spot. "All business for a seagull."

Dar looked up at the creature. Was it just an odd local variation of a normal bird? Or was this a Gulull?

Dar heard the answer to his unspoken question in his head: *Yes*. At that, the bird seemed to wink at him. Could it really be? As he stared at the creature, he saw a small hand appear out of the plumage on its breast and give him a quick wave. Before Dar could move, the hand was hidden away again.

"You okay?" Deek asked. Apparently, he'd seen Dar twitch out of the corner of his eye.

Dar took a moment to respond. "Yes. I was just thinking that things may not be what we think they are…"

Zander put down his book. "The Abbey is not what we think it is. I'm certain of that."

Deek looked at his brother strangely. "Where did that come from?"

Zander crossed his arms, tucking the book under one of them. "I've seen too much weirdness from Ocktur coming back from the place for it to really be an abbey. Ocktur is as religious as I am a squid."

The Gulull quickly turned its head and sized up Zander.

"So maybe there is something going on there. What can we do about it?" Deek mirrored his brother by folding his arms. "I'm too busy trying to stay alive to worry about if the Abbey is an abbey, or if it's a tavern, or even an illusion."

Zander got excited at that. "It could totally be an illusion."

Deek smiled. "It's probably not an illusion."

"It's a little big to be a tavern," Dar commented.

"There's only one way to find out." Deek turned to face Dar. "I think our commanding officer should pay the place a visit."

Dar sighed. "An unofficial one, of course."

Deek smiled. "Can I come too?"

Zander answered for Dar. "No."

FOURTEEN

Escape

Nothing ruins a good illusion like reality.
—second bylaw of the Hierarchy of Illusionists

"Dar." Zander was shaking him awake from the sleep he was getting before his adventure. The Vanander brothers had the overnight shift on guard duty, so as soon as it was well dark, they'd agreed to get Dar on his way.

"I'm up." Dar rubbed his eyes. He had hoped to talk to the Gulull while the brothers were out but felt the sleep more necessary. He gathered up his sword, took what money he had, and put on his boots.

"Taking a sword?" Zander whispered. "Isn't that dangerous?"

"Going without one is more dangerous." Dar winked at him, but in the darkness, of course, Zander couldn't see it.

Luckily, Dar could see better than his friends at night. His mixed elven-human heritage meant he could see heat signatures as well as the visual colors. On a night like this, that meant he could typically see people a minute before they could see him.

"If I'm not back by dawn, tell Drots I was summoned back to the headquarters in the middle of the night. If I'm not back by another day, release the bird, and head across to the enemy and surrender to them."

"Surrender? We've been told they will kill prisoners." Zander clearly couldn't believe what he was hearing.

"You're more likely to survive the war in their prison than over here." Dar put his hand on Zander's shoulder. "That's the most import part of this, Zander. Survive. Promise me."

Zander took a moment, but then put his arm on Dar's shoulder. "I promise."

"Good. If Drots gives you trouble before the second day, just move everything up and get out of here."

"Good luck and safe journey, Dar."

"See you before dawn."

Dar took off running toward the Abbey. He was able to keep up a good pace, and he covered the distance pretty quickly. Along the way, he passed a footman unit in reserve and two units with horses, one of which was probably a heavy cavalier unit.

After what seemed like three hours but was probably closer to four, Dar arrived at the Abbey. Even at night, it was an imposing building. Flying buttresses, spires, and giant glass windows dominated every side. The building was at least four hundred feet long, probably one hundred feet wide, and at least twice that high. Dar could see guards stationed at a pair of fancy, detailed doors, which, in his mind, made them the front doors. He could see two guards, heavily armed, and a collection of people entering and exiting the building. Away from that door was another opening, and as Dar watched a single, gaunt-looking form opened the door from the inside and placed a big barrel outside. This person jammed the door open, then walked outside, picked up the barrel, and started to work their way to a ditch a good fifty feet from the building.

Dar figured it was a servant using a side door to dump some garbage, so he ran to the door and used it as cover. After a quick glance to make sure the servant was facing away, Dar stepped inside.

Dar blinked once or twice to let his eyes adjust. He was in a kitchen, and there were various races of individuals working at making dishes, some of which looked delicious and others disgusting. Knowing the manservant would be back in a moment, Dar took a risk and joined the queue of various creatures carrying trays of food out of the kitchen. He grabbed a beef-looking dish and followed the rest of the creatures into a hallway and then to a breezeway with a small staircase against the outer wall. There was a person there issuing orders. As each server reached the man, he would inspect their dish and then spout some number. Dar was worried he wouldn't know what do to with the number, but he got lucky and got the same number as the person in front of him.

"Three."

Dar kept up with the human in front of him, which was easy, given the fact that Dar was six inches taller than the guy. The thing behind him was an orc. The orc had some disgusting dish and had been assigned not a number but a word: "Basement."

Dar followed the server up the stairs, looking around as much as he could without being obvious. At the first landing, on the second floor, he had to walk around to the other side to go up the next flight. He could see a wide hallway lined by doors on one side and a rail on the other side. Leaning up against the rail were women of all shapes and sizes—but mostly larger and less delicate looking—most of them naked. Some were old enough to be grandmothers, with haggard features, shaggy hair, and missing or misshapened teeth. Among them, some partially naked men could be seen haggling with them. The men were in worse shape than the women, some looking like they had never bathed. Then a bag would be exchanged—gold coins, no doubt—and the pair would head into a room.

Dar looked around for the guy before him and noted he was quickly getting up the stairs. So Dar keep going and made it up to the third level.

This level was laid out like the one before it, but the railing was in better shape, and so were the women and clientele. This level was full of officers, and the women were all human, shapely, comely, and young. Clearly this was a more expensive wing.

Dar closed the gap with the guy in front of him, and now he could see where he would need to drop off the dish: a large serving area at the end of the hallway. As he passed down the hallway, the women acted like he wasn't there. Dar kept his eyes down, but the shapes of the more naked bodies were hard to ignore. His delivery mission completed, Dar followed his guide in turning around and heading back toward the stairs. But just before he got there—and just after his leader descended them—Dar darted into a dark room with an open door.

He needed to think. These clearly weren't nuns. At least not nuns of any religion he had ever heard of. He wasn't sure what to do next, but getting out of there sounded like a good start.

There was a rustling noise in the back of the room.

Dar turned and searched the area with his night vision. He could see the outline of a body. By the size and curvature, the body was female, and the signature was still fresh, so she was alive. Dar drew his sword and crept toward her. She was hiding under a window dressing, her heat signature still clear through the sheer cloth.

Dar shut the door and figured out how to lock it. He pulled out a coin and cast a light spell on it. With the light he could see her. She was mostly naked, young and thin.

"I can see you. Come out." Dar spoke quietly enough for his voice not to alarm the girl.

"Go away, I'm not seeing anybody tonight." There were tears in her voice. "I've had enough for tonight."

"I'm not here for pleasure." He softened his tone. "I want to help you."

She peered out from behind the fabric. "Help?"

"Tell me your name."

"Janelle."

"Have you eaten lately, Janelle?"

"If you don't to tricks, you don't get fed." She leaned up against the wall and let herself slide down. "I can't do it. They try to make me, but I can't do it."

"Stay here."

Dar pocketed the coin, and the room went dark. He opened the door, which unlocked it. He stepped out into the hallway and shut the door behind him. He walked over to the table where he had just dropped off the tray of food and started loading it up with various other things he found there.

Salad greens, meat, bread, vegetables, all in modest portions so he could get a variety onto the plate. Walking down the hallway once more, he swung his sword around to the front to clear the way; the women still paid him no attention. He quickly made his way back into the room with Janelle.

He locked the door and pulled out the light coin once again, then went over to her and handed the food to her. "Here. Eat."

She took the plate and started eating large mouthfuls.

"Take your time. You don't want to shock your system," Dar cautioned. He let silence descend on the room so she could eat in peace. After she had finished half of the plate, he started to talk again.

"Can I ask you something?"

"Here we go," Janelle said. She placed the plate down on her lap, apparently in an attempt to preserve what little modesty she still had.

"Nothing like that." Dar stood and got a blanket off the bed. With his sword, he cut it in two, and then he cut two slits, one for each arm. He tossed it to her. She grabbed it and quickly used it to cover up.

"I want to know what this place is, exactly." Dar turned away from her and looked around the room.

"It's a whorehouse. What are you, blind?" She put the bread into her mouth.

"So it isn't an abbey?" Dar examined the art on the wall, which featured fancy paintings, gold leaf candelabras, and exquisite woodwork. "It's a little fancy for a house of ill-repute."

"It was once an abbey, but the owner claimed that the nuns and monks owed back taxes and kicked them out. He made it his own house, and then when the war came, he turned it into a whorehouse. He gets a cut of all the transactions, or for people like me, he gets it all after the floor lady gets her take."

"You don't get any money for giving your body to the men here?" Dar tried not to make it sound too harsh.

"I was stolen from the city and forced to work here." Janelle started to cry. "I never gave anything to anybody." She sobbed heavily. "They always took it. I fought them."

"Stop." Dar wanted to comfort her, but he wasn't sure how she would take it. "That is over. When I leave, you're coming with me. I will get you out of here."

It was clear that she couldn't believe the good news. She sat there crying into her food and chewing until she swallowed hard and cleared her throat.

"What will it cost me?"

"Nothing more than a smile, and maybe your thanks." Dar held out his hand.

"Why are you doing this for me?" She reached up to his hand but stopped short.

"I'm not doing it for you. I'm doing it for me. If I was to leave you here, I wouldn't be able to bear it."

"You're not like the other men in this army." She took his hand.

"I've heard that before."

"What is your plan?" she said.

"I don't have one." Dar couldn't help but grin at his own comment.

"That might not work." She cast a glance at the curtain, apparently considering hiding behind it again.

"I figure we get you to the kitchen and then out from there."

She pursed her lips, her eyes darting around as she chose her destiny. "Let's go."

Dar cracked the door open a bit and looked around. If they were going to make it to the kitchen, their best shot was to act quickly. He might have trouble with the routing person, but he had a bluff ready. He took Janelle's hand, and they quickly ran down the stairs. When he got down to the router, the fellow looked up and started to say something, but Dar cut him off.

"She wants to order something special, and the colonel told her to go down to the kitchen and make it herself."

The router nodded and watched them walk by.

Dar bluffed his way to the back of the kitchen but lost his sense of direction. He looked at Janelle, but her vexed expression showed she hadn't been down here. He stepped into a back doorway. There were no lights on in the room. Dar looked around and swore under his breath. He pulled out his light coin, which revealed a desk. This appeared to be the office for the kitchen—and unfortunately, it had no other exits. Janelle stood behind him, and they closed the door. Janelle looked as if she could use a break. Dar was happy to take one too, and they rested for a couple of minutes.

Then the doorknob started to turn.

Quick as a flash, Dar jumped behind the door and waited for person to come in. It turned out to be a wispy man, probably the one who'd been dumping the garbage earlier, holding a candle. As Dar eased out from behind the door, he decided on his course of action. In one quick motion, Dar handed the light coin to Janelle, blew out the candle, and took hold of the man, with his sword to the fellow's neck.

"Don't move and you'll live."

"Don't hurt me!" squeaked the man. "I've got no money on me."

"I don't want your money. I want information," Dar snarled at the man.

"I'll talk, just don't kill me." The man was shaking.

"Where is the way out?" Dar kept the man pointing away from them both so he couldn't identify them if it came to that.

"The front door is at the other end of the building."

"I meant the secret door, the one you dumped the trash out of." He jostled the man to help refresh his memory.

"That one? You pull the third light sconce from the end, and it will open the door." The man swallowed hard. "Please don't tell anybody else about it."

"Where did all the treasure in the house come from? This isn't a house of holy folk. Nuns and abbots don't need gold candle holders."

"When the master took over this place as his country house, he brought his extra items as a way to make the place look nicer. Plus, as people paid influence to the master, that gave him extra money to put into the house."

"Bribes? Interesting. Go on."

"Influence has its price."

"Still, keep going. Where and when did the whores show up?" Dar squeezed the man a little to remind him of the urgency of the moment.

"The ladies joined the house once the wife of the master left for the city when the war started. He started sharing with the commanders after that, for the right price. And that led to having excess baggage. They've had trouble getting enough wagons together to get the items of value out of the house, and without the lady of the house around, master has…" He paused. "Contracted for more and more ladies. Once he saw the value they were adding to his life, he decided to keep them all."

"So the armies are defending a whorehouse full of bribes for your master?" Dar could feel a retch building. "What is his name?"

"My master is the Lord Protectorate."

Dar was shocked. He paused for a moment too long—the guy knew something was up.

"You're from the army, aren't you?" The man's tone had changed, and some of the fear was gone. He sounded like he felt he had some leverage now. "If you're from the army, I can arrange some of the better ladies to spend some time with you. No first- or second-floor girls for you. Third floor the whole way. One, two, maybe three of them at the same time. You can do anything and everything you've ever dreamed of. Just let me go, and I'll make it happen."

"What size are your shoes?" Dar shook him again.

"What?" The man was confused.

Dar looked at Janelle. "Put out the light out and take his shoes."

The room when dark, and Janelle dropped to her knees and started to feel around for the man's legs.

"A little more to your left," Dar called out, using his vision to help her. She found the man's legs and pulled at his feet. He lifted his foot to kick her, but increased pressure on his neck from Dar's sword stopped all resistance.

"Take your shirt off," Dar said to the man.

They fumbled in the dark, with Dar giving both parties directions. Dar took everything but the man's underwear, and

Janelle put it all on. It was a little big, but a tuck and fold here and there kept any surplus fabric out of the way.

Finally ready to go, Dar pushed the man hard toward the desk. He sprawled every which way and tumbled over it to the other side. Quickly, Dar opened the door, grabbed Janelle's hand, and guided her out into the kitchen. The service line paid them no attention, and soon Dar found the sconce that opened the secret door.

With that, they were outside.

"I can't see anything." Janelle clenched his hand tighter. "I'm scared."

"You're free," Dar said softly. "Just hold my hand, and let's get out of here."

They ran as much as Janelle could take, and at times Dar carried her to keep the pace up. Dawn was coming quickly, and she needed to be on her way to the enemy lines before the sun was up.

"Why aren't we heading to the city?" Janelle looked up at the stars. "We're heading the wrong direction."

"If you go back to the city, people might see you. You might get caught again and be forced to go back there. Or worse."

"I'll take worse. Those horrible men forcing themselves on me, I would rather die." She seemed about to break into tears again.

"The people laying siege to the city aren't evil, I know that now. I'll get you to them, and you'll be out of the war until it's over."

"Can we stop?" She sounded weary.

"No." He scooped her up and put her weight on his shoulder. He jogged as fast as he could, but after a mile, she protested again.

"Put me down."

"Will you run with me?" Dar pleaded with his eyes.

"As best as I can." Her faced showed that being carried was almost as hard on her physically as it was for Dar.

They reached the outskirts of the camp just as the sky had started to turn from black into a blue hue. Dar signaled for Janelle to walk silently, but she wasn't very good at it. Just as they got to the opening in the palisades, Dar heard Zander.

"Halt and be identified."

"Zander, it's me, Dar."

"Don't try that. What is the code word?"

"Avalon." Dar tugged at Janelle's hand, urging her onward.

The fire in the center of the campsite area was providing enough light that Zander could see Dar wasn't alone.

"Who's your friend?"

"I don't have time, Zander." Dar kept walking, pulling her along. "I'll explain later, just keep your mouth shut."

"Explain about what?" Deek said from his position on top of the wall.

Dar rolled his eyes and picked up the pace. Janelle struggled to keep up.

"I can't keep going," she said, finally. She pulled her hand from his and dropped to the ground.

Dar looked to the horizon and saw the first rays of sunlight. He pulled out his sword and stuck it down the back of her shirt, between her skin and the cloth. He pulled up, and the sword sliced the shirt and her thin undershirt completely in half.

"What are you doing?" she screamed, struggling to her feet. She clutched the remnants to her chest, trying to keep some of her modesty.

"Motivating you to get moving." Dar pointed at the enemy lines. "You show up there fully clothed and they'll think you're a soldier. You show up in tatters and they'll know you're a refugee."

"You're a monster like the rest of them." She looked at him as she walked toward the enemy lines. "I knew I shouldn't have trusted you."

Then she took off running. As soon as she was clear of him by about fifty feet, Dar could hear the all too familiar whistling of arrows. He took off running in the other direction and didn't stop until he reached the palisades. He ducked for cover and sank to the ground to catch his breath.

He wasn't down for long before the Vanander brothers showed up.

Dar could hear Deek's smile. "So, tell us about your friend."

FIFTEEN

Taken

A good thief only takes what he needs. This is,
of course, everything.
—"Lefty" Rightfingers, Master Thief of the
Free City of Holin

Dar had answered the brothers' questions about Janelle
as much as he could. He didn't have as many answers
as they had questions, and they asked very different kinds of
questions. Deek seemed more interested in the bribery operation, while Zander worried about the mistreatment of the
women inside the Abbey. Dar quickly got exhausted after
the adrenaline of the whole night finally faded. He headed
over to the sergeant's tent—even though he still stayed with
the brothers most nights, he could bivouac inside. It would
be quiet and dark in there, and he could get a nap while the
brothers went on with their duties.

He stretched out on the cot and was soon asleep. But
his rest was fitful; dreams of the Abbey filled his mind. The

women, the smells, the utter betrayal of their purpose as an army. Finally, Dar couldn't stay asleep any longer, so he rubbed his eyes and opened the tent door.

Drots was standing there.

"Heard you had a hard night." Drots was smiling. "Heard you went to the Abbey."

"You've been hearing lots of things." Dar sighed.

"Ocktur took me there once. I had a great time. Did you have a great time?" Drots winked at him. "Did you know what to do with one?"

"Don't go there, Drots."

"This one new girl showed me a nice time after I taught her a lesson on how to…"

"What did you say?" Dar clenched his fist, but it was clear that Drots didn't see it.

"She had to be taught to let a man do what a man wants to do, but I enjoyed the challenge. I think her name was Janelle, blond…"

Dar shut Drots's mouth with a brutal right cross to his jaw. The blow sent him flying. Dar picked him up by the scruff of his neck and put his fist next to Drots's face.

"I don't take kindly to rapists, Drots. I hear you doing things like that again, and I'll make sure you can't ever harm another woman. You get me?"

Drots had tears forming in the corner of his eyes, and his nose was bleeding. His cheek was already turning red and puffy.

"You get me?" Dar shook him. "Or you need another lesson?"

"I get you," Drots said feebly.

"Paying for it wasn't enough, you had to force yourself, you had to take." Dar dropped him down to the ground. "You disgust me."

Dar noticed a small crowd had formed.

"Nothing to see here. A disciplinary issue that has been addressed," Dar said to them, waving them away. "Unless others want the same lesson, we are done here." Dar was taking a page from Ocktur's leadership book, but it didn't feel right.

"Behind you!" a voice called out.

Dar turned to see Drots coming at him with a crude blow. Dar pivoted and struck at Drots with his right hand again. With Drots's added momentum, the blow had extra force. Drots reeled from it, and Dar followed up with a leg sweep, dropping Drots to the ground. Dar pulled his sword and pointed it at Drots's nose. The tip was barely an inch from the tip of his nose.

"Are we done yet?" Dar said. "If you don't learn your lesson soon, I'm sure I can find another corporal for the unit."

"I'd be careful from here on out if I was you, Dar."

"Drots, we don't have to like each other, but if you and I can't get along, you'll be the one regretting it, not me. You did a wrong in my book, and it wasn't fair for me to hit you like that, but like I said, I don't like rapists. Why rape a girl when you could easily have found another woman who would happily take your money for pleasure?"

Drots held his tongue. Dar knew why.

"I'd find another pleasure, then, since my policy is, hopefully, crystal clear."

Dar looked around the crowd.

"If I hear any of you men are violating women, you'll answer to me, and you'll be far worse off than Drots here. I don't put up with that, and having been warned, your punishment will be severe."

Dar looked around the crowd. He saw some shock, some sadness, and some dejection. Jusin nodded in support and looked in disgust at some of the less enthusiastic reactions.

"Dismissed!"

Dar stood in the center of the tent area with his sword still out. He watched Drots stand up again and scamper off to his tent to treat his wounds. The Vanander brothers came up together.

"Wow. What happened?" Deek said, keeping his eye on Drots's tent.

"Drots raped Janelle." Dar put his sword away.

"That girl from last night?" Zander shook his head.

Dar turned and walked away from the two brothers. Deek called out. "Where you going?"

"To see Ocktur and get some answers."

Dar took his time walking to the battalion headquarters. He had little idea where it was, but after he found the light infantry reserves that he had seen the night before, he stopped and asked them for directions. The pointed him in the right direction, and by noon he was at the encampment.

"I have come to see Colonel Ocktur," Dar said to the guard at the front of the cordoned-off area.

"Do you have an appointment?" said the man. His build was slight, and he didn't have any weapons.

"I don't. I have an important military question that I need the colonel to answer." Dar started to walk past the man.

"You can't go in unannounced." The man stood in Dar's way and put his hand on Dar's chest. "What is your name?"

"Dar."

"What unit?"

"He'll know."

The man wrinkled up his face in a way that indicated people who barged into Ocktur's tent without appointments came out dead. But all the same, the man turned and walked into the tent. A brief second went by before he came out.

"You may enter, the colonel will see you." His disappointment was obvious, but Dar paid it no mind.

Dar stormed past the orderly and went inside. Ocktur was relaxing in a chair, a goblet of something in his hand.

"What can I help you with, Dar?"

"Why is the Abbey a whorehouse?" Dar jumped to the point.

"Why do you care?" Ocktur took a sip of his beverage.

"Why is the line extended around the Abbey when we could defend the city beyond it with half the troops if we didn't have this massive spur in the lines?"

"We have a mission, and we do it." Ocktur put the goblet down. "What we defend, or why or where, isn't for us to decide. We do our duty, and I expect you to do yours."

"How much money have you spent there?"

Ocktur laughed. "Too much. But that doesn't matter. Time in the Abbey is a perk of the job. You keep the company defending that flank like I did, and you'll get time there too."

"I don't want time there." Dar was disgusted.

"Not into the ladies?" Ocktur laughed. "I knew there was something wrong with you."

"I don't pay for love."

"It's not love you're paying for, foolish boy." Ocktur took another sip. "And what goes on there is worth it, I can assure you."

"Did you know Drots raped one of the women there?" Dar shifted his weight back and forth.

"I know he selected a newcomer, but I had my hands full." Ocktur stared off into the distance, lost in some memory that Dar was sure he didn't want to know about. "I know he went to the third floor. I like the second floor better. They can take a man of my size." He laughed.

"I didn't come here to talk about your recreational activities." Dar put his hands on his hips. "I think what we are doing is wrong, and we should pull back the troops behind the Abbey."

"That isn't going to happen."

"I want to go on record," Dar chirped at him.

"I'm telling you to let it go." Ocktur sipped his drink. "I have my orders, and I follow them. It says defend the Abbey. Me and my units will do that until the enemy has failed or we have been relieved of duty."

"We are losing, aren't we?" Dar stared at Ocktur, who wasn't meeting his gaze.

"I've seen better, but I've seen worse." Ocktur smiled. Apparently revisiting memories of his times in the Abbey. "But I hear we have more recruits coming, so that will be nice. Hopefully, more people like you and fewer like Modo."

"Don't send any Modos my way." Dar moved toward the door.

"By the way, I'll let you get away with it this time." Ocktur was staring at him—Dar could see fire in his eyes. "But you'll address me as Colonel, and show me the respect of the rank, or you'll be dead before you can say another word. And if I hear you're not doing your duty, I know Drots can run that unit."

Dar opened the door. The orderly rushed in. Ocktur addressed him. "Cadge, schedule a trip to the Abbey tonight, and an early meal here at the camp."

"Yes, Colonel."

Dar looked at Ocktur. He was smiling.

"Good afternoon, Colonel Ocktur," Dar said, venom dripping from his every word.

"Dismissed, Sergeant Dar."

Dar walked back slowly, taking his time to think over what his next move would be. He clearly couldn't maintain his role in this war, which left him questioning what else could be wrong about what he knew of his new life. He was just in sight of the camp when he noticed some action up ahead. Picking up his pace, he ran into the camp. The enemy was everywhere. The few defenders he could see were clumped in a couple of groups, some near the palisades, some near the tents.

The first foe to attract his attention was a heavily armored female warrior, spinning and slashing, yet drawing little blood. She would parry and attack a defender until they were unarmed, then she would strike them with her fist or with the pommel of her sword. Then she started a somatic motion, which Dar recognized as a sleep spell. She finished it before he could get to her, and as Dar closed to engage with her, Dar could see her targets: the Vanander brothers.

"Zander! Deek!" Dar called out.

The she-warrior turned and faced him. She blocked his first blow with her sword. Dar struggled to keep up with her, but she wasn't pressing the attack on him. Behind her Dar could see more attackers, all dressed in heavy armor like her.

They didn't join the fray against him, but took up a position next to the Vanander brothers.

"Turn around and leave," Dar said, "and I'll let you live. You don't want this site. Just leave the prisoners, and we'll let you leave without conflict."

"I'm not leaving without my brothers." The voice came from behind the mask.

"What?"

Dar didn't see the mace that hit him in the back of his head.

Sometime later, Dar awoke to the sight of a rather fat man on an overworked horse. The heavy cavalier unit, Dar reasoned. His head pounded, and his vision was still a little blurred by the blow.

"You're lucky to be alive, friend," the fat man said.

"Thanks." Dar rubbed the nub on the back of his head gently. "I am Sergeant Dar, who are you?"

"Cyral, Knight of Merit."

Dar didn't recognize where that was in the chain of command. "Pardon my question, as my wound has left me disoriented, but what rank is that an equivalent to?"

"Major." The man was not amused.

"My apologies, sir." Dar started to stand, but his head wasn't up to it.

"The blighters must have seen us coming. They were heading out of here just as we arrived." Cryal moved in his saddle, and the horse shifted under him. "I figured we could have added to our tally had they stayed."

"Did you see a female warrior with two prisoners?"

"What? A she-warrior?" The knight looked disappointed. "I did not. If it's the one I heard about, she doesn't normally leave survivors." He glanced out into no-man's-land before looking back down at Dar. "Perhaps you got hit harder than you thought. They had their wounded with them, that much I could tell. Once we got out in the open after them, they started with the arrows, and we had to come back here."

"How many dead?"

"Our boys? Or theirs?" the knight said.

"My men."

"Not my problem, chap." Cryal looked down at Dar. "You able to assume command, or should I leave my lieutenant behind?"

"I'm good, sir," Dar lied.

"Right." Cryal raised his right hand and waited for his lieutenant to arrive on horseback from a few steps away. "Get the men ready to leave. Seems everything is under control now."

"Aye, Major."

Dar took a deep breath and rubbed the back of his head. It still stung.

The major wheeled his horse around and glanced over at Dar. "Good luck to you, and please don't take this the wrong way, but I hope never to return here."

"Thank you, Major. I hope my men will not need your unit's service."

"Cavalry!" The Knight of Merit bellowed so loud it seemed to bounce around the palisades and through Dar's head. "Back to base!"

Dar sat for a while as his unit started to assemble around him. Only then did he consider standing again.

"You able, Sergeant?" Dar didn't have to look at Drots to know a sneer of envy was there for all to see.

"I leave for a few moments, and the corporal in charge lets all matter of disasters break loose, and I'm sure we're missing some men." Dar reached out his hand to get a hand up.

Jusin reached out his hand and braced for Dar's weight. Dar came up slowly, but he maintained his balance.

"I want the company to muster. We need to figure out how badly that just went." Dar walked slowly to the center of the area where they would normally muster. "Look around for bodies."

"Which is it?" Drots queried. "Do we muster, or do we look around for bodies?"

"Muster in five minutes."

Drots said something under his breath, but Dar was more focused on getting into his tent to rest for a few. Maybe Zander had something in the supply hammock to help with the pain. Dar turned and looked out into the camp. He knew neither brother was anywhere to be seen, but he looked for them anyway, hoping they would appear. He sat on his bed and took a look around. He noticed the empty cage, pondered about the missing Gulull. He hoped it had escaped, but he would know the next time he saw Jesper. The thought of how that would go caused a moment of dread.

He could feel the echoes of the brothers lurking around him, and it weighed on his heart. He could hear the men outside looking for them, and in his heart Dar knew they would not find them. He searched his heart for strength, knowing that if he started to cry, it might not stop. He just couldn't go on. Drots, the war, Ocktur, and now the fat knight, the she-warrior, and the loss of the brothers—it was all too much for him. He was just a simple apprentice, not made for this. It wasn't his destiny. Dar realized he was blinking too much, his eyes trying to will the woozy feeling out of his head. The room started to spin, or maybe it was him. He wanted to lie down—he wanted the world to lie down. It was hard to focus, hard to breathe, hard to think.

"Is the master of the unit about?" The voice was from the yard.

"He's in there," came another voice, one he should have recognized, but didn't.

Dar felt the door open and a person approach him. He could see it was the man who brought the cart around. His mind couldn't find the name.

"What are you doing here?" Dar said to the man. The room started to spin, and the man seemed to be moving very slowly.

"I could ask you the same question." A smile formed on his lips. "A little birdy told me to come over." Dar stared at the man, unable to make his eyes focus on anything for long. "You've gotten a nasty blow to the head, haven't you?"

"I've been all right." Dar leaned back and used his arms to help hold him steady.

"Your pupils are different sizes, and your head isn't evenly shaped anymore."

"And?" Dar was already tired of the conversation.

"And you'll die if you don't get it treated. Right now, the stuff behind your eyes is bruised as bad as your top of your head is. Unless you get help, you'll drop in and out of consciousness and finally quit waking up at all." His eyes lit up with his trademark humor. "You know, probably."

"My friend with healing powers was taken by the enemy, so unless you have some potions or magic for me, I suppose it's not looking good for me."

The man's lips smiled. "I have both." He moved in close and whispered so only Dar could hear. "I'll give you the potion, as the magic spell would attract too much attention. Not many spell-casting peddlers in this neck of the battlefield, are there?"

"What of my men?"

"Put one in charge. You'll need some time off, even with the potions."

"Which…"

"Ah, drink first." The man produced a potion flask from his belt and handed it to Dar, who took it. The other man pulled the stopper and helped tip it up to Dar's lips. And then the fluid cascaded into his mouth.

It tasted like rays of pure sunshine on a summer's day. Dar could feel his vitality returning to him as the liquid flowed down into his body. And his mind returned.

He was drinking a strange potion from the cartmonger. He trusted the man—Jesper, his mind finally resolved—but a potion could have easily have been poison. He paused, a bit of the drink still left on his lips.

Jesper grinned. "I guess enough of it has gotten into your system to make you realize the folly of drinking a potion from a relative stranger. But I have done you no wrong so far, so you're wondering, do I keep going, or do I hope that what I had won't be fatal?"

"Not anymore." Dar wondered if Jesper could read minds. He hoped he couldn't.

"So what is it now?"

"That I owe you a great deal, Jesper." Dar took in more of the potion. "And I wonder what you are, since clearly you are not just a seller of wares."

Jesper moved toward the door. "It is not the time for that now. Keep the potion with you; it will fill itself again after midnight. Leave some in the bottom—just a drop or two, mind you—and it will magically return. Keeping drinking some for a couple of days and you'll be like nothing happened."

"You must let me pay you."

His smile was back. "It is not time for that either." With that he left the room.

Dar finished as much as he dared to drink and put the stopper back into the flask. He looked around the room again. Out in the yard beyond he could see the unit at muster, waiting for his return. He stood triumphantly, sure of his footing, albeit with still a slight soreness in the head, and strode out to the unit.

"Report." He came to a stop next to Drots.

"Zander and Deek are missing. Banes is dead."

"Enemy losses?"

Drots stood silent.

"Enemy losses, Drots?"

"None, Sergeant."

Dar looked out at the gap in the palisades and contemplated the fate of the brothers. Something had been said to him during the battle. He couldn't remember what it was, but he knew it was the answer to the mystery.

"Normal duty cycle. I want a sentry on watch at all times. Dismissed."

SIXTEEN

Clarity

"The only thing that is clear in hindsight is what
not to do."
—Elader the Old

Dar settled into his hammock and wondered about the
day. Dinner had been the usual blandness, and the pain
in his head was just about gone. Though the sun had yet to set,
it was dark outside. He could hear the drops of rain start and
then the predictable sounds of flowing water echoing across
the camp. He wondered about the guard on the palisades, but
he wasn't as concerned about it as he should have been. While
the pain was gone from his head, his heart still hurt. He still
wanted to cry. So he extinguished the last light in the tent and
let his emotions flow through him. Wave after wave of rain
came down both inside the tent and out, only stopping inside
when Dar drifted off to sleep.

It wasn't long before he was in the throes of a dream. Vivid
colors, echoing voices, and soft wisps of clouds were balanced

by severed limbs, bloodied warriors, and the oddest collection of things from Jesper's cart. Dar could feel his body floating across the land in his dream when suddenly a woman appeared.

Dar opened his eyes. It was still dark, but the rain had stopped. The dream still lingered in his mind's eye, and he could see the moments from the end of it like they were still happening. The woman—he'd been sure it was Janelle at first—turned into a beautiful woman in chain mail. She was tall, powerful, and full of purpose. Her aim, he could tell, was to kill him.

It was both love and fear at first sight.

Dar swung out of the hammock, heading out of the tent and toward the guard post. He might be having a crisis of conscience, but he still had a job to do. Jusin was manning the guard post.

"Hi, Dar."

Dar could tell he was tired and bored. "How you doing, Jusin?"

His face brightened a bit at the mention of his name. "Just trying to survive."

"I know what you mean."

The two stood in silence for a moment. Jusin broke it.

"What you doing out this late at night? You don't have a shift."

Dar smiled. "Just couldn't sleep. I thought I'd see how things are going at the front."

"We're all at the front."

Dar laughed softly. "You know what I mean."

Silence again.

"You think we'll survive this?" Jusin looked out over the palisades at the enemy beyond.

"We've gotten this far, haven't we?"

"How far is this, exactly?" Jusin mumbled.

"What?" Dar tilted his head.

"Nothing, Sergeant." Jusin straightened out a bit.

"I understand." Dar put his hand on the other man's back. "We're doing nothing but surviving, aren't we. No counterattacks, no feints, nothing but sitting here waiting for a miracle that I bet isn't coming."

Jusin nodded. "Sometimes I wonder if we're just in purgatory, getting a little bit of torture every day, waiting until it's our time to die."

"I had a life before this, and I will again after it. So will you." Dar squeezed Jusin's shoulder a little, but the armor diffused the gesture. "What did you do before the war?"

"I was the shepherd of a flock just near Frearea. I come from a wandering tribe. I was supposed to be wed by now."

"Let me guess, an Ogre Magi knocked you out, and next thing you knew, you were here."

"I didn't realize that brute was an ogre." He looked at Dar. "But yeah."

"And you were told the Abbey we are defending is full of…?"

"Nuns and refugees?" Jusin said softly, not sure he had the right answer.

Dar smiled. "You have family other than your fiancée?"

"Three sisters and a brother."

Brother.

Brothers.

Dar stared off into the distance.

Finally, Dar came out of it.

It all made sense now. He knew what he must do. He looked around and saw that Jusin had wandered off a bit. He walked over to him.

"Sorry about that."

Jusin shrugged, clearly not sure what, if anything, to say.

"I'm going to give you an order, and I need you to follow it to the letter. You'll need to be creative about it, but I need you do to this for me."

"Yes?" Jusin looked a bit afraid but also honored that he was being trusted with this obviously solemn duty.

"I haven't forgotten how you made sure I got some water in those harsh early days. Today, I'm making good on your request to pay that kindness back to you. Talk to the men— gently—and figure out which have joined the unit via the ogre versus those who were recruited by pay or other means."

"What does being recruited by the ogre mean?"

"That you are most likely good of heart and noble of origin." Dar smiled.

"And those who weren't?" Jusin sounded a bit hesitant to ask.

"Modo, Ocktur, Drots—those are the ones called here by money, greed, power, and worse."

"Evil?" Jusin swallowed hard.

"Most likely." Dar looked him in the eye.

"We aren't on the good side?" Jusin struggled to keep his emotions in check.

"The Abbey is a whorehouse full of stolen and otherwise ill-gotten goods." Dar put his arm on Jusin's shoulder again. "I just discovered that a couple of days ago."

"So, if we are on the wrong side of the war, what are we going to do about it?"

"Once you figure who was pressed into this army, tell them, privately, the code word 'navigator.' When they hear that word, they must lie down and surrender immediately, no matter what they are doing or where they are. Even in the middle of battle."

"So once you get enough troops from the other side inside the palisades to defeat the evil, you'll have the good ones among us tip the scales. I get it."

"Something like that." Dar held Jusin's eye. "I can't do much about Drots being second in command, so do what you can to keep off his bad side and keep yourself safe. If you see Jesper, trust him. He's a good man."

"Jesper?"

"The peddler."

"Oh." Jusin watched Dar as he pulled away and headed back to the campsite. "What are you going to do?"

"Better if you don't know." Dar looked at him a last time. He smiled, trying to assure both Jusin and himself it would work out.

"Probably true. Good luck."

Dar paused at the guard post next to the palisades. His gaze darted to the opening, a lightness in the dark of the night. He turned and walked back to the tent, then fished out one of Zander's white shirts. He didn't put it on—it wouldn't have fit anyway—but rather balled it up in his and started back to where he had left Jusin. His strides became longer the closer he got to the opening and turned into a light jog as he crossed out into no-man's-land. He stopped after a while, unsure of the width the area. Just to be safe, he unfurled Zander's shirt and started waving it over his head before he started forward again. He glanced over his shoulder, but he was too far away to see the guard post from where he was. Dar had only taken another two steps when the unmistakable sound of an arrow hitting the ground in front on him made him stop.

"Halt!" came a voice from the night.

Dar stopped, raising both hands high into the sky. "Hold your fire!"

"I'll do the talking." The voice was stern and forceful but somehow very quiet.

Dar let out what he hoped was an agreeable-sounding grunt.

"Good."

There was a long pause. Dar didn't move.

"What is the passphrase?"

"I do not know."

"So, you wish to surrender?" It was another voice, like the first, but slightly different.

"I wish to switch sides."

Dar wasn't sure if he heard a bunch of people talking or if it was a breeze kicking up suddenly. His arms were getting tired. "Can I put my arms down?"

"No." It was the first voice.

"Ask Zander and Deek. They will tell you about me. I know you took them. My name is Dar."

Dar was sure this time the sound he'd heard was talking. He lowered his arms.

The silence got to Dar after a while. He hadn't counted on surrendering taking so long. He guessed it didn't happen that often.

Finally, he heard a voice. A woman's voice. "How can I trust that you are Dar?"

"I have Zander's white shirt. I can tell you how Deek almost drowned and how Zander saved him. Deek snores but won't admit it. Zander got his book from Jesper the peddler."

"You may step forward until we tell you stop." Dar figured the voice belonged to the she-warrior that he and the Vanander brothers had battled.

"Do you have the Vanander brothers here still?"

"Keep walking."

"I want to make sure they're all right." Dar searched the darkness, looking for something, anything. He heard a scuffling noise behind him, but as he turned to look, the bag was already over his head and being pulled down past his elbows. His natural reaction was to fight, but after lifting his arms, he stopped. "Just please try to be gentle? I won't fight back, I promise."

"Then go limp and let us do the work." The first man's voice came through the burlap.

Dar complied and lowered himself to the ground. His captors tugged the bag all the way down and rolled him over onto his back. Dar got poked in the head by a stick twice—they seemed to be mounting some loops built into the sack onto some poles. He felt the ground drift away from him as they lifted him up and started to walk at a steady pace.

"This seems like a lot of work for you. I could have walked myself to wherever we're going."

"Until we know for a fact that you're who and what you say you are, I don't want you knowing anything about our operations." The first sentry's voice was broken by the strain of the work.

"I hope it's not far. This bag isn't very clean." Dar was trying to stave off boredom. Being dragged around in a bag wasn't part of how he had figured this would go.

"I would rather not parley, if you don't mind. This isn't very easy."

"Sorry."

He tried to get comfortable, but it didn't work.

Dar figured it was about an hour later when the bag was set down. He had hit three rocks along the way. He'd also heard a small brook and birds starting to sing, meaning dawn was close.

"We there now?"

"As there as you're going to get." It was the woman's voice. "You can get out of the bag."

Dar found the opening of the bag, made his way out of it, and blinked at the brightness of the light. He was inside some sort of building, and all the lamps were facing him. His eyes hadn't adjusted, so he blinked, squinting.

"It's a bit bright, if you don't mind."

"Dar!"

The next thing he knew, he was in a bear hug. The voice rang true in his ears. "Zander!"

"Deek too," said Zander's brother. He chuckled, then addressed the sentry. "That's him."

"Troops dismissed," came the woman's voice.

Dar still could barely see in the brightness. "You boys going to introduce me to your sister?"

Zander stood next to Dar, shoulder to shoulder. "Dar, Katowyn Vananader. Kat, Dar." Dar held out his hand, not sure where she was.

"Hello." She didn't take his hand.

"She's normally much nicer," Zander chimed in. "But wars make her grouchy."

"They make me itch." Deek smiled at his own joke.

"Why are you switching sides?" Kat's voice was clearly to his left side.

Dar faced her general direction. Her form was starting to come clear, despite the brightness of the lights. "After your troops nearly killed me when you took your brothers, I did some thinking and put the pieces together. Once I figured out I was on the wrong side, I figured I'd correct that."

"I don't trust traitors."

"Kat!" Zander scolded her.

"Katowyn, Zandy." Her tone chilled the room.

"What about Janelle. Did you talk to her?" Dar crossed his arms. He could see her well enough to make out her features. She was as tall as he was, still in her chain-mail armor, and filled the room with an energy that could not be ignored. She had charisma and sense of grace and wisdom about her that was obvious to anyone who engaged with her. And he could see her clearly now—she was the most beautiful woman Dar had ever seen.

"You cut her shirt to take her modesty from her. Or worse." Kat crossed her arms. The chain mail made no sound.

"I motivated her to leave. She was getting hysterical, and she couldn't stay." Dar looked Katowyn straight in the eye. "If I was going to take her modesty, why not pay for it in the Abbey? Why not cut the front of the shirt instead of the back? Why would I wait until we'd nearly reached your camp, where it was the most risky? Why not just have my way with her on the trip back from the Abbey? "

"Good points." Zander nodded.

"Shut it." Katowyn turned to her brother. "Whose side are you on?"

"The truth." Zander looked at Katowyn. "You've heard our stories about him, and still you question him?"

"Like I said, I don't trust traitors."

Dar sighed. He looked at her accusing eyes. They were blue like gemstones. He gathered his thoughts and started in, force building in his voice.

"I was taken into this war without my permission. Beaten and forced to defend what I was told was a holy building. When I later found out it was whorehouse, I saw the war for what it was, and I corrected the situation. I did not come here to be badgered by you. I came to lead a strike into the heart of the protectorate's forces and end this war. I want to destroy the evil that exists on the other side of the lines, and I know the best routes, the best tactics, and the best times to make it happen, with as little bloodshed as possible. I can't be a traitor to a cause I didn't agree to join, in a war I never knew existed. If you can't trust me, that's your problem. If you can't use me to end this war, then you're just as evil as those you claim to hate and fight against. I have a life I want to get back to, so either let me get everyone back to their lives, or free me so I can restart mine."

Dar spotted a free chair with its back to Katowyn. He walked over to it and sat down.

A moment passed. Then another.

Dar figured Zander would have said something by now, but clearly both brothers where waiting for their sister to say something first.

"I'll ask the chain of command."

Dar turned and caught a glimpse of her heading out of the door. Zander and Deek both snuffed the brightly glowing lamps and came over to sit next to him.

Dar looked them both over critically. "All that time we spent together, and you never mentioned you had a *warrior* sister?"

"Zander?" Deek left the question hanging.

"Katowyn is nine years older than we are. She left home when she was eighteen and I was only nine. So we really grew up without knowing her. "

"We hadn't seen her for five years." Deek jumped in. "She's part of an order called Journ…"

"Deek!" Zander jumped in.

"What?" Deek put his hands in the air.

"She doesn't like people knowing things." Zander's look shot daggers at his brother.

"Sorry I asked." Dar tried to smooth things over.

Deek started again, sounding a little sheepish. "We decided when we woke up in the hay bale that we wouldn't talk a lot about ourselves. Until we could figure out what was what." Deek seemed to build up some confidence when his brother didn't interject. "But now that we're safe, we can share a little more."

"Understandable."

Zander nodded.

"So, the Abbey is full of prostitutes?" Deek smiled. "Didn't see that coming."

The three made small talk for a while to kill the time. Deek and Zander told of their years before the war. They told tales of youthful visits to bazaars, how Zander once startled Deek's horse and it ran for ages, long summer walks, and a blissful if unfocused life. Dar was chiming in every now and again, but he was not paying much attention. He was thinking about how he would attack the lines he had defended for so long. His thoughts occasionally drifted off to Katowyn's eyes and long black hair. Finally, they ended up dwelling on food.

"Can I get something to eat?" Dar jumped into the conversation as Zander took a breath between sentences.

Deek looked to Zander. "She didn't say we couldn't feed him."

"What do you want?" Zander smiled from ear to ear.

"What?" Dar looked at Zander. "Do you have a chef here?"

"Better than that." Zander stood up and walked outside, pausing in the doorway. The first rays of sunlight peeked into the building. "We have clerics who will create food and drink for you magically."

"Two rashers of shoulder bacon—cooked, of course—two tattie scones, hot, and two fresh sourdough buns with cheddar cheese. Please."

"Tottie scones?" Zander quipped.

"A thin potato-based griddle cake, unleavened and only as thick as a slice of cheese. A treat from my youth."

"Oh, a potato scone." Zander smiled.

"Sounds perfect. Me too, Brother." Deek nodded at Dar.

"And to drink?"

"Fresh, pure milk. Tall glass."

Zander looked to Deek, who just nodded.

"Consider it done."

Zander had only been away for a few minutes when the door opened—apparently, these cleric chefs of theirs were quick. "Ah, good," Dar said, "I'm starving."

"I'm afraid you're going to have to wait." It was Katowyn. She had a group of people with her. "That's the one, Colonel."

The three men behind her were a motley bunch. One was clearly a knight, his plate mail reflecting the outside light until the door shut tight behind them; the tallest appeared to be a cleric; and the last didn't seem to have any weapons or instruments to denote his profession. Dar was glad to have had his request to switch sides taken seriously. If he warranted the personal attention of these three, it could only mean good things.

The tallest started a spell. Dar knit his brow, and Deek met his eyes—they were unusually stern. Deek slowly nodded, lowering his eyes. Dar turned to the cleric, awaiting the end of the spell.

"In his heart he is a good man—he cares not for Law or Chaos; both suit his goal of making the world a better place." The cleric turned toward the other three. "He is skilled in the arts of magic but isn't practiced enough to be in the Enclave. He is thereby free of the Cloture dictum. He radiates a strong sense of being a warrior, yet there is clearly the power of the beyond in him. Jesper is right to think he would be a candidate."

"Jesper?" Dar stood. "Is he around?"

"Don't get excited." Katowyn motioned for him to sit again. "Where he is or isn't doesn't matter to you." Dar remained standing.

"He isn't going to betray him, Katowyn." The unarmed man spoke with a deep voice.

"Whether Dar is going to be a candidate is between Jesper and myself."

"I beg to differ." The unarmed man smiled. "I believe that, despite my retirement, I still have a say in the matter." He put his arm on Katowyn's shoulder. "I recommended you in my first year of retirement, and that worked out just fine."

"I think we should judge him by the content of his character. See if it is lacking." The knight's voice seemed higher than one would have expected for a man of his size. "If he wants to end the war, I say we let him."

"I agree." The unarmed man reached into his belt and pulled out a sack. He opened the sack and reached inside, much deeper than seemed physically possible. "From my bag of holding to your arms." He looked at Katowyn.

"Dar," Deek answered quietly.

"Dar." The man nodded at Deek. "I present to you my second-favorite weapon." He pulled out a half-inch-wide, six-foot-long strip of willow wood with a string dangling between its two ends. "Elves give names to their most powerful weapons. It is known as Weeper, and do not be fooled by its appearance." He placed the wood between his legs, pinching his knees together to hold it from dropping. He cinched the sack he'd drawn the device from and placed it back on his belt, then grabbed the stick in one hand and the string in the other, which he pulled back like it was a bow. As he did, the willow strengthened, and the string went tight. As the string nestled under the man's chin, Dar could tell it was bow of great power and strength.

"It takes the strength of the wielder and turns it into its own power. Draw it like a bow, and it will become a bow. Wear it around your body like harness and it will survive all but the most damaging spells, such as disintegration. This power allows it to survive where a normal bow could not. I have taken it into many a raid, and it has suffered many a crushing blow, but here it still works, some twenty years beyond the day I received it."

The man slowly let the tension out of the string, and as it went slack, so did the wood. He tossed it to Dar, who snatched it out of the air. Dar looked at each person in the room in turn, starting with Katowyn, trying to read their reactions. Katowyn wasn't jealous, as he'd thought she'd be—there was many things swirling in her eyes: guilt, sadness, pride, desire, honor, and a sense of hope. Which of these Dar was simply projecting onto her and which were really in her heart, he couldn't determine.

The three men of the command were easier: pride, and a sense of both satisfaction and doubt. Dar wasn't sure why the cleric doubted him; perhaps he wasn't happy about the blood that Weeper surely had shed.

"Nice." Deek made his thoughts clear.

"You honor me with this weapon." Dar tested it out, only pulling it back until the wood stiffened and the strip of wood showed its true colors. "I'm not sure I deserve it."

The unarmed man spoke again. "End the bloodshed, and it will be a fair price for the service rendered."

The knight cut to the chase. "What is your plan?"

"At night most of the chain of command goes to the Abbey to enjoy the services of the women who reside there. My company is down three men and won't receive replacements until two days from when I left, if the man in charge even reports the losses. I know some of the men in the unit won't fight me, further weakening the point of attack."

The knight was still not convinced. "That gets us through the palisades, but what then? They have a mounted reactionary force."

"The whole salient around the Abbey is to just defend it. We push a concerted attack on the far side, and when my unit area collapses, we storm the Abbey and kill all of the commanders. "

"Cut the head off and body dies?" The cleric chimed in. Dar wasn't sure he had been listening up to that point.

"We rouse the inhabitants, making sure to set the willing mercenaries on their way, freeing those held against their will, and then burn the building to the ground."

"Burn it?" The unarmed man didn't seem to believe what he had just heard.

"It is the simplest way to break the morale of the whole army. They will see it in some form or another across the whole line. Destroy what they are there to fight for, destroy who they are fighting for, and they will fight no longer. Only the purest of evil will still have motivation, and even that will be flagging."

"I like it." Dar turned to see Katowyn smiling. "Aggressive and absolute. It will be totally unexpected."

The cleric closed his eyes and lifted his hands to his face. Dar figured it was some sort of prayer or communion with his deity.

The unarmed man took a seat on a nearby chair but said nothing.

But the knight didn't need to think further. "I'll lead the force on the opposite side, and I'll use our reserves to make sure that even if you don't break through, one of us will. The force that doesn't get countered by the mounted reserves will get the Abbey." He turned and headed toward the door.

"Wait!" It was the cleric. "I will help you." He glanced at the unarmed man. "Hinelim?"

"I'm too old to fight with a sword, and my magic left when I married." The unarmed man stood. "But I agree with the plan."

The three walked out of the cabin.

Not a minute later, Zander walked back in carrying a tray full of the items Dar and Deek had ordered. He noted that Katowyn had returned and Weeper was sitting on Dar's lap. "What did I miss?"

Dar grabbed one of the rolls and put the potato scone and the bacon inside of it. "Not much, just the planning for the end of the war." He took a big bite and smiled as he chewed.

SEVENTEEN

Action

"When swift in action and bold in thought, the
true path comes easy."
—the motto of the Qro'elle, an elite elven com-
mando unit only rumored to exist

Zander had brought two rolls for each man, and Dar ate his
as Katowyn led him to another building in the complex.
Dar felt he should have been looking around the area more to
get a sense of his location, but he couldn't take his eyes off of
Katowyn. They walked around the camp, weaving in and out
of tents, formations of men, and wagons. Finally, he couldn't
take it anymore. "Where are we going?"

She didn't turn to address him, nor did she slacken the
pace as she answered. "We are heading to my unit. Our numbers are no greater than the enemy's, but if you're correct
about the strength of your old unit, we won't need much more
than them anyway."

"How many people are in your unit?"

"Twenty at full strength."

"In my short military experience, you're implying that it is not currently at maximum." Dar wished he could see more of her face to see how she took his comment.

"They are used for many purposes, so it will take a few hours to get them all back from their assignments. Once they are back, the unit will be at full strength."

"Who is the leader of this army?"

"His name is Vaynor, and while he possesses rank equivalent to that of a general, he is a wizard and leaves the war to the Council of the Three." She glanced over at him. "But I wouldn't concern yourself with that. Tonight is the only focus."

"Sure. Sure." Dar was glad that she didn't seem annoyed by his comments or questions.

"I'm going to let you billet down for a couple of hours, as I doubt you got a full night's rest before coming over to us."

"Plus, there was that whole head-crushing thing that happened."

She didn't appear to notice his comment. Finally, they came to a collection of tents, most of them just pup tents that would barely shelter his frame. "Pick a tent and try to sleep for a while. If you want, I can use my powers to help that along."

Dar nodded. "I'll take that one." He pointed at a tent off to his left.

Katowyn moved to the front of the tent and dropped to one knee. She reached inside and pulled out a couple of backpacks. "Fine. Here you go."

"Will you tell the owner of this tent that I'm sorry?" Dar moved past her as she stood back up.

"It's my tent." She cast the spell of Sleep with her free hand and smiled as Dar's face hit on the floor of the tent.

Dar opened his eyes. He started to sit up, stopping when the roof of the tent reminded him of his surroundings. He crawled out of the pup tent and was greeted by an elven warrior.

"I am going to be your assistant, Dar. I'm the conductor of the unit." The warrior held out his hand.

Dar shook it. "What is your name?"

"Conductor, if you please." He motioned for them to start walking. "Easier that way. By tomorrow I'll be some faint memory, so no need to cloud your mind with extra names that won't matter soon enough."

Dar paused, about to press the issue, but then thought better of it. "Fine. So, Conductor, what is your role, and what are we doing?"

"The conductor is in charge of all nonbattlefield activities of a major command unit. I direct transportation, catering, pioneer duties, ammunition, construction, and supplies."

"So your rank is equivalent to…?"

"Command sergeant major."

"So you outrank me? I was only a sergeant." Dar frowned. He wasn't sure if he should throw in a *sir* or *Conductor*.

"They appointed you a rank of major for the operation. You outrank me, but we aren't very much into the sirs and ma'ams out here at the edge."

"What rank is Katowyn, if I might ask?"

"Major." Conductor took a sharp turn, and Dar had to catch up to him.

"And where are we headed?"

"Back to the front."

"I have no supplies"—Dar tugged on the bowstring of Weeper—"other than this."

"There will be weapons and armor waiting for you at the front."

"Conductor, how long to the front?"

"Getting tired?" Conductor looked over his shoulder at Dar.

Dar wrinkled his lips. "Just ready to end this."

"About an hour." Conductor looked ahead again. "Just give us thirty minutes to get you suited up before dark settles in."

"I know Ocktur would travel toward the Abbey just as the sun was setting. Given travel time, time to eat, and time to pick out a companion, that's no more than one hour."

"We can hit that window."

"I hope so, Conductor."

Dar couldn't help but rub the chain mail he'd been given by Conductor. It was the color of silver but was lighter than leather armor and made no noise. It lengthened itself to accommodate his larger shoulders and superior height as compared to his assistant.

"What is this armor, Conductor?"

He was behind Dar, checking the fit for himself. "It is elven chain mail. Magical chain mail, to be exact."

"Does every elf have this?" Dar shook his arm up and down to see how silent it really was.

"Only the elite units receive magical chain mail as standard issue, but everyone who serves the elven communities can petition for it. A petition has never been turned down."

"Do I get a magic sword?"

"We don't have any of those." Conductor moved around to Dar's front. "Well, to be more correct, we don't have any right now. I have some back at our operations base, but we don't have enough time to go back there before we launch the operation."

Conductor was approached by another elf, who gave him a quiver full of arrows and walked away. Dar reached out and was handed the quiver.

"I haven't really used a bow much," he said. "Not since before I went into apprenticeship for magic."

"A wizard warrior?" Conductor chuckled softly. "A combination not usually seen outside of my race."

"My tale is longer than the time we have for it."

"Aren't they all that way?" Conductor laughed. "Sorry, elvish joke."

Dar smiled politely, not exactly getting the joke.

"Use it if you need to," Conductor said. "Don't worry, its magic will improve your aim."

Dar drew his sword and swung it around. A longsword with long handle, it felt well balanced and easy in his hand. "Is this magical?" he asked, focusing on the movements of the blade.

"Just high-quality steel and expert craftsmanship."

"I would hate to see what your magic swords can do."

Conductor smiled. "You have to remember that with our longer life spans, we don't see taking a month to produce a single blade as a sacrifice, or even a duty. Our materials, weapons, spells, our art and music—they all get more of our time and souls than you humans put into anything save your children."

"So why do you risk that longer life on wild and dangerous adventures like this one?"

The earlier smile gave way to a more troubled look. "That longer span also brings us wisdom. We know that if you do not stop evil, it will not stop. Ever. So we must risk our lives to have lives worth living."

"Amazing." Dar sheathed the sword and looked to the night sky. It was a purple black, with delicate hints of the blue that had departed just minutes before. Dar rubbed his hands together. "Time to start the end of this evil."

"I'll summon the troops, and it will begin."

Dar could barely see the edge of the palisades. It was true that he had strong night vision, but it was nothing compared to that of the elves of the unit he was heading into battle with. They seemed to see as well in the night as they did in the day, and they moved making just a whisper of noise. Dar walked behind one of the unit's corporals. At least, he assumed the man was a corporal. He led the squad but not the unit. Dar felt a little lost by it all. The elves didn't really talk to him—well, other than Conductor—and things like rank were difficult to ascertain from their uniforms, let alone in the dark of night. Dar could see a torch flickering inside the palisades, which gave off a little light but didn't help enough to illuminate much at this distance.

"Shall I have an archer kill the guards?" the corporal asked Dar.

"Some of the men are good." Dar was going to continue when the elf held up his hand and nodded, which Dar took to mean the conversation was over for now.

It was confirmed when the unit took off toward the line again.

"How about the torch?" Dar said as quietly as he could.

The corporal just nodded. He waved his hand around and motioned with his fingers. Dar took it to be some sort of hand signal, because the instant the gesture ended, it seemed, one of the others unleashed an arrow. It flew true and knocked the torch down and into one of the many puddles that dotted the tent area.

Dar awaited the call to arms, but it didn't come right away. So he took off, making sure to nudge the corporal forward, which got the whole unit moving.

They had reached the gap in the palisades. The guard apparently moved over to see what had happened to the torch. Once they'd seen the arrow, the game had changed, which was apparent now from the racket.

"Alarm! We are under attack!"

Drots. Dar recognized the voice.

The elven unit started sprinting to close the distance, but Dar's old unit was pouring out of their tents, ready for battle. Dar drew his sword and readied himself. The yard area was full of men and elves, and it was time to spring the trap.

"Navigator! Navigator!" Dar yelled so loud he feared it would wake up the next unit over or the Abbey itself.

There was moment when Dar was not sure it was going to work. He heard the sound of a handful of weapons being thrown down, followed by thumps and low-toned cursing. The sound of steel hitting steel came next as the elves assaulted the remaining defenders. Dar struggled to tell friend from former friend, so he left his sword out but unused. He wandered around, wanting to check on those lying down, but he needed to keep an eye out for trouble.

Suddenly, a light shot out of the dark. Dar turned to see the source. Drots held a stone that was the source of the illumination. In his other hand was the bag he had just pulled the stone out of. Dar rushed him.

"Dar!" Drots discarded the bag and took up his sword again. "You're with them?"

Dar let his sword speak for him. Drots was able to block his first blow, and the next, and the one after that. But Dar didn't have something in his other hand, so he had the edge. Drots parried a blow and threw the stone at Dar. It clanked up against his armor—a duller, lower note than Dar had expected—and fell to the ground. The effect of the light was lessened, and the extra shadows gave the elves, already superior in numbers, another edge.

Both hands now free, Drots counterattacked, and Dar gave up a little ground. "Ocktur was right to take me to the Abbey," Drots said, "and to give me special treatment. I'm better than you are. He just put you in charge so he could keep an eye on you and to help motivate me."

Dar spun around and let the whipping action of his arms direct a heavy blow toward Drots's midsection. Drots blocked it, but that left his side exposed. Dar drew back the sword— from the look in his eyes, Drots knew he was in trouble, so he shifted his weight to the right, bringing his body back to center. Longsword met longsword as Dar redoubled his efforts. Dar could hear the other battles around him coming to an end, and he knew that Drots could too. Drots angled his blows to force Dar to give ground, which would allow him to flee. Dar refused to yield. Getting desperate, Drots lunged at Dar, who parried the blade away and countered with a pushing stroke straight at Drots's chest. The blade tore through the armor and cut into flesh underneath. Dar had barely removed the blade by the time Drots's legs would no longer hold his weight. Drots's face went ashen, and he slumped forward, landing facedown in the dirt and mud. Dar stood there waiting for his opponent to do something, but it was over.

Only when Conductor came over to check on him did Dar realize that he was panting and covered in sweat.

"You knew him?"

"Hated him, really."

"There can be no joy in killing, but it is okay if some deaths make you less sad than others." Conductor flipped over the body, making sure the eyes of the dead were closed. "That is the elven way."

"The part of my soul that he killed doesn't feel joy over his passing, just relief."

Conductor nodded. "What is next?"

"We send the surrendered troops out of here, leaving this place abandoned, and we push on to the Abbey itself."

"How do we know the surrendered troops will honor the truce?"

"I'll show you." Dar turned and looked around. "Jusin? Jusin? Where are you? Stand and be counted!"

"Over here!" came his voice. Jusin was rising to his feet over by the entrance.

Dar and Conductor trotted over to him. "Good that you were able to tell those who should survive the code word."

"I tried to work fast." Jusin was talking past them, clearly not able to see them very clearly. "I was next to Drots when the torch was hit."

"You were on duty again?" Dar looked surprised.

"Lucky for you Dar was with us," Conductor commented.

"Who are you?" Jusin turned to the source of the strange voice.

"That doesn't matter, Jusin," Dar said. Conductor looked sheepish and retreated a step away, as if to remove himself from the conversation. Dar continued, "What is important now is that we move you all away from the palisades and out across the lines."

"Makes sense." Jusin seemed to be seeing them better now.

"Conductor?" Dar turned toward the elf, who took a stride forward at the same time. "I want a guide to move these men to a human sector of your army on the other side of the lines. I think there will be less culture shock if they are among their own."

"A wise move." Conductor paused for a moment, then walked over to another elf and started to converse with him in their native tongue.

"What language is that?" Jusin spoke softly, trying to keep his comment between the two of them.

"Elvish." Dar walked over to the light stone that Drots had hit him with and picked it up.

"Drots is dead?" Jusin's eye were open wide.

"He earned the wages of evil." Dar went back to where Drots had fallen, wishing the Conductor had left him face-down. Then he stopped and turned toward the open area of the palisades. "Attention, Ax Company!" He yelled as loud as he dared. "All survivors who hear my voice come to the light for further instructions. This is your commander, Dar, and reporting for muster at my position is an order."

Dar held the light stone high, and out of the corner of his eye he saw the elves retreat to the shadows. Dar nodded toward Conductor. Having the elves out of sight would help keep things a little more tidy.

After a few minutes, just five more men stood around Dar. They were dirty from being in the mud, and their faces showed the strain of not knowing what was going on. The bodies of their comrades lay all around them, and it was clear they were wondering if they were next.

"The war is over for you. You survived." Dar looked each one of them in the eye in turn as he spoke. "You have fought well and with honor. Now it is time for you to start to return to your families, your homes."

Dar could see a few tears forming. Clearly, several hadn't thought they would get to this moment. Ever.

"Jusin is in charge now, as I have more things to do before I can return to my home. Jusin will lead you to a unit of men on the other side of the lines. Do what they tell you do to, and you will be taken care of well. I know trust is something in very short supply here, and it may be hard to consider those that you thought your enemies yesterday your friends today. But let that hatred stay here, where it belongs, and start to heal."

Dar let that sink in for a moment. He knew they had to get moving again, but these men were still in his command, and he felt the need to keep providing them with some leadership.

"No weapons, no violence, and until you arrive amongst men, the less you say the better for all. This is still a war zone, and those on this side of the lines might not treat you any differently from the enemy. Once among the men on the other side, you can talk freely, and they will help you home."

After a long pause, Jusin spoke up. "How can we trust these people to help us?"

"There will be but one guide, and he will keep his distance. You do not need to like him, just follow him. He wants you to get to the human units as badly as you want to get there."

"And why no weapons?" Jusin spoke again, and the rest nodded approval.

"Trust is to be earned by both sides."

Jusin looked at the ground. "But we are safe, aren't we?"

"You have my word."

"And mine as well." The elf spoke loudly as he came out of the shadows. "I would be honored if I could reward your brave service with helping you back home. I give you my solemn word to keep out of the way, quiet, and be ready with help should you need it."

Jusin looked back at Dar. A long moment passed, and he wiped a tear from his cheek. Finally, he said, "I accept." Then walked toward the elven warrior, dropping his belt to remove his weapon.

The rest followed suit. Just before they walked out of the sphere of light, Dar called out. "Jusin!"

Jusin turned, and the group paused. "Yes?"

"You'll need this." He threw the light stone to him, and he caught it. "Be safe, my friend."

Jusin held the stone over his head. "You too. I hope we meet again in this world, and if not, we will be meet in the next."

"Have a good life, Jusin."

Jusin nodded, and the group left.

Conductor left Dar to his thoughts for a minute or two before walking over to him. "You ready to move on to the next phase?"

"Did the knights in reserve commit to a direction yet?"

"Nobody knows this part of the line has been compromised. Our agent ahead, who is near the knights, reports no movement from them."

"Jesper."

Conductor nodded. "Our agent should remain slightly secret, just in case."

"Agreed." Dar started to walk toward the Abbey. "Can we outflank them, avoid them altogether, and still get to the Abbey?"

"Probably."

"What if once just slightly past them, we set this encampment on fire? The blaze will attract their attention, and they'll move away from us and the Abbey."

Conductor smiled. "A capital idea. Keep marching toward the Abbey on the best route, and I will rejoin you." He then turned and disappeared from sight.

Dar could see the faint glow that the Abbey always imparted to the sky around it. The torches along the bottom of the building gave it an eerie glow that could be seen for miles.

Dar appreciated the time alone on the walk. It seemed like the first time he'd really controlled his own destiny since he'd joined this accursed war. Lost in such thoughts, it felt as if he covered the whole distance to the Abbey in just minutes. Dar kept to the road, and once he decided to stop, he quickly found himself surrounded by elves. They were just at the edge of the darkness near the Abbey.

Conductor was at his elbow. "Plans?"

"This is easy and hard at the same time." Dar looked at him and then back at the Abbey. "The place is full of workers;

I can only assume they are noncombatants, unless they are an orc, goblin, or some other inherently evil creature. The women should be spared, but if they attack you, I would defend yourself as needed. Men in uniform I would put to the sword quick. And once in the higher levels of the building, put it to the torch. Let it burn up and down."

"Why not burn the way up?"

"It will let those who have a shred of innocence some time to escape."

"The evil will too," Conductor said through pursed lips.

"They will already have known our blades by then."

Conductor thought about it for minute. "Do you not think it would be too easy for an officer to impersonate a waiter or other worker and escape our assault?"

"Would you rather slay an innocent or let a disgraced leader escape? If you want to kill them all and let the lords of the heavens see who deserves torment, you might find yourself on the wrong side of the scale of justice."

Conductor smiled at Dar. "I was hoping you would say something like that."

He turned to the troops, and while he addressed them in Elvish, Dar studied the side entrance where he had once entered the building. They would have to force it, but that would be their way in.

"Move fast, move silently, kill without pause, and once on the fourth floor, set a fire and make your way back to here. Combatants only," Dar mumbled, not sure if anyone other than him was listening. He waited until Conductor went silent.

Dar waved his arm towards the Abbey. "Let's go."

EIGHTEEN

Collision

"Time knows no favorites."
—Nki, the Duchess Priest of Chronum, the God
of Time

Dar moved at full stride, his heart racing as he shoved the
secret door wide open. The same man was there, but
apparently, the rage in Dar's eyes, the glint of steel in his hand,
and the number of elves behind him gave the man pause.

"If you want to live, I suggest you run, and run quietly."
Dar didn't look at the man; his eyes were locked on the door
at the other end of the kitchen. "Otherwise, you will not see
the dawn."

"I'm…" Dar could hear the panic in the man's voice.
"Yes, sir!"

The man shot through the door and didn't look back.

The elves split into teams and spread out across the bottom floor. Dar knew where he would find most of the cadre,
so he sprinted toward the stairs, where he encountered an orc

with a tray full of food. A quick lunge with his blade and the creature was no more. Dar caught the tray and set it down on the floor.

Now on one knee, Dar could see a mix of servants, officers, bouncers, and prostitutes down the long hallways that stretched along the sides of the Abbey. Using his sword would give them too much warning. They would see him coming, and either they would fight or flee. In ones or twos, that wouldn't be bad, but as the word and the noise spread, one and two would turn into ten and twenty.

That wouldn't be good.

He sheathed his sword and pulled Weeper off his body. He tugged an arrow from the quiver on his back and notched it on the string. He continued up the stairs and stopped just short of the landing; this vantage point allowed him to peer out at the floor without exposing anything but the top of his head. He spotted an officer downrange.

He was with a woman, and the man's hands were all over her. She seemed to be only tolerating the moment, probably because of the price he was paying, Dar figured. They were heading toward him. The woman saw him; he stepped to the top of the stairs and let the arrow fly.

By the time the man was on the ground, the woman was three steps away from him. She screamed. Dar looked to his left, along the short side of the Abbey. Nobody was there. He turned back to the long side, waiting for a door to open, as surely someone had heard her scream. Out of the corner of this eye, Dar saw the face of an orc peering down from the level above. He pulled another arrow and placed the shot through the left eye of the monster. It plummeted to the bottom level.

Dar pulled another arrow.

A moment passed. Then another. Time to go, Dar said to himself. He turned and climbed the next flight of stairs. Dar could just barely hear the screams of the woman now. It was hard to hear over the sound of his own heart beating.

He stopped short again. This level was empty on the long side. He climbed to the top of the stairs and looked to the left. What he judged to be a human servant was cleaning up a mess of some sort. Dar pulled his bowstring back, then paused. The servant looked at Dar. He looked barely old enough to tend a flock, let alone be in a place like this. Dar squinted at the kid.

"You need to leave here."

"Who are you?" There was a touch of bravado in his voice. Dar could hear the fear underneath.

"Who I am doesn't matter. This place isn't safe for civilians. We are just here for the officers and soldiers. We don't want to kill the innocent."

Dar could see the kid hadn't seen a bath in while, but his eyes showed he had seen plenty else. "Was that scream your work?"

"She's fine. The soldier she was with, well, you'll need to ask his thoughts about it in the next life."

"You mean it, don't you?" The boy stood. "You're going to kill them all."

"I'm not asking you to take sides. I'm telling you to save yourself. Just get out. Go anywhere else, just don't stay here."

"What I want to know…" Dar noticed the boy's eyes darted to his left, then back to him. It wasn't a long look off, and it wasn't very far off, but he clearly saw something.

Dar wheeled around and took in the scene. Partway down the long side, a door had opened up and a soldier stepped out, still putting his pants back on. Dar could just hear what he was saying. "Next time, when I say what I want, you do it quick, or you'll get more than my fist." The man muttered something under his breath and started to fix his belt. The sound of the sword on his belt clanked down the hallway.

He never saw the arrow that killed him.

When Dar turned back, the kid was already running the other way.

"Alarm!" the boy shouted. "Alarm!"

Dar pulled back the string and took aim.

He couldn't do it.

He turned to face the center of the Abbey and walked slowly backward so his back was up against the wall.

"Alarm! Alarm!" The kid ran along the far long side. "Alarm!"

One of the doors near to him opened up. It was a woman. Dar turned to look along the near side.

A door opened. It was a soldier, no armor, epaulets on his shoulders. He had no pants on and had clearly stopped in the middle of the action. "Who called the alarm?" the man yelled out.

Dar stopped him short, the arrow sticking out the other side of his chest. Dar could hear the woman inside the room he'd stepped out of start screaming.

Dar peered down the length of the Abbey to the far end of the short hallway. He thought he could see a couple of teams of elves working their way up the stairs. He waved at them. They waved back.

"Alarm! Alarm!" Dar turned and watched as the kid headed into one of the rooms. Either his father was an officer or his mother a whore, or both. Dar pitied the kid.

A door close to him opened.

Dar aimed at the opening.

It was a woman. She reminded Dar of Janelle. While she looked around the Abbey, Dar held still, waiting for the moment to play out. A moment later, she saw something that caused her to dart back into the room. Dar scanned the hallways, taking a moment to look up and down to the levels above and below.

This time the woman stepped out of the door with a dagger in hand. It was red with blood. She was dressed now, and she ran toward the stairs that Dar had just come up. She was only a stride or two away from the stairs when she spotted Dar.

Dar wasn't sure how to respond.

"You killed him?" she said.

"I'm not interested in harming anybody who isn't an officer." Dar aimed at her, but his eyes pleaded with her to not make him do it. "You're free to go, but I suggest you ditch the weapon."

She looked at the dagger—it seemed for a moment that she'd forgotten it was there. She tossed it back toward the doors. "I killed that fat bastard who kept coming back and doing disgusting things to me."

"I'm sorry." Dar started to scan the hallways for more movement. Most of the men must have been too drunk or too busy to care.

"It felt good," she continued. Dar could see the mental armor she had worn for so long starting to fall away. She sobbed, softly at first, but then harder. "You will protect me, won't you?"

"You must flee the building," he told her. "There's an army coming from the west of the city. Head that way, and you'll run into them. They will clothe and feed you. They can help with the wounds in your heart and mind as well as your body."

"You won't…"

On the floor below them, Dar spotted movement—a door was opening. He waved his hand to get the woman's attention, and she stopped. He waved her off, but she stayed rooted to the spot. He looked sternly at her, then motioned more vigorously for her to get moving. "Get moving," he said. "It only gets worse from here."

But then he saw the sense of distrust and betrayal cross her face.

"I'll escort you past the second floor, but you must find your own way out."

She nodded.

Dar led the way, his bow and arrow at the ready. They reached the landing in one quick rush. Going up the stairs protected him, but going down left him exposed. He could see the person who'd come out of the door. It was a tall, scraggly-looking jumble of a man. He had his weapon out, scanning for action.

Dar let fly an arrow.

The man's armor stopped it cold. But the woman, apparently deciding to take advantage of his distraction, turned to the staircase and took off running down to the bottom and freedom.

The man motioned toward a doorway. Dar pulled another arrow and aimed a little higher. He waited a moment and shot.

The arrow grazed the man's head, and he leaned back into the doorway.

"You get out of here," came a woman's voice. "I've already got one in here, and I don't do teams."

"Shut it, you fat whore!" the man bellowed.

Dar aimed another arrow at the man's head. It missed by flying wide to the left.

"You best not say that to my woman!" Dar thought he recognized the second man's voice. The first target held fast in the doorway, struggling to stay out of the arrow's eye.

Dar took off running, stowed Weeper, then pulled his sword.

He just needed the man to stay under cover for another moment. The man peered out of the doorway, and then quickly ducked back in. Dar's footsteps made a bounding noise on the old stained mahogany floorboards. The man peeked out again just as Dar got to the door, then stepped into the hallway, his weapon at the ready.

Dar lunged an attack at the man's midsection, which he easily dodged. He countered with a swing at Dar, which Dar easily countered with his sword. The clanging noise echoed through the hallways. Dar swiped at the man, who blocked the blow with his sword. Dar could see the man's head turning slightly to the side, and he could smell alcohol on his breath.

Dar turned and ran back toward the stairs.

His foe took the bait and took off after him.

Dar stopped short and swung his sword with both hands back behind him. The blade cut the man across the gut, forcing him to drop his weapon. Dar could see blood and fluids everywhere as the man's life started to ebb. He was clearly in a great deal of pain, so Dar silenced his scream with a quick blow to neck, killing him quickly.

"I'm going to kill you for saying that about my Bessie," barked the voice from in the room.

"I told you, it's Beth!" retorted the woman's voice.

"Shhhh, woman, men are talking."

Dar could clearly hear who it was now.

"Come out, Ocktur, and meet your destiny."

"Dar?" There was the sound of clothes being put on. "I would not have guessed you would be the type to call a lady fat."

"I didn't, that was somebody else."

"Now you lie too?"

Dar stepped into the room. It smelled of food, alcohol, and sex. He could see the woman; she was morbidly obese and very homely. The sights, the sounds of her struggling to get out of bed, and the smells of the room made Dar wince. But he shook these distractions from his mind and turned his attention to Ocktur. His former commander was trying to pull on a chain-mail jerkin but clearly wasn't sober enough to do it.

"I'll take you barehanded!" Ocktur threw the jerkin at Dar. It wrapped around his blade and clung to Dar's arm.

Ocktur leapt at Dar. The distance was more than Ocktur had figured, though, and Dar bought himself some time by chucking Ocktur's sword and armor at him. The sword landed near his feet, and Ocktur had to adjust his stride to not end up on his face. Dar took that moment to dodge to the side. Ocktur couldn't compensate and rushed past Dar, but then settled his momentum and turned to face him.

Dar worked his way to the center of the room, his weapon at the ready. He could sense the woman nearby. She was crouching near the large bed that dominated the room. "My battle is with Ocktur. Stay out, and I won't hurt you."

"You help out, Bessie, and I'll pay you triple every night for a month."

"I'm warning you, stay out of it." Dar was stern, but his tone was pleading. He didn't want to shed any more blood than he had to. But he could not have her as a threat.

"You come at him from that side, and I'll come at him from this side." Ocktur wiped his mouth. "He won't hurt a woman. He's too good for that."

Dar reached to his dagger with his left hand. He pulled it out and threw it at the woman. His throw placed it into the wall behind her, right at the level of her head.

"Your choice, Beth." Dar faced Ocktur. "I won't miss again."

Beth ducked down, trying to hide behind the bed. Dar could see her naked bottom peeking above the level of the blankets.

"Fine, whore." Ocktur started to rub his knuckles. "You'll get the wages of failure, then." He smiled at Dar. "Once I'm finished with him."

Dar raised his sword, placing it between Ocktur and himself, and watched for the sign that his adversary was going to charge.

Ocktur swiped at the side of Dar's sword with his hand, pushing it out of the way, which left Dar struggling to hold onto his weapon as Ocktur made his next move. Realizing that the sword wasn't going to defend him, he spun in the direction Ocktur had sent it. This moved Dar out of the way of

Ocktur's charge, but not by much. Dar swung at Ocktur, but he didn't have the right grip on his sword. He hit the massive half-ogre with flat of his blade, making a lot of noise, but doing little real damage.

Dar jumped up onto the bed. It was softer than he had figured and slowed his movements.

Ocktur grinned again and lunged at Dar, both arms out in front of him. Dar jumped up and back while bringing the blade down. The flat hit Ocktur square on the top of the head. Ocktur's hand had Dar's leg for moment before it went limp. The bed groaned and creaked as the full weight of the half-ogre came crashing down on it. Dar ended up back by the headboard, crashing into it with his full weight. The violence of both actions caused the bed to come apart, with pieces flying around the room.

Dar paused, letting the moment settle.

Ocktur wasn't moving, and Beth was screaming; splinters of wood from the bed covered her.

Dar moved over to Ocktur, intent on finishing the battle. He placed his sword on the man's neck and paused.

He could smell fire.

Dar looked at Beth. She could smell it too.

Dar looked down at Ocktur. He was still breathing but clearly out of it. Dar pulled his sword away and headed to the door.

"I suggest you leave him to his fate and get out of the building. It will be burnt to the ground before dawn."

Dar didn't wait for her reply. He headed into the hallway.

The hallway was full of people scrambling to get somewhere else, with most picking the stairs at each end of the main hallway. Most were women, and most of them nearly naked. For the most part, they ignored him. Dar kept to the edge of the flow until he saw a man in uniform. Dar adjusted the pommel of the sword in his hand and struck at the soldier. The man fell to the ground, but the mob didn't stop. A few of the women near Dar reacted in horror, but when he didn't attack them, they just kept moving as they pushed toward the steps.

Dar turned and looked toward the back of the pack, where he spotted another soldier. The crowd was quickly thinning, so Dar started to walk toward him. Seeing Dar, the man went to his belt, finding nothing. As Dar was letting the women go by, the man rushed to the banister. He looked at the floor below, then leapt. Dar rushed to the railing and looked down at the man below. He had landed awkwardly on the main floor and seemed hurt. The man struggled toward the end with the large main doors, where it appeared—judging from the large crowd that had gathered there—most people had sought to make their escape.

Dar looked up. The fire was spreading quickly, and the smoke billowed above and below the flames. The fourth floor was engulfed, and most of the third wasn't fit for man or beast. Even on the second level, the smoke was starting to get thick, so Dar decided to make his exit. He turned to the stairs and quickly made his way down to the first floor, and from there to the side exit.

It was clogged with people, some of the larger women just barely able to make it out the small doorway. Women and manservants were starting to fight over who would get out first. This brought the flow of traffic to a complete halt.

"One at a time!" Dar yelled, banging his sword against the wall.

That got the attention of the crowd. An obese woman turned away from the manservant she was abusing and looked at Dar.

"Get moving!" Dar yelled again. The manservant took a step back, struggling against the weight of the crowd, and let the woman go first. As she passed halfway, he pushed her, and the way was open again.

Dar waited toward the back of the pack, but the progress was slow. He had no idea how to make things go faster, and he could smell the smoke building: the fire was closing in. While the flames were still a ways away, the fatal effects of the smoke would only continue to increase. The crowd thinned far too slowly. Some were going to make it. Some would be trapped.

"Need help?"

"Conductor!" Dar almost hugged the man who'd appeared by his side. "We need a bigger opening."

The elf started a magic spell, and as he concluded it, a large portal appeared on the wall. It was larger than the door it was relieving, and the doubling of the escape routes made the crowd seemingly evaporate into the smoke.

"The spell won't last long, so keep it moving," Conductor commented.

Dar ran back to the stairs to see if anybody was still inside the building. The smoke was thick, and while he could hear cries of pain, nobody was actively moving out of the building. He looked for Ocktur's large form, hoping and fearing at the same time he would see him.

"The passwall spell's portal's closed!" came a yell from below.

Smoke billowed and flowed, and nothing stirred.

It was time to get out.

Dar flew down the stairs, reaching the door as fast as his feet could take him. He didn't pause until he was clear of it and at least a hundred paces from the burning building. Looking away from the Abbey, he could see the huddled masses of women, no doubt struggling to make sense of the evening. There were some who straggled in the direction he had pointed the first escapee, and it seemed like the elves were shepherding them toward the oncoming human army.

Feeling better about the noncombatants, he turned back to the Abbey. Flames had shattered all the windows above the second floor, and most of the second-floor windows as well. Smoke ate at the brilliant glow of the fire, but it couldn't dull the massive conflagration. To Dar it was like day, hot and dry. The fire coaxed the wind on faster, enticing it to join the dancing flames. This helped to create a sirocco-like wind that stirred against Dar's cheeks and ears, demonstrating the fire's force, even at this distance. Dar looked around again. None of the elves were looking at the fire. They looked to the stars, or to each other, but not to the flames. Conductor approached him, looking down at the ground.

They walked slowly away from the fire. The sound of the flames and the crackling of the wood ate up all other noise in the area. Dar keep looking around. Finally, Conductor asked him, "You okay?"

"I wonder how many innocent souls are in that building right now."

"There are a lot more of them out here now, thanks to you. Consider that before you torture yourself over those who ended up on the wrong path."

"I'm not sure I see it that way." Dar cast a glance at his companion.

"Because you're not sure you're one of the innocents?"

"My innocence was lost when I got here." Dar stared straight ahead.

Conductor reached up and patted him on the back. "Not all lost innocence is a bad thing." He smiled. "Otherwise there would be no children, and the marriage bed would quite boring."

Dar looked at Conductor and wrinkled his brow.

Conductor just laughed.

NINETEEN

Prudence

"While the war might be over for the body, for
the mind it may continue a lifetime more."
—General Silvaetra

Dar and Conductor trailed the mass of people working
their way toward the palisades that he had defended
for so long. Even though they could no longer see it, they
heard the Abbey collapse behind them. It was an amazing
and horrific noise that rolled like thunder and shook the
ground like an earthquake. It was over as quick as it had
started, and suddenly all was quiet, except for the sounds
of the group ahead reacting to the destruction behind
them. The sky behind them remained bright, until the sun
finally chased the light of the flames into obscurity. Once
dawn firmly established the sun's dominance, the smoke
became the telltale sign of the work they had done overnight. Dar kept an eye out as he they walked, scanning for
the retreating enemy forces.

But as they drew closer to where his time in the Army of the Protectorate had begun, Dar was startled at the changes. Look as he might, there were no enemy forces of note. There were signs of a hasty retreat—such as dropped weapons and occasional marks in the dirt were somebody fell as they ran—but otherwise there was no proof that armies had clashed nearby. He could see stragglers around the edges of the area, but none of them approached the group of refugees. The strays didn't appear armed, and they must have elected to stay away from the large body of people based on sheer size. The horde he was in was composed mostly of women, and all but the elves were unarmed, but Dar imagined it would be hard to tell that from any sort of distance.

"What happens next?" Dar said to Conductor, without looking at him.

"All the refugees head to the human sector to be dealt with, you included, and you all figure out where your best destiny lies. Then you get on with it."

Dar turned to look at his walking partner. "What about you?"

"Me and my people will go back to our lands behind the Elvish Great Wall and rejoin our families." He met Dar's eye. "Or do whatever we must do. Same as you."

"Why don't elves and mankind do more together?"

"Good question."

They walked a while more, silence between them.

"You didn't answer," Dar said, looking sheepishly at Conductor.

"You're right." He looked straight ahead. "I don't have one. So I had nothing further to say. To say more would be a waste of time."

"A man who will live for a thousand years is worried about wasting time." Dar furrowed his brow.

"Your time is precious. I wanted to save it." Conductor smiled broadly at Dar. "Looks like the first human troops are encountering the band from the Abbey."

"What do you think they'll do?" Dar squinted ahead, but couldn't make out the details that Conductor could. "Soldiers and prostitutes are a mix for trouble."

"Katowyn's at the ready. She'll make sure things go right."

Dar squirmed a little. "Is Katowyn nice?"

"No." Conductor smiled. "She's tougher than a turtle's shell and just about as friendly. But she is a great force for good in this world, and her word is true until the end of days."

"She seems a bit rough to get to know."

"You're basing that on the conflict between your immediate physical attraction to her and the distance she keeps between herself and everyone at all times."

"Tell me what you really think, Conductor." Dar favored him with a look of mild shock.

"For a human, she is very attractive, I'll give you that, but her family and career come first. That is the source of the distance."

"I know her family." Dar looked ahead. "What is her career?"

"That is up to her to tell." Conductor stopped walking and held still.

It took a moment for Dar to respond, but before long he stopped too and turned to face the smaller man. "Why did you stop?" he asked.

"It is my time to go." Conductor looked Dar in the eye. "My unit must help close out some areas of resistance, and you have done enough for this war."

"I can help." Dar took a step toward the elf. "You know how good I am in a fight."

"Dar." Conductor put his hand on Dar's shoulder. It was over the smaller man's head, and the gesture brought the two very close. "This is not your war. Your time has been served."

"I'm afraid to go back," Dar said softly. He wasn't sure where that truth had come from, but it felt good to get it out there.

"Because you like killing people?"

"Because I like helping people. I like not always knowing what is around the next corner, and I like being outside with nature. The feel of steel in my hand and honor in my heart. Doing what must be done with the clarity of purpose. When the purpose is just."

Conductor smiled and took his hand off of Dar's shoulder. "Tell Katowyn I told you to have her conduct you home."

With that, he turned and started to trot away. Just at the edge of earshot, though, he turned around and spoke one last time.

"She'll have some of the answers for you."

And then Conductor was off and running. Several other elves came out of nowhere, it seemed, and joined him as he raced off to the next battle.

Dar took a deep breath and sighed. He turned to face the refugees from the Abbey and started walking toward them.

He could use some answers.

When Dar reached the inner circle of the band of refugees, he could see the three Vananders at work. Katowyn was clearly in charge of everything, Zander was tending to the wounded and abused, and Deek was handing out supplies and just trying to be useful. Dar stood a couple of steps away and didn't want to interrupt any of them as they tended to their duties.

But then Zander waved to him. "Dar!" He spoke a few soft words to the woman he was tending and then raced over to see his friend. "I'm so glad to see you."

"Hi, Zander." Dar forced a smile. "I'm glad to see you too."

"Really?" Zander gave him a doubtful look.

"Survivor's guilt, dear brother." It was Deek. "Blanket?"

"I'm not feeling guilty." Dar waved off the blanket. "I would like some food."

"Yes, yes." Deek turned to another helper and waved at him. "But did you…" He paused. "You know."

"Did you battle any of our old unit mates?" Zander asked Dar.

"I battled and killed Drots." The helper arrived with a tray full of hard rolls with meat and a stone cup with some sweet-smelling liquid. Dar helped himself to both.

"That's sweet water—it will clear up any food-borne illnesses you might have." Zander smiled but then turned serious. "Ocktur?"

"I fought him in front of the whore he was with, but I couldn't kill him. He passed out on the bed, collapsing it, and we left him to the fire." He paused and took a bite of the roll. "I'm pretty sure he's dead."

Zander looked at him with a scolding scowl.

"What?"

"No matter what they did in the Abbey, they're all free women now."

Deek joined in. "They don't like using the *w* word. It's a pejorative term that doesn't fit them as free women now."

"Katowyn's doing?"

"Yes, I did outline that rule." She came up from behind Dar. "Let me guess, you were using *that* term to describe one of our refugees."

"Until I helped free them a little while ago, that is what they were."

"Is that what you would call Janelle if she stood here now?" Katowyn narrowed her eyes at him.

"She was forced into it." Dar crossed his arms. "So, no."

"Many of these women were forced into it once upon a time, and now it is all they know. They're offended by that term. Just like I think you would be offended if I called you mercenary or brigand. Until a little while ago, that is what you were too."

"Point taken. I concede to your wisdom." Dar took another bite of the roll. "How is Janelle? And Jusin? And Jesper?"

"You can eat first, instead of speaking around your food. It's bad manners." Dar found her tone even more scolding than her words.

"Sis." Zander looked at her disapprovingly.

"Jusin is fine," Deek said. "He is resting, and we are trying to arrange a route home for him." After a pause to let Dar take a drink, he continued. "Janelle was already sent back to her family."

"She'll be all right with some guidance." Katowyn crossed her arms, mirroring Dar's stance. "Jesper has already moved on to his next mission."

"Guidance?" Dar blushed when he realized he had a mouthful of roll again. He raised his hand to his mouth as he finished the thought. "And mission?"

"Janelle and the other rape victims aren't just going to be cast back into society," Katowyn said. "Most of these women turn to selling their bodies because being raped or being forced into the prostitution has destroyed their self-worth and their view of the world. When offered guidance, most don't return to their former occupation. Most find the way back to the path they wanted to live before the horrors."

"Glad to hear it." Dar was done with the roll. It was perfect, like all the food he'd had from the kitchens of this army. "You didn't say anything about Jesper."

Zander looked at his sister, then looked at Dar. "She said he was fine, so let's leave it at that."

Katowyn held up her hand. "Jesper should know. He is a Journeyman, and he's gone to help correct another wrong somewhere else in the world."

"Is Conductor a Journeyman?"

"Who?" Katowyn tilted her head a little to one side.

"General Silvaetra," Zander stated. "I saw him walking with Dar out of the camp."

"Yes, he is." Katowyn could probably see the look of shock on Dar's face, because she raised her brows. "And so am I."

"The general said you should conduct me home. Do you know what that means?"

Deek smiled. "I do! Road trip!"

Katowyn smiled. "My brothers and I will take you back home. Where is your home?"

"I was in training with a mage near Palaidius. You can take me back there."

Katowyn nodded. "In a few days, I will come get you, and we will make the journey together. Until then, find a palisades disposal team and work with them." She turned her attention to her youngest brother. "Deek, you go with him."

"Sure thing, Katowyn." He turned to his brother. "See you later, Zander."

"Keep him out of trouble, please?" Zander spoke as he turned away.

"I will," said Deek.

"I meant that comment for Dar."

Dar and Deek found their old tent and joined the crew taking down the palisades to pass the days away until it was time to go home. Deek would question Dar at length about his time in the mage's tower and what it was like to be a wizard in training. Dar would ask about Katowyn, trying not to be too obvious about it. What were the Journeymen like? What did she say about it? The questions kept coming, but there wasn't much in the line of answers. Deek wanted to help, but Katowyn had joined the Journeymen when the brothers were very little and she had said about it little since.

The time with ax and shovel did Dar good, but clearly, it wasn't for Deek. At the slightest sign of a callus or blister, he would stop working for a couple of hours. That would free him up to field more of Dar's questions. Dar worked and worked, almost to the point of ruin. Deek would tell him to slow down, and he would, but just for a while.

Once the palisades were down—a fairly straightforward job—they began turning the large timbers into wooden boards for houses and shelters, a much more taxing line of work. They started with a handsaw, cutting off the rotting bits that had been in the ground, then using an adz to remove the outer, pitch-covered layers of wood. They would then roll the log over to another team that was using a magic saw and Cantrips—minor spells, as Dar explained to Deek—to set the logs into boards. Dar knew he didn't have to help, but the cutting team was happy to have the extra hands. They saw Deek as a necessary evil, it seemed.

The day fell into a nice routine for Dar and Deek. Up with the sun, breakfast, (food would arrive on a cart for the whole disposal team), and then work until lunch. They would break during the hottest part of the day, then resume work until dinner arrived at sunset. They sat around a fire made of leftover wood from the palisades and discussed everything and nothing all at once. Each man had a story to tell, and although Deek usually ended up doing most of the talking, each got to know the others as time went by.

At the time of the fourth day's midafternoon rest, Katowyn and Zander showed up at the camp. By that time, the palisades had been completely denuded of all the logs, turning the former fortified area into a wide-open field. Another team had come by and filled in the pits in front of the walls, and whatever they didn't need—such as the extra tents—had come and gone.

"You ready to go?" Zander asked Dar.

"We need to get our stuff together." Deek spoke for both of them, it seemed.

"What about my armor and sword?" Dar headed toward his billet. "And the bow, Weeper? Am I supposed to give those back?"

Katowyn looked around—Dar could see it in her eyes that she had recognized the area. "You can carry them for now. Just in case we run into any trouble." She fixed her gaze on Dar. "You can wear the armor, if you like."

He had felt a little naked without it. The elven armor was like a second skin. "Thanks, I will."

It took Dar a moment or two to gather his possessions, but Deek straggled behind, as usual. But then, finally, they were saying their goodbyes to the other members of the disposal team. Dar looked back on the area and drank it in once last time. He then turned to Katowyn. "Take me home."

They entered the Union of the Free on the third day of their journey and kept moving at a brisk pace, despite Deek's protests. Dar mostly talked to Zander, hearing how his life had come into focus once he got to talk to a few of the clerics who had been in the encampment. *The Book of Miracles* had shown him the way, and he was certain, after helping the huddled refugees, that his calling was to serve all of Holimoren through prayer, healing, and an open heart. Dar listened in earnest, asking Zander about the different gods, and ignoring Deek as he made faces (until his sister corrected the situation). Dar wanted to talk to Katowyn, but somehow always lost his voice when it came time. So it went each day until they crossed into the Dire Lands.

The Dire Lands were a political and ethical no-man's-land in the middle of an otherwise good and lawful part of Holimoren. The area had become a colony for the evil army from the Venge Kleptocracy and the Chaotic Disunion, far to the direction of the setting sun. The two evil states had put together a massive force to try to force the Free City of Holin and Palaidius into submission. But a force of men, dwarves, and elves—all hailing from the Frearea and the lands the Vananders and Dar had just travelled through—had become the Anvil to the Holin/Palaidius force's Hammer. Too large to destroy outright, but crippled beyond being a real threat to local rule, the Kleptocracy and Disunion forces had settled a horrible little town called Gulch.

Considering how beautiful the surrounding region was—it was known as Eagle's Glen—Gulch was twice as horrible as it would have been anywhere else. Over time the evil that had established it had been diluted, and the Anvil and the Hammer disbanded into history. But though the area lacked the villainy and evil of those that had formed it, it still was a place of desperation and malice, and not one to cross unaware. Katowyn kept them in a close formation and would badger anybody who got more than a stride away from the group. Dar found himself close to her, and slowly the confidence in him built up.

"So, how did you end up a Journeyman?" He was walking with his sword out, as per directions. Well armed was well left alone in these parts.

"I was in training for the sacred arts like Zander, but something wasn't right. I wasn't sure I wanted to be a cloistered cleric. So I went on an adventure to see if maybe being an action cleric—doing by deed instead of word—was more my taste. And it was."

"That's when you quit coming home." Zander glanced over his shoulder at her.

A moment of regret flashed across her face before her resolute expression returned. "Yes, that's true. And it was out on one of those adventures that I was attacked and captured by some brigands. They had killed or driven off the rest of the adventurers in my party, and I was held by them for a while. They violated me, and each spent a time taking me by force." Her voice didn't waver.

Zander stopped. "Katowyn, I didn't..."

"Keep moving. It's the past, and I've dealt with it. It happened." She pushed Zander to keep moving. "Now, let me finish answering the question."

"Sure." Zander looked a little sheepish.

"After the second day, the survivors from my group had collected a few more people from a nearby town, and they came at the brigands. One was a master swordsman, and he alone killed half of the brigands. My compatriots freed me, and I extracted my revenge on those that had defiled me." Her eyes darted down before returning to the horizon. "I couldn't trust anyone. All men were suddenly my enemy. Except the swordsman. His words soothed me. He spoke of a woman who would come and help me. So I abandoned my adventuring days and waited. I was sure the swordsman had lied and all but swore myself to the cloistered life, where I would never be touch by a man again. But then she arrived." Kat took a moment in the story to take a deep breath and let it out as soft sigh.

"You okay?" Zander queried again. He kept the pace this time.

"She would say if she wasn't, brother." Deek elbowed Zander.

Katowyn smiled. Clearly the story got better for her from here. "The woman was an angel. We walked and talked for over a month. When the nightmares struck me, she would hold me, and when the tears wouldn't stop, she would bring me water and tell me to let them keep them coming. We talked of when I picked up a sword and killed those who had attacked me. I hadn't used that weapon before, but it felt right. She gave me a weapon, and we started to practice with it. The better I got, the safer I felt. The swordsman came back, with a suit of armor for me, and then she told me that she was once a Journeyman. And that the swordsman was still in the order."

"General Silvaetra, wasn't it?" Deek guessed.

"Yes, it was." Katowyn smiled. "The woman was once his wife, Jilvare. They had married before joining the order, and while their souls were still connected, being in the Journeyman brotherhood means you must forsake those types of relationships. They hadn't been one flesh since the summer before I was born, and they still loved each other."

"Journeymen don't feel love?" Dar asked quietly. Hoping.

"We do, but there isn't time for it. Plus, as part of the magic that is being a Journeyman, you must choose magic over the needs of the heart. When we are ready to come off of the road and stop being Journeymen, love will find us. Everyone who has quit the order has done so for love."

"Did Jilvare?" Zander queried.

"She did," Katowyn said with a touch of remorse.

"But I saw the general cast a spell," Dar ventured.

"I did say she *was* a Journeyman. Past tense." Katowyn frowned slightly. "Jilvare's heart was lead in another direction, though the general's didn't change. She bore her new love a son, and they live somewhere in the Protectorate of Palaidius, last I heard. When she visited and helped me, she wasn't in the order anymore. But she knew my soul was right for the path of the Journeyman, and the attacks had hardened me for the travels that lay ahead of me. I wasn't a frightened girl anymore—I had become a woman, and a Journeyman. Since then, I've been all over the land. Barbarian lands in Frearea, Palaidius and the Tyrant Fiefdoms. No one takes me against my will, and I sleep well at night in peace."

"Against your will? That implies you still have physical relations?" Deek asked.

"Deek!" Zander turned red. "You don't ask about your sister's love life."

"It's not about love, brother," Katowyn replied. Zander turned a deeper red as she continued. "Sometimes there are needs that must be met, and when they are, they are on my terms."

"Next subject!" Deek yelled. He pulled out his book and started to leaf through it.

"How did you know the Journeyman path was right for you?" Dar asked, although he was tempted to seek more stories about the last subject.

Katowyn's face softened into a slight smile as the memory came back to her. "I lay awake one night, looking up into the stars and deep into my heart. Like the sun as it came up the next morning, what I had to do was clear." She looked at Dar. "Jesper and Silvaetra both think you could be in the order, but that is your choice."

Dar wanted to ask more, but he felt he had to honor her honesty and willingness to share. "Thanks for that."

She surveyed the area around them—they were deep into the Dire Lands now. "We should keep quiet for a while."

A while turned into the next day. Deek and Zander were obviously in shock over their sister's tale, so Dar kept to himself as he thought about his next steps.

Once into the free lands that surrounded the Free City of Holin, they started talking again—light fare this time. They caught a ride on a passing wagon after a quick negotiation with the driver. There were two halflings (not related, as Deek found out), a young human couple trying to elope, and two migrant worker dwarves in the back, and the Vananders talked to them all over the day. Dar kept to himself, and though he was polite when spoken too, but he didn't initiate any conversations.

Finally, they stopped the wagon and climbed out. Over the hill away from the road was the tower. They still had an hour's walk ahead of them, though, made worse by the sudden onset of rain. When they reached the bottom of the tower, Dar was happy to see that it was still intact and the drawbridge still closed. He walked up to the bridge landing and yelled out, "Master, it's Dar."

Nothing.

Dar looked over at Katowyn. "Is the Cloture over?"

TWENTY

Journeyman

"You are welcome to return to your lives, and
please embrace the new normal."
—traditional end of Cloture

They were locked out of the tower.

"Do you have any spells that would let you get into the
tower?" Deek asked Katowyn. Dar was shaking his head even
before Deek could look his way.

She smirked. "I haven't studied my spells in days. Those I
remember wouldn't help us."

"How long do you have to study a flying spell, or Open
Portal?" Deek quizzed her.

"Overnight, brother." The smirk became a smile. She
seemed to know what his next remark would be.

"In this weather?" Deek frowned.

"We'll set up camp and make do." Zander turned to Dar.
"Is this place highly travelled?"

"It can't be seen from the road, so it's pretty rare that someone would pass by." His mind flashed back to the punch of the Ogre Magi that sent him into this journey. "But it does happen."

"So the three of us will take turns keeping guard, and Katowyn can rest and study the spell to get us into the tower."

"That's a good plan, brother," said Deek.

"I agree." Katowyn nodded.

They set up a lean-to to give Katowyn room to study under its shelter. She ducked under it and sat down—Dar knew the sight of a spell book as soon as she pulled it from her pouch. Magically, the small volume expanded to the size of a huge tome, with the glyphs of the language of magic covering every side. The boys kept quiet as she poured herself into her studies.

Around midnight the weather broke, and Deek even took a guard shift. Katowyn had worked until nightfall, then turned in for the evening. The answers about his life still hadn't come to Dar, so he was happy to stay awake as much as needed. His mind raced, and only when Zander forced him to rest did he get any sleep. When dawn came, he was already awake and ready.

"I want you to fly into the tower, Dar." Katowyn surveyed the outside of the tower. "You know the tower, and you know the safest way around."

"Plus, if your wizard master is in there, you won't get a lightning bolt or turned into a lizard for breaking and entering an occupied tower," commented Deek.

"A true insight from you, brother." Zander laughed.

Dar readied himself and nodded at Katowyn. She cast the spell and touched Dar. Instantly, he could feel the pull of gravity let go, and he took to the sky.

"Nothing fancy, please, just get in and unlock the door," Katowyn called out.

Dar headed into the sky and landed on the top of the tower where the familiars like the Gulull were welcomed. He looked around and saw the tower was still in good shape. He started toward the stairs and made his way to the front door. He was just about to open the door when he heard the chime of the Master's talking spell.

"I hear my master, and I obey."

"Dar, I'm home," came the Master's voice. "Come meet me in the kitchen."

Dar raced down the stairs to the kitchen.

"Master, I have a tale to tell," he said with excitement.

"Master, I have a tale to tell" came his voice again, almost like an echo.

"You have to turn off the talking spell," the Master said, his face frumpy and his pipe hanging out to one side.

"You have to turn off the talking spell" echoed the spell.

"My master is finished with me, and I obey." Dar instinctively looked at the ceiling.

"Dar, you have been doing nothing the whole time I was gone?" The Master gestured around the room at the dust all over the pots and pans. "You will clean every inch of every room!"

"But what about my tale?" Dar's mind race to Katowyn and the rest of them outside of the tower.

"Boring drivel of a child." The Master didn't even make eye contact with Dar. "Back to your work."

Dar swallowed hard. It had all became clear to him in a heartbeat, and the words exploded out of him. "I'm leaving you, Master." The dam broken, the words kept coming.

"I'm joining the Journeymen, and my new master is waiting outside."

Master turned and looked Dar in the eye, a smile spreading across his face. "I was starting to think I was going to have to beat you to get you to honor your own destiny."

Dar was stunned.

"Pack what you need and go with my blessings."

Katowyn was running out of patience when the drawbridge from the tower creaked to life. Not sure if it was going to be Dar or his master, she prepared for the worst. Her face naturally went stern in moments like this, her resolve showing across her brow. But she smiled when she saw it was just Dar, looking happy.

"I'm now free." He stopped in front of Katowyn. "I'm no longer a wizard's apprentice. I'm now a Journeyman."